Guns of the Temple
Volume 1 of the Polaris Chronicles

Bryan Choi & Erica Carson

Guns of the Temple is a work of fiction. Names, places, and incidents either are a product of the authors' imaginations or are used fictitiously.

Published by Delphinium Press, LLC.
www.carsonchoi.com

To Domo

Table of Contents

Acknowledgments

Thanks to Shay, Whitney, Greg, and Colby for being my beta readers and providing feedback. You told me what was good, what was stupid, and what deserved death by dog pits. I received help and inspiration from the Frequency writers' community in Providence and from the gamers of Ninpocho Chronicles. I will always be grateful to Jason Yarn for his time and valuable insights. And finally, I couldn't have done any of this without the skill, love, and sick burns of my coauthor, Erica. – Bryan

Thanks to everyone who encouraged me to stick with it, especially the Thunderdome team. Double thanks to my inimitable parents, abeonim, and eomeonim for encouraging and supporting our efforts. – Erica

1

Taki chewed the cuticle of his thumbnail as he scanned the river of fighters that wound slow and dusty around where he crouched. Nearly every able-bodied squad and company was headed toward the gates of the Cloud Temple. From there, the men and women would start their marches north to relieve their peers from months of restless vigil against the Imperial hordes. But Taki was not part of this congregation—at least not today. Instead, he was on the lookout for a deserter from his squad: a senior corporal who had lost his mind and was now trying to make a run for it. *Draco Emreis, you stupid ass,* Taki thought. *I haven't even met you and you're already ploughing my career.*

Unexpected pain made him realize he had bitten a bleeding divot into the root of the nail. Taki sucked at the wound and chastised himself. Biting was a nervous habit he had picked up even before academy training, with multiple bouts of remission and relapse. Until today things had been going well and his fingers had begun to heal. He had graduated third in his class and had been promised a rare posting in the capital. There, he would have worn white livery with braids and brass buttons and have had little chance of seeing combat. But he had turned the job down, and in just a few hours of post-academy life his fingers looked like raw bark again. Two weeks of disciplined progress undone.

"Newboy! Are you blind or just slacking off?" Hadassah snarled. "He's approaching you now. Next to the cornet in red brigandine!"

Taki winced. Though she was actually meters away in a steeple overlooking the street, the effect of the *Phon* sutra made it seem as if she was yelling right in his ear.

"My name's Taki," he muttered.

"I don't *care.* Go stop Draco or we're really in the shit."

"What does corporal Emreis even look like?"

Hadassah grunted with displeasure. "Muscular, dirty blonde hair. Tall," she said.

"Can you be more specific?"

"He's *pretty*. Now go!"

Taki clenched his jaw and continued to scan the crowd. Garish standards proudly flapped in the wind atop pikes and splashed color against the dust. Light glinted from polished helms and mail armor. A cart loaded with cannon and shot pushed its way through, accompanied by cursing and spitting from driver and pedestrian alike. He found the cornet wearing red brigandine.

Hadassah was right about the man next to the officer. Draco *was* a pretty specimen, with blonde hair, high cheekbones, and thick calves. He chatted gaily but his smile was forced and he glanced backwards too often, as if aware that his squadmate had him in the sights of her crossbow. Taki hopped off the boxes he'd been sitting on and started to make his way forward.

"I just realized," Taki said. "He has no idea who I am. Won't that be a problem?"

"That's why we put you on the street. He's less apt to run away," Lotte said.

Taki's back stiffened at the sound of her voice, though she was also far away. Lotte was a regimental captain and the leader of his squad. He had met her only a short time before, and she had immediately ordered him to search the Temple grounds for Draco. Strangely, she did not seem to have lieutenants, and had issued commands to Hadassah and Taki directly the entire time. "Just keep him occupied for a bit," she continued. "We'll nab him soon."

"Yes, Captain," Taki said.

He slowly shook his head. Depending on the circumstances, an attempt at desertion usually earned a heavy flogging followed by hanging. It was easy to understand Draco's motivation, and hard to sympathize with him. Taki had never wanted to be a polaris of the Temple in the first place, but the fact that he could use what the alchemists called *prana* gave him no other choice. Everyone, especially polaris, knew that they were dangerous and unfit for life on the outside. It was their just penance to be confined to the Temple and atone for centuries of sin by fighting for the Argead Dominion. If Draco couldn't accept that then he deserved what he got.

Scenarios ran through Taki's head for how he would distract his target. He could always be rude and try to entice Draco into fisticuffs. Or pretend to be an old acquaintance in need of a loan. Or just flirt with the man. The latter option made Taki fuzzy in his stomach, anxious that perhaps Draco would simply scoff at and dismiss his smile.

A Dominion priest grabbed his wrist and Taki glared. One of the many pestilences afflicting the Temple was the sheer number of vagrant ascetics who trolled the streets exhorting for holy war and begging for alms. Hitting them was frowned upon, as was refusing to donate. Taki tried to wrest his limb away but the wizened priest held firm.

"I bless thee, brave polaris!" The priest swung his censer dangerously close to Taki's face. Thick, fragrant smoke washed over his hair and caused him to cough. "Know that it is *not* a sin to kill the degenerate sodomites of the Osterbrand Imperium! They serve none other than Shaitan Himself in the guise of man."

"Thank you, Father, but I cannot stay here," Taki said.

"*Payment,* dear son. I have given thee my blessing!"

"I didn't ask for it!"

"It is thy *duty* to repay God for thy destruction of His earthly kingdom! Just one bullet will do."

Draco was about to pass by. Hurriedly, Taki dug his free hand into his belt pouch and thrust a steel-cased .25 caliber round in the priest's face. The holy man smiled jaggedly, snapped up the cartridge, and let go. Taki swore under his breath and turned just in time to almost collide with his target. He tried to fake a familiar grin but it came out as a grimace instead. Draco cursed, turned on his heels, and dashed away into a side alley.

"He's running!" Taki snapped, forgetting how loud the sutra amplified his voice for the recipient. He could almost *feel* Hadassah recoil.

"Ow! Not so loud, damn you!"

Taki bounded after his target over hastily-overturned bales of trash. Draco had already begun to climb to the rooftops near the far end, and swung from jutting pipe to protruding brick with practiced grace. *Prana-enhanced physique. An Achilles,* Taki realized. *I can't match him for speed or strength, but that means he's probably not a good caster.*

"Slow him down. Attack him if you have to. I'm almost there!" Lotte shouted.

Taki thrust a hand forward and opened his prana gates wide. He was a decent swordsman and a passable shot with a firelock, but his real talent, rare even among his kind, was elemental channeling. Under any other circumstances he would have been flogged for using destructive sutra on Temple grounds, but his captain had ordered it.

"*Khala!*" he intoned. A biting chill enveloped his arm and frosted his fingertips. Pressurized air lanced forward and hit his target squarely in the back. Draco slammed face-first into stucco, lost his footing, and tumbled to the ground. Taki froze. He hadn't intended to make Draco fall from such a height. He hadn't intended to break his senior corporal's neck.

Like a cat, Draco twisted a meter off the ground and landed splayed on all fours. The cobbles under his feet and fingertips cracked and the air shimmered against a dusty corona. He hopped to his feet and drew a fighting iron. Invented by the Chung Kuo far to the east, the kau sin ke was a brutal and yet simple device: three solid bars of steel jointed together with a single chain link between them, a leather-wrapped handle, and a nasty bludgeoning end. Draco whirled the spiked head in the air so fast that it became a blur, and slowly advanced.

Taki backed away in terror. He had a knife sheathed at his side, but was not wearing armor or a helm. He could attempt to use sutras, but against an agile opponent in close quarters he was dead. A rifle would have been useful, but those were all locked away.

"Skipping the court-martial and going straight for the execution, are we?" Draco growled.

"I'm sorry! I didn't mean to hit so hard." Taki said. He extended his hands in surrender. "I'm in your squad. The captain told me to stop you. I'm just following her orders!"

"*My* squad? I've never seen you before."

"My name is Taki Natalis. A corporal, like you. I just joined today."

"A likely story, that."

"It's true!" Taki paused and jammed a hand against his right ear. "Look, Hadassah is telling me to tell you to stop being a damned potato or she'll put one in your left nut. I'm sorry! These are *her* words, not mine."

Draco frowned, but his menace melted away quickly.

"I just can't win, can I?" he said. "The captain's close by, isn't she?"

"Will you put down your iron?" Taki asked.

"Oh, right. Sorry," Draco caught the swinging end of the kau sin ke, folded the bars together, and holstered it at his waist. "Just so you know, I wasn't *actually* going to attack you. Just wanted you to run away."

Taki exhaled. "It's fine. I'm sorry I went too far with the sutra."

"So you're new, eh? It's been a while since we've had a fresh face."

"Why did you try to desert?"

"It's a long story, but I'll tell you if you've got the time."

Lengths of weighted rope cut the air with a whooshing sound, wrapped around Draco's torso, and squeezed the wind from him. Taki whirled around just in time to see a woman charge past and tackle the hapless corporal to the ground. She rolled him onto his back, drew back a fist, and punched him in the face. Blood spurted from his nostrils onto the cobblestones.

"Stupid bastard!" Lotte huffed. She rose to her feet and wiped her knuckles on the hem of her blouse.

"Captain?" Taki asked, grimacing in awe.

"Hey, want me to plug him? Just a flesh wound?" Hadassah asked. She strode into the alley with her crossbow leveled at Draco's leg.

"Did anyone follow us? Did anyone see?" Lotte asked.

Hadassah looked back at the street and shook her head.

"Thank God," Lotte whispered. She lifted Draco to his knees by the front of his gambeson and fixed her steely eyes on his watery orbs. "Corporal Emreis. Do you know that the punishment for desertion is death?"

He nodded. Taki held his breath. Hadassah spat.

"*I own your ass,*" Lotte growled. "*I*, not *you*, decide when you live or die. *Is that clear?*"

"Yes, Captain," Draco gasped.

"Good," she said with an unexpectedly sweet smile. She drew him forward, as if to plant a kiss, and slammed her forehead into his with a dull thud. His eyes rolled back into his head and he went limp. Lotte let him down gently before turning to Taki and Hadassah. "Natalis and Mikkelsen, get him back to quarters and chain him to the radiator. If he complains, stab him. Then report to the kitchens for regular duty. We've fallen behind thanks to these shenanigans. Natalis, I hope you're good at peeling potatoes."

* * * *

Days later, Draco seemed to hold no animosity toward his compatriots for the earlier beating. Rather, the discussion had turned to the Ursalans, whose skirmishes with the Dominion had ended under terms of armistice only a year ago.

"So what would you do in my place, then?" Draco asked Taki with a grin. "You've got a chevalier taking a piss with his back turned and all you have is a rusty dirk. If he cries out, his squires will rip your guts out through your bunghole. Your rifle's gone tits up, and just as a bonus, you're *naked*." He stabbed a potato with his peeling knife for emphasis. The chain between his manacled ankles clinked merrily on the floor.

Severed carotid: five seconds till incapacitation and twelve seconds till death, Taki thought. *Heart strike: near-instant death depending on depth of cut, but access from the back highly limited by ribs and vertebrae.*

This place smells. I wish I were out fighting somebody.

"Wait, you were *naked,* too?" Hadassah groaned. "If I'd known I'd *definitely* have blown your cover."

"Spiteful much? I had *circumstances.* Anyway, your answer, Natalis?"

"I'd slice his throat." Taki shifted in his seat and mimed grabbing a target from behind and drawing a knife from ear to ear. "It's the standard takedown, right?"

"That's what everyone thinks, but it doesn't *work* on a real person." Draco waggled a finger at Taki. "They'll bite you when you try to muffle 'em, and it's easy to slash yourself instead. Happened to me." He tapped the back of his left hand. Purple scar tissue snarled between two knuckles and his small finger did not extend all the way as the others did.

"But what else can you do? Won't the target make too much noise?" Taki asked. He reached into the tub in front of him and took out another potato to peel. Number two hundred forty for the day.

"Not if you go for the kidney. It'll cause so much pain that all they can do is gasp. And it's better if you step on the back of the knee. Make them fall onto the blade." Draco wiped his brow with the hem of his shirt before also reaching for a potato and setting to work on it.

"It has to be a *quick* thrust, though," Hadassah said. She jabbed the air with her peeling knife and slapped the opposite hand against her thrusting arm for effect. "You can't expect someone to stay still while you inch it into him."

"She's right about that. Oh, and another thing, too. Just because you've put a man's eye out doesn't mean he's done for. I stabbed a Templar right in the socket and the bastard nearly put a mace in my skull. You need to open an artery."

"Yeah, and wherever you go, make sure you stab a few times after that, or at least twist around a bit," Hadassah added. "All you virgins think it's just 'stick in once and leave it.' You have to be *vigorous* to satisfy your partner."

"Now you're just being disgusting."

"And you're being a spoiled princess. If we don't show this kid how to do things properly he'll make us all look bad. What is he, like a day out from the academy?" She dug a potato eye out and flicked it across the room.

"Eight days," Taki said, to her great disregard.

"The *best* place to go is right here and stab down," she continued, pushing a finger against the base of his throat. There, the top of his breastbone made a deep valley underneath surprisingly thin skin and her poke induced nausea. "No one ever bothers to wear a gorget, so it's like you're sticking a pig. You've done that, right?"

"Er, I... No."

"Really? How useless are you? Are you some rich merchant's kid? Did you have servants licking your-"

"Dassa, lay off him," Draco said. "He just wanted to hear about when we were fighting the Ursalans. And I was having fun telling him. Especially since we're never going to battle again."

"*Don't!* Don't remind me of that."

"Right. Sorry." Draco cleared his throat and was silent.

An involuntary frown crossed Taki's face. His senior's words were only the latest additions to the mounting strangeness of his life since graduation. Like how the first time he had met Draco was during the man's attempt to desert. Or how Lotte seemed to be stuck peeling potatoes alongside her grunts. Or how they had spent all of their time in the kitchens rather than in battle rotation like every other company of foot in the Temple. His reservations finally overwhelmed, he raised a hand.

After a few silent heartbeats he put it down when he realized the others were staring at him. This wasn't the academy anymore.

"Sorry, Emreis. What did you say about never seeing action again?" Taki asked, trying not to seem embarrassed. "Aren't we at war right now?"

The others exchanged a look.

"Is he an idiot?" Hadassah groaned. "I thought we didn't take the touched ones."

"Wait a second. Captain, haven't you told him?" Draco asked.

"I thought the Major did. Or that one of you lot would," Lotte said.

"You *had* to bring it up, Draco!" Hadassah buried her face in her hands.

"I'm sorry, I wasn't told *anything*," Taki said, shrugging helplessly. Sweat stung his eyes and his stomach turned. What sort of hidden taboo had he just brazenly exposed?

The door to their sweltering storeroom opened. Though the air it brought in was redolent of grease, it was at least somewhat cooler. A scullion stepped in to grab the potato bowl and replace it with an empty one, not bothering to acknowledge Taki and the others. It was enough of a reprieve that Draco could take in a breath and compose his thoughts.

"We had to tell him eventually, Dassa. Okay, Natalis, I'll start from the beginning. You remember what happened to Berlin?"

"Sorry, what does Berlin have to do with anything?"

"Humor me."

"Okay, Berlin. Didn't their king torch it just 'cause?'"

"You're oversimplifying it. What really happened was that a few years ago, the Sanctissimus Rex Ursalus looks over the maps and concludes that the Imperials will end up banging down the walls in less than a year. They'd already sacked Krakow and Gdansk a few months before, so the Capital was next up for a siege. But if there's anything the Ursalans hate more than us, it's the asiatic horde. So, the Rex orders half his godrotting army to the sole task of bringing every single tire in the land to the capital-"

"Wait, you mean those ancient dark orbs that spawn bloodsuckers?"

"Yes, those. Back before the Fall, everyone wore at least four tires on their person when leaving the home. Kind of like a codpiece, hat, and bodice all in one. Anyway, the Rex has his men pile all the tires up till every single city block was about a man's height deep. Then he has it all set on fire."

"That's an odd choice for fuel."

"No, tires burn *forever*. That's why it's called 'The Great Tirefire of Berlin,' because the most glorious city of the old world—the *only* place untouched by the mushroom clouds of the Fall—will still be a flaming rubber crematorium long after we're all dead."

"I thought the Ursalans called it 'The Beacon of Triumphant Strength' or something."

"Well, they *do*, it's just that everyone else calls it what it really is. Regardless, it turns out to be amazingly effective at stopping the enemy. The million-strong Liberation Army of the Osterbrand Imperium sees this gigantic smoke column in the sky and just *stops*. They've been laying around in Silesia cradling their manhoods ever since."

"Why can't they just...go around the thing?"

"Beats me. Maybe they have some kind of deep-seated fear of fire? Or maybe they felt like the Rex was too much of a mad dog to fight? After all, this is a guy who'll turn the crown jewel of Queen Europa to molten rubber just to spite you."

"Good point. So what does this have to do with us?"

"I'm about to get to that. You remember our basileus tried the same thing, right?"

"Yes, on Santorini."

"Except we don't have so many old tires lying around, so His Grace makes the legions find what they can and ferries them all to the island. They make a pile about twenty meters high or so and then light it on fire. It kills every fish in the sea for ten kilos and now the coast smells like burning hair."

"'The Triumphant Light of Argead Defiance.'"

"Also called 'Tirefire the Lesser.'"

"Which is… Which is the name of this squad! I remember now. It was hidden in the papers that the Major had me sign. But isn't that kind of *blasphemous?* Why is that even allowed?"

"Good, now you're getting to the root of the problem. The basileus made *his* tire fire to show everyone how clever and strong he was—really had a lot of pride in the thing is what I'm told. But the Imperium just declared war on us the next week."

"I thought they had a fear of burning rubber."

"Maybe our fire wasn't big enough? More likely, we're just a small buffer state in between them and the Ursalans. Knock us aside, cross the Alps, and you're in Versailles before you know it. Bottom line is, our squad's name is a direct affront to our liege. I don't think His Grace really knows about it, because otherwise we'd all be swinging on the gallows by now. But our exarch sure as hell does. The punishment for insolence is a flogging, but since no one has the guts to whip *that woman...*" Draco's expression grew dark at the mention, "...we lowbies get the shaft instead."

"So *that's* why I've been doing nothing but peeling potatoes every day since I got here?"

"*You've* been peeling less than a week. *We've* been doing this for the last year."

"The last *year*? When will this end?"

Draco arched an elegantly-manicured blonde eyebrow at his junior corporal, as if unsure whether to be derisive or sympathetic.

"Natalis, this won't *end*. As long as our name is 'Tirefire the Lesser,' we're stuck in the kitchens peeling potatoes from dawn to dusk, forever. We won't sally forth to battle, and we certainly won't partake of the spoils. Our lot is to suffer. I've lost so much skin off my fingers doing this crap that everyone in the Cloud Temple is now a cannibal, and I'm seriously thinking about ending it all."

"I'm sorry! I didn't mean to open a wound or anything," Taki said.

"You say 'sorry' an awful lot. Look, it's fine, I said too much," Draco said, waving dismissively. "Honestly, we're a bit surprised you waited this long to just *ask* us why your life went to shit for no reason."

Taki let out a laugh which he quickly stifled. The last thing he had wanted was to make the burly man-at-arms start spouting off about bloody endings again, or try to escape. "I guess I didn't want to make waves," he said with resignation.

"I get it. You're not a complainer. No wonder you got shanghaied into our squad. Weren't you one of the top initiates this year?"

"I wasn't at the bottom." *But I might as well have been,* he thought.

The academy had been a constant slew of fencing, shooting, sparring, and most onerously of all, hours submerged in lightless liquid meditation sucking air through a stingy tube. Most of his classmates were destined to end up dying in the mud of some horrid battlefield holding their guts in. Because of his talent, Taki had been pronounced as one of the rare students with an actual future. He was someone to keep far away from the front lines. With the luxury of hindsight, he now realized that turning down an offer to join the Praetorian Guard of the basileus had been foolish, but the woman—*that woman*—had made a very compelling argument at the time.

"The major sought you personally, didn't she?"

"Yeah, she did. I couldn't really refuse." His fingers unconsciously brushed the side of his cheek where she had whispered honeyed promises into his ear, her actual words now forgotten and replaced by the gratification of her exotic brusqueness. He couldn't help being easily hoodwinked by the first mature female to call him a pretty little thing and praise his skill. Especially not after she had scruffed him by the neck, dragged him into a closet, and swatted him until he signed the papers.

"Sorry to hear that. So anyway, now you know."

Speech gave way to the chalky grind of rhythmic slicing. Taki frowned again. Now he could really stand it no longer. Did none of the others see the fundamental gap in the logic of this twisted situation? Were they really just that stupid or ignorant? He chose his next words carefully. Fostering resentment could be fatal.

"Uh, look, I really don't mean to offend anyone who's thought of this before, but why can't we just, you know, change the name to something else?"

"Because it's not for us to change. The Major put it on the official ledger and none of us have the authority to change it. Besides, she chose it with...love and care," Lotte said. Taki stared at her. The silver aiguillette hanging from a shoulder board on her blouse definitely identified her as a regimental captain. Someone who should have been long-removed from this sort of grunt work.

"What she *means* is the major gets really horny at witnessing the suffering of others. Kind of like touching yourself while pulling the wings off a fly," Hadassah said. Her expression had at least changed from despair to disdain.

"Not another word, Mikkelsen, or I'm chaining you to Draco and tossing the key," Lotte warned.

"Then how the hell am I gonna pee?"

"What part of 'not another word' did you misunderstand, lance corporal?"

"Captain, go easy on her, she's got brain problems after all," Draco snickered, earning a kick to the shins. Taki stifled a laugh.

"*Something funny, Newboy?*" Hadassah spat at him, prompting him to reflexively look away from the angry girl.

"All of you be quiet and pick up the pace," Lotte said, rolling her eyes. "If we don't peel another fifty kilos we'll be locked in here all night. Then we're *all* holding it in."

"Captain," Draco said after a long pause. "I mean no disrespect, but Natalis is right, and his brain hasn't been softened by a year of torture. Our suffering is *entirely* the fault of one person. But this...person," he spat the word, "also has the power to end our torment, and you have the standing to convince her. So I'm asking you once more. Just make her change the name. Please."

"I can't!" Lotte exhaled in frustration. "I've begged her over and over again. The answer is always 'no.' She's stubborn."

Draco rose and attempted to pace despite his manacles. "Are you sure you've tried *everything?*"

"Yes! She just doesn't feel remorse. Or mercy," Lotte said.

"Have you tried offering her..."

"A bribe? I'm too poor."

"Then how about-"

She knew what he was going to say. "Sex? She laughed at me."

"That's horrible! I... I wouldn't have laughed."

"That's very sweet. Now return to peeling, Emreis."

"I've always liked you, you know."

The tips of Taki's ears turned red to hear Draco's words. *Did I just hear some sort of love confession? How loose is the discipline here, anyway?* He reached for another potato and surreptitiously glanced at his captain to see what her reaction might be.

Lotte rolled her eyes. "You've always liked everything with a vagina."

"But yours is special!" Draco stopped, as if forcibly swallowing his own tongue. "Anyway, would you mind undoing my irons?"

"No. That is, I *do* mind."

"Come on, *please?*"

She crossed her arms. "If Natalis hadn't stopped you, you'd have been shot at the gates. Actually, I think they wanted to shoot you anyway but didn't want to hit me...much."

He looked close to tears. "I'll run faster this time. *I promise.*"

"Besides the obvious issue of you dying, I can't just let you desert again."

"Then I have no choice." Draco tossed his half-peeled tuber into the communal pile and resolutely straightened his posture.

"Damn it, Emreis, not again," Lotte groaned.

"I'll save everyone the bullets and off myself right here. Sorry, Lotte, I *really* tried." He gripped the handle of his peeling dirk in both hands and pressed the tip against his throat where it would penetrate the carotid artery. "See you in Hell, Major *Hecaton Kheiris Mezeta!* Goodbye, world!"

He squeezed his eyes shut and his arms tensed. No one heard the door to the room open and close in that instant.

"Don't cut yourself. It dulls the knife," a woman's voice hissed in Draco's ear. His torso was stock-still but his legs began to quiver.

"M-m-major? I uh, didn't realize you were right there, and…"

"If I *really* thought you were about to contaminate my dinner, I'd knock you on your ass, but you don't have the sand to complete the job. Stop preening like an idiot and pay attention."

"All rise and salute, you dogs! There's a flag officer present!" Lotte snapped, and kicked Draco in the shin.

The newly-arrived woman exhaled in disappointment and stepped around him to put a booted foot up on a nearby bench. She lit a hand-rolled cigarette and focused a feline stare on her subordinates. Crow's feet framed a pair of sun-flecked eyes that probed the innermost recesses of whoever she fixed her gaze on without regard for consent.

Strange, Taki thought—when she had accosted him a few weeks ago those golden irises had seemed so enchanting. Now, the silver-haired woman was pushing him to the verge of nervous incontinence.

"H. K. Mezeta: the Hundred Arms of the Mountain," he murmured under his breath.

Hecaton's ears pricked up. "The 'H' is for annihilation."

"But that's not the right spelling," Hadassah said.

"You've got a big mouth for someone who can barely read," Hecaton said.

The redhead fumed with anger and shame.

"Major, do you have *orders* for us?" Lotte asked. It was the captain's role to serve as a buffer between high command and the grunts. That job was doubly important when dealing with this particular major.

Hecaton actually visited her squad in the kitchens on a regular basis, though it seemed that she only did so to gloat. However, she was also tasked with assigning them to missions. Battle orders were a rare and precious event that meant the chance to leave the Cloud Temple and potato duty, at least for a short while. They meant keeping Draco and all the others from suiciding, deserting, or going stir-crazy. War with the Imperium was the best thing to happen to Tirefire the Lesser in a long time.

"Mmm, yep," Hecaton said, and handed a calfskin envelope to Lotte. "Details in the folder. Bottom line is that you infants are on guard duty at the Vergina town armory, and I'm babysitting you. The bigwigs think the Imperium will try to take the stupid rock. Rumors are they'll send their new crop of spetsnaz. What a *stupid* name. Anyway, your job is to spank them and drive them away. Like you would a cat pawing and purring at you in the morning because it's being a little shit."

"Understood, Major. Thank you... And, speaking of cats, how is Babu doing?" After Hecaton's third refusal to change the name of the squad, their mascot privilege had been revoked.

"Don't worry, I'm keeping that useless male fed, but he's become annoying the way he carries on and humps everything with four legs. I know a woman who has a way of dealing with that. She ties a string really tight around the little sack and just leaves it there until everything dries up and falls off."

"How charming." Lotte cast a sideways glance at Draco. "And, one more thing. Considering that my senior corporal just tried to off himself over potato duty, would you consider changing the unit name?"

Hecaton exhaled in annoyance as she regarded the tub of peeled potatoes.

"You lot *are* polaris of the Cloud Temple, are you not? You are inheritors of the power that destroyed the Golden Age of mankind. Each of you is worth an entire *legion* of the regular army. So I'm sure you can handle killing a few potatoes. Look, they don't even shoot back!" She picked one up and crushed it. Starchy gore dribbled between her fingers and spattered on her boots and the floor. "Anyway, haven't you ever considered this as a valuable training opportunity? You should *thank* me for my gift."

She was rewarded with stultified expressions as she departed the room. "You all need to take a good, long, hard look at yourselves in the mirror." The door to the storeroom shut on her words.

"A... gift. This is... a gift?" Draco whispered.

Hadassah raised an eyebrow.

"Should we, uh, report him to the surgeons or something?" she asked.

Lotte's open palm smacked into Draco's face with a resounding crack before she crossed her arms.

"Draco Emreis, why *shouldn't* I have you lobotomized for that?" She pierced him with a glare. He guffawed, rubbing a hand over the welt on his cheek.

"I, ah, wouldn't be a useful member of the squad, then. You know, you need your brain to strategize, right? I reason it's all or nothing. Either all my brains are in my skull or they're on the floor. Besides, it's all fine now, we're finally getting some action! And more importantly, getting out of this place!"

"So basically you're saying," began Hadassah sagely, before windmilling her arms. "*Oh GAWD! I'm an angry little zit and when things don't go my way I'll spray you all with my disgusting body fluids!*"

"Shut it!"

"She's *right*," Lotte said. "How do you think that selfish little outburst made us feel? Made *me* feel?"

Taki's knees weakened. At this point he would have gladly taken a week of peeling in silence over this. There was nothing in the world he hated more than witnessing an argument or a scolding. Such displays had always made him feel embarrassed by proxy.

"My apologies, ma'am!" Draco said, saluting. "But admit it, this really sucks! I mean, more than a year on punishment detail over the name of our squad? It's all the major's fault. We're all laughingstocks of the Temple. I can't get a date to save my life! I mean, I'm a *man* and I have *needs*, and when we can't even get leave to go to the brothel what am I supposed to do?"

"Deal with it!" Hadassah said. "You think the captain and I are doing any better? I'm completely unmarriageable at this point."

"You can't get married because you're a nutty mutant."

"Rotten asshole! Tie a string around your nuts!"

Taki started to smirk at their exchange, but a glance at Lotte quickly squelched his mirth. His captain was silent, but the look in her eyes sent fear coursing down into his nether regions. In the academy, instructors had tried to teach him how to read bodily cues to better assess an enemy. Though he had forgotten most of it, he remembered that another human's willingness to kill was never subtle. *She's going to murder them,* he realized. *Their antics have driven her mad and now she's going to stab Emreis in the throat, break the loudmouthed girl's neck, and put a round in my gut. It's not fair. My career's just beginning. I've never been kissed!*

"Oh, Emreis! How did you find out what the major's full name was? I just knew her as 'H. K.' and thought that was it," Taki blurted out, blatantly trying to change the subject. Draco seemed the type who liked to show off his knowledge. *And my godrotting life depends on it.*

"Ah, well, I wish I could say it was the result of great planning, but it was actually spontaneous. I snooped around in her office a bit when I came to deliver her meal and she wasn't there." Draco cracked a grin at his own derring-do and blew smoke away from an imaginary pistol.

"That's *illegal,* Corporal." Lotte sighed. The wild-eyed despair Taki had seen in her features seemed to have vanished. His knees buckled as the tension left his body.

"Well, it's not like I could read much," Draco said. "Most of what she keeps laying around is written in this weird squiggly text, not even pictograms like the Chung-Kuo use. But in any case, I saw some documents from the exarch addressed to her and they had 'Hecaton Kheiris' on them."

"For all you know, that's a fake name. She's never told me that, and I've known her the longest."

"You say that like it's a point of pride, Captain."

"Shush."

"Maybe her name really is, like, 'Hannihilation' or something? Wouldn't put it past her," Hadassah said, sucking her teeth. Her earlier spat seemed to have been forgotten as easily as it had started.

"How long have you known her, Captain?" Taki asked.

"Two years, so far," Lotte said. "The others, only a year."

"Oh God, and what a time it was. I came in as a private and got promoted to root vegetable," Draco said.

"And what a greasy latke you'd make!" Hadassah chuckled. "Dumbass, you can't even cook."

2

Deep in the heartland of the Osterbrand Imperium, the last traces of spring were dying beautifully around Lucatiel von Halcon. As she made her way up a winding trail hewn from the exposed slate of a mountainside, the air tasted more and more like nectar, and pink cherry blossom petals fluttered through the air to litter the stones around her. And yet, all of this elegance only provoked a familiar pang of dread.

"Those damnable trees are in bloom again." Her older brother spoke her thoughts even as she formed them.

"I still curse them every season," Lucatiel said, pleased. Such occurrences affirmed their bond, just like the softened noses and charcoal-black hair inherited from long-forgotten parents. It was a secret point of pride for her that even their scars were well-matched.

"I'm told that the citizens love it."

"But they were never made to clean every single petal off the ground," she said. Lucatiel brushed a silky fleck from between the cinches of a sleeve and watched it fall to the ground. She fought the urge to snatch it from the air along with its numerous brethren. They were no longer the old man's property, she reminded herself.

"Why *did* he ever do that to us in the first place?"

"To teach us the importance of small details, of course," she replied, poking her brother in the arm to show how aghast she was. "The little things always change the course of battle. You *should* remember that."

He smiled and patted her on the shoulder. "My apologies. I was simply complaining for its own sake."

"Don't complain too loudly, dear brother. We owe *Ba'gshnar* everything. Our lives, our skill, our commissions. The very fact that we can be together," she said, shaking off the thought of separation like an evil aura.

"Yes, I know full well how much he has done for us, and I will always be grateful. That is why I look forward to seeing him again. Even when I remember all the times he punished us for silly reasons."

"To be fair, you *were* quite rebellious. It's a wonder he never outright strangled you, especially after you tried to desert that one time."

Her brother laughed. "You don't know it, but after I got back, the old man made me rub his smelly feet for days on end. I'd take a strangling over that, any time."

Lucatiel giggled before stopping to look up at the gentle drizzle of pink and white from the treeline above. "I know it may sound like betrayal, but after that damned desert I'm even glad to see the blossoms falling. I feel like I can finally appreciate their beauty."

With thoughtless grace, she ran a hand through her hair to dislodge small shards of color. They floated gently to the ground, joining the others to accumulate like clouds of fluffy pink. Her brother held his breath while he watched her, before obviously averting his gaze. Lucatiel did not mind, however. His praise and attention were fair recompense for the protection she provided him.

"I've said it before, but it's good to have hair again, and to see yours, Luca," he said, extending his hand to her.

She took his hand in hers and gently kissed it before intertwining their fingers together and drawing closer to his side. The two progressed up the steps hand in hand and reached the top of their ascent. They passed under a gate of crudely hewn cedar within a copse of fragrant pine, and returned to the place they had left a year ago.

The bihara was a study in color for all who entered. Lush green from the forest canopy gave way to brilliant hues of pink and white from the cherry trees outlining a path to the interior. A cluster of yurts maintained vigil in the center, outwardly crude in appearance but meant to withstand any temblor or misdirected sutra. Construction of the entire complex had been directly authorized and funded by the padishah, the king of all kings and supreme ruler of the Osterbrand Imperium. It was an uncontested crucible of martial power, where the absolute best of the Imperium's deadliest warriors received their training.

The von Halcons were among this cadre and knew little other way to live. They had spent their early childhoods within the high-walled fortress of Sheol, where blood and iron were pillars of life. Because the siblings had showed the signs of control over prana, life had constantly alternated between grueling days spent chained up in the lectorium, frenzied spars against their comrades, and countless hours of suffocating darkness and silence within sensory deprivation tanks. By the time they had been selected for the bihara, they had thought it odd to not be confined to sterile cells at night.

"Strange."

Lucatiel blinked. "Aslatiel, what perturbs you?"

"It's just that morning meditation isn't usually held inside…"

Lucatiel's mouth opened to respond, when she saw someone's foot swing toward the back of her brother's head. Every prana gate in her body flew open and energy surged through her consciousness. She brought up a fist reinforced with enough power to obliterate a suit of plate and aimed to intercept her brother's attacker. Then, she abruptly stopped. The greeting hadn't been meant for her.

Aslatiel ducked the roundhouse, whirled, and slammed an open palm into the acolyte who had attacked him. The boy flew back a few meters and landed, barely-conscious, in a dusty heap. Aslatiel dodged an overhead strike from another assailant and answered with a snap-kick to the girl's thigh right where her tunic ended. To Lucatiel's relief, her brother had been careful to not to shatter the trainee's vulnerable knee. Leaving a major joint unguarded was a rookie mistake and one the girl would have to learn from. The acolyte collapsed on the temporarily useless limb before rolling away to recover. A third tried to grapple her brother from behind received a nasty throw in compensation.

A dozen acolytes now circled Aslatiel with longswords and spears. In the bihara, there were no dummy weapons: all steel was sharpened and oiled for battle. Aslatiel reached to his scabbard and drew his kriegsmesser to face the onslaught. The curved blade was not a weapon suited for restraint, but it was the only steel he had on his person.

"*Ba'gshnar*, the cherries are especially annoying this year." Lucatiel turned her head and flashed a brilliant, sapphire-eyed smile at the old man next to her. She'd only now detected his presence, but was positive that he'd been watching the fight alongside her from the very beginning.

"Be careful how you talk about my favorite trees, or I might make you join the others and sweep them up again," the man retorted, although not unkindly. Short-statured in comparison to most, he nevertheless radiated a serene and absolute power from every aspect of his being. He wore a mane of thick, gray-white hair gathered in a loose tail, a patch over a long-lost right eye, and no other ornamentation to identify his origins. He was called *Ba'gshnar* by his students, and Chronicler by everyone else. It was he who had built the bihara in the first place and trained all of its students.

No one knew where Chronicler was from or why he had volunteered his service to the Imperium, and he had never deigned to answer those questions. What was indisputable, however, was the fact that because of him, the spetsnaz evoked all-consuming terror with the mere whisper of their name. Chronicler answered only to the padishah, and only when he felt like doing so.

"For you, Lord, I would sweep the courtyard with gratitude, a thousand times for a thousand seasons," Lucatiel countered, batting her eyelashes innocently as she leaned toward him.

"You sound like the worst love ballad, played on the saddest lute, sung by the drunkest student in Nova Muscova," Chronicler snorted as he flicked her dismissively on the forehead. "Come back and try to be flirty with me when you've read some more Li Po."

"I prefer Master Kong."

"Kongzi was a humorless hack. Whenever I read the Analects I feel like he's stepping on my neck. Figures that you'd like his work."

"Well, I just can't respect a poet who drowned himself trying to grasp the moon's reflection," Lucatiel said, crossing her arms as she pouted.

"Oh? Is that not hypocrisy on your part, Lucatiel van Halcon? Don't you still find yourself reaching for a beautiful illusion despite not knowing how to swim?" Chronicler fixed a knowing look at Aslatiel, and then at Lucatiel. She averted her eyes, bile rising in her throat.

"But I *do* know, *Ba'gshnar*. You taught me everything I needed to know to survive," she muttered.

"Just to clarify, I was speaking metaphorically," he said, gently winking at her.

"*I know that!*" She balled her hands into fists and scrunched her brow.

With a fluid rotation of his hips, Chronicler pivoted on the balls of his feet and nonchalantly intercepted a downward heel strike aimed at where his neck joined his shoulder. The old, one-eyed man's perpetual smirk widened as he faced his attacker. Bruised and battered acolytes lay scattered on a circle in the courtyard, most barely conscious. A small minority struggled vainly to their knees.

"I was wondering when you'd come to help your dear little sister," Chronicler said. He peered at the heel of Aslatiel's boot, and gingerly pushed the protruding, spring-loaded blade back into its slot in the heel.

"Don't you think you've rattled her enough?" Aslatiel shifted to maintain his balance. If he were at all fazed by having his leg in the old man's iron grip, he did not show it.

"Perhaps. However now that you are officers of Alfa Gruppe," Chronicler said, tapping the maroon cherry blossom emblazoned on his former student's shoulder, "you cannot always rely on each other. I have always, always told you that one day, you will be separated from each other." The old master let go of Aslatiel's foot and slowly shifted his stance to invite open combat. "Lucatiel can take care of herself. That is why I did not risk my students attacking her. However, I worry about *you* sometimes. Now come, strike me!"

His expression grim, Aslatiel drew his blade again and assumed a menacing high guard stance. Air rippled around him, and like shadows fleeing the dawn, the grains of sand at his feet scattered before his aura. As he swung at Chronicler's head, thunder roared in from the sky.

And just as abruptly as it had begun, the fight was over. Chronicler nonchalantly brushed a speck of blood—Aslatiel's—off of his cheek and stretched.

"Aslatych!" Lucatiel swore under her breath as she ran over to her brother's dusty, supine form and knelt by his head to cradle it.

He groaned in response, his features a picture more of disappointment than pain. "Luca, I'm fine. I swear to the padishah. You don't have to act like I'm dying or anything." He chuckled and turned his head to spit a wad of brown-speckled mucus into the dirt.

"I know, but..." Lucatiel grit her teeth. "Do not resist me. You breathe like you've broken a rib."

Before her brother could object, she had already placed her palm over a deformity on the left side of his chest below his armpit. All of Chronicler's disciples were instructed to visualize the energy within their bodies as a flow of clear, glowing water, and the major prana gates of the body as valves running alongside arteries and veins. Her brain was the wellspring, and her heart provided the driving force. She reduced the flow going to

Bryan Choi & Erica Carson

her other extremities, and opened the gate to her right arm. Droplets of prana began to form at her fingertips like sweat, and she willed them to seep into her brother's wounded firmament and quench the fire of pain that raged from fractured rib and bleeding muscle. Only a little was needed, for Aslatiel would eventually block hers out of his desire to not see her waste resources. She pulled her hand away, and opened the rest of her gates, feeling whole again.

"Thank you, Luca," he said, patting her cheek. "It'll take a little time to heal, but at least I won't fall to a catarrh now."

Lucatiel flushed despite her best efforts to stay cool.

"Ahem." Chronicler cleared his throat as he dusted off his jacket. "Aslatiel, you need to meditate more often—only then will you be able to shake off the mind's limits and join the all-awareness. I could predict every single one of your strikes, whereas you could only predict a minority of mine. I thank you, though, for not killing or maiming my students. Some of them might serve you later."

"I live to serve, *Ba'gshnar*." Aslatiel rose to his feet and managed a stiff bow.

"You made well of yourselves during that little spat in the Caliphate. But while you sailed back here, we finally declared on the Argeads. The first strike in the campaign will be at their citadel, Vergina, at the northern border. It's a taxation point more than anything else, but well-guarded and a visible show of strength for the Dominion. Take it for the glory of the Imperium."

"Yes, Milord, but I am afraid our company lacks for numbers."

"Which is why I will accompany you, along with a legion of janissaries. After our triumph, Alfa's future will be assured, and you will never lack for eager men and women willing to die under the banner."

"*Ba'gshnar*, I'm so happy! You'll finally see us on the battlefield." Lucatiel said.

"We will carry out our duty to the fullest extent of our abilities," Aslatiel said with a note of finality.

Chronicler gave them a sideways look, deepening the lines of his already craggy features. "Then why do you still tarry here? Go forth, and kill."

23

3

In grudging acknowledgment of their upcoming battle and probable agonizing deaths in the service of the Dominion, the most unfortunate squad in the Cloud Temple was free from the kitchens for a day. To celebrate, Lotte permitted them to sleep late in their quarters as long as everyone made muster by the end of morning watch. Having been so used to getting up by the end of middle watch, however, no one found themselves able to sleep for that long. Before the sun could crest the horizon, the ready room was a bustle of groggy activity born out of habit.

Temple barracks were a squalid affair, with the most common arrangement a communal living space ringed by sleeping cells and a small powder room with latrine. The spaces were cramped and there was no way to change, bathe, or eliminate in privacy. There had been concerns in the past about the behavior this would incite in squadrons of young men and women, but reality was different. There was only so much living together that one could tolerate before temptresses and bravos became unpalatable to each other.

Taki sat at the ancient wooden spool table in the center of the ready room, nibbling on the end of his quill while jotting down and appending notes on a ledger. To his displeasure, he noted that the nib was starting to curl, which would soon render it useless. He would have to get another soon, and even the lowest-grade nibs carved from plastic were overpriced. *The most plentiful remains of the Golden Age of Man, and they're really just the droppings,* Taki thought to himself. Plastic had neither the strength of metal nor the density of wood, and was mostly unsuitable for use in crafting. However, its one redeeming quality was that it could be found nearly everywhere, and often in great quantities.

Next to Taki, Draco carefully trimmed back stubble with a greased stiletto stropped to a razor's edge. In his free hand was a much higher-grade relic: a small circle of flawlessly reflective mirror. Taki wondered who Draco had killed to acquire such a piece, but quickly chastised himself for covetousness. When Draco wasn't speaking, it was easy to mistake the senior corporal for some sort of mythic prince with his flowing gold hair, high cheekbones, virile jaw, and broad shoulders. Taki, on the other hand, could never manage so much as a credible mustache let alone an authentic combat beard. Before his envy could crest further, the boy caught sight of the manacles still around Draco's ankles and decided he was probably better off overall.

"Already working on that, Natalis? How diligent you are!" Lotte said, peering over his shoulder while she cleaned her teeth with a pick and cloth. Taki turned to reply, only to blush and shrink when he realized she wore nothing but her smallclothes. She raised an eyebrow in confusion but quickly realized the reason for his consternation. "Ah, I've forgotten how cloistered the academy was," she said, and withdrew to finish her morning toilet.

"Still embarrassed by boobs?" Draco asked with surprising compassion. "No worries, it's natural when you're so fresh out of that monastery. But I promise you'll grow jaded at the sight of those two. Now, *my* perfect, chiseled body on the other hand..."

"No one wants to see *you* in the buff," Hadassah said, plopping down at the table. Draco snorted. Taki remained uncomfortably quiet, trying to concentrate on the ledger. Miffed that he paid no attention to her, Hadassah's lips curled into a devilish smirk. "Hey, Newboy, you want me to make the captain have an 'accident'? So you can see what you wanna see?"

"Don't bully him." Draco flicked her ear.

"Ow! Shithead."

"An accident? Oh my, it simply wouldn't do to have a cute girl like you dunked in the *latrine!*" Lotte said as she returned fully dressed. Hadassah vehemently shook her head in protest of her innocence. "Well, Natalis, what do our stores look like? I haven't seen our books for months."

Taki sighed, glad the subject had shifted back to work. He decided not to ask her why she had abandoned all responsibility of the squad's finances. Perhaps, he mused, that was the real reason the major had been so keen to recruit him. He had learned to read, write, and factor before entering the academy, making him a rarity among the mostly unlettered lower ranks. Hence, he was the unit's purser from now until his death.

"Since the squad hasn't been active for the last year, we have a goodly amount. Sixty rounds of old Nayto, thirty-five Sovietskij Rimmed, eighty-five Luger, and fifty Murrikanian ACP, all virgin pre-war surplus. There's an abundance of common dirty rounds for our use as well. We also have around a kilogram of loose powder and three kilograms of minie ball of various sizes," he recited.

"That's a lot of ammo," Draco said, greed glinting in his eyes.

"Yeah, we could buy the exarch's tower with that. Or eat bacon every day forever!" Hadassah said.

"I thought you were a Jewess."

"I told you before, I don't do the whole *kashrut* thing."

Draco shot her a dirty look.

"I'm obligated by the Hoplite's Code to remind everyone that the less we shoot, the more we end up getting back in our pay," Lotte said. Inhabitants of the Temple had a few privileges that levy troops of Dominion nobility did not. "Of course, I expect you to shoot as much as necessary to accomplish your mission. Anyone holding their fire just because you want to hoard is going to catch a beating."

"Emreis, your pistol uses black powder, so I'm giving you a hundred grams and thirty-six balls for this," Taki said, marking down ammunition assignments for the group. "Captain, you will get your standard combat load of twenty-eight Murrikanians. Mikkelsen, you get twenty rounds for your Nagant and sixteen Luger for your pistol. Finally, I will take thirty rounds of old Nayto."

"Make sure my rounds are flat-nosed for use on infidels," Hadassah said.

Lotte ignored her. "Make sure you control your trigger finger, Natalis. Old Nayto is expensive, and you're only being allowed to fire it because your gun uses naught else."

"I will, Captain. I can throw wind and fire instead, and if nothing else I can handle a sword," Taki said. Like any Cloud Temple initiate, he had been compelled to prove proficiency with sword, pike, and crossbow before being awarded expensive and dangerous training with firearms.

"And remember, everyone, we're not the sole company responsible for guarding the fort. It has its own men at arms, and the river overlook is constantly patrolled by carronade barges. We're merely there to shore up defense in case the regulars are overwhelmed. Plus, we have the major."

"I don't know if that's a plus," Draco said. He lamented that he could not spit in their quarters.

"I'm surprised I didn't have to account for any ammunition for her," Taki said. "Actually, come to think of it, she doesn't really use a firelock in general, does she? Does she have any weapons?"

"Have you seen her fight? She doesn't need to use any ammo," Hadassah said, shaking her finger at him. "If you haven't seen what the major can do with lightning, you're missing out. No one else can do that, not even the exarch."

"Dassa's not japing with you for once, Natalis," Draco said. "If you see the major get annoyed, you'd best run in the opposite direction."

"I'd prefer *not* to see her do that ever again," Lotte said, shaking her head.

"Indeed," Draco sighed. "I'd rather face a horde of rapey landsknecht."

"Like the ones that tried to jump the major as she was taking a shit," Hadassah said.

"Mikkelsen, you're talking about our flag officer here," Lotte warned.

Hadassah blinked in feigned innocence. "But Captain, I'm pretty sure she has an asshole, and possibly lady-parts."

Lotte replied by sharply rapping the girl's head with her knuckles.

"Sorry, I don't follow any of you," Taki said. "What did the major do to those Ursalans?"

"Okay, ever seen a guy just...go *plorp*?" Hadassah said excitedly, miming an explosion with her hands.

"What?"

"I had this Kingdom asshole lined up in my sights, and all of a sudden, *zap!* Pink mist, smell of burnt leather everywhere. It was awesome as hell! Anyway, the old hag's a pain, but she'll kill everything that moves. Including you, Newboy."

Taki raised an eyebrow and decided to abandon further inquiry.

"Captain, we're going to be facing something more than the usual Imperial harassment unit, though. Didn't the major talk about them using spetsnaz?" asked Draco.

"She did," Lotte said. "And they are a formidable enemy, too. They've got stronger armor, harder steel, more guns, and better bullets than we ever will. But we have the backing of righteousness in our actions. The Imperium is overreaching, and they will realize that once we reach in and pull out their entrails. Still, though, all of you be cautious…and don't hoard all of your *good* bullets," she said, patting Hadassah's knee.

"Let's get to the shrine and get our ammo, then. I haven't had a chance to hold my iron lady in a while. This'll be fun," Draco said. Jauntily, he pushed the door of the ready room open and stepped into the cloudbank outside just as the first rays of sunlight pierced the horizon.

Taki's pupils constricted too late as a stray sunbeam hit his face and turned his world searing white. The same thing had happened to him years ago, right after he had crossed the threshold of the Cloud Temple for the first time in his life.

The men who had retrieved him from the orphanage had called themselves "polaris," and had told young Taki that he would also become one if he survived the trials ahead. Though the Temple was far away it was always watching out for children like him, who had caused the ruinous events known as the Gotterdammerung, or more colloquially, the Fall. It was the Fall that was responsible for every malady of the present day, where scores fell to the sword or starved to death in the uncaring shadows of ancient, crumbling skyscrapers. The knowledge and progress of the old world had been mostly forgotten, except this time everyone knew who was to blame.

Taki's ancestors had racked up such a burden of sin that even eight centuries later, he was hellbound the moment he'd exited the womb. His only chance to escape eternal damnation was to serve the basileus of the Dominion as a soldier, and never leave the Temple without the permission of a lord of the realm. When Taki had asked the men how he had been noticed, they had been surprisingly honest. The presbyter had noticed the boy's propensity to set fires without the aid of flint and steel. Taki was lucky, they had said. A more ignorant guardian might have had him drowned.

After making their way on horseback for what seemed like countless leagues, the two escorts and their unwitting charge had joined a larger group of children and chaperones. Some had worn manacles, while others had seemed to journey of their own volition. A few of the youngsters had died on the ensuing march and the subsequent hike up a frozen mountain road, but Taki had survived to stand before the gates. He had stared mutely up at the high concrete walls emblazoned with dire warnings against unlawful transit, and had realized there was no going back to life as a human. Still, he had reflexively taken a look behind him, just to make sure.

And the sun chastened me for doing so, Taki reflected as he rubbed his eyes to drive out the floating purple afterimages clouding his vision. *But I'm about to go on a mission, so why am I being punished now? This had better not be an omen.*

Draco whistled as he jogged down ancient stone steps and through claustrophobic alleyways and thin overpasses with his companions in tow. The Cloud Temple had little space to spread laterally and so expanded vertically for the most part. No one was quite sure how old the fortress was. Everything seemed to have been built atop something else which was built atop ruins which were built on yet more ruins. Alleyways led to nowhere and staircases could simply stop in midair to drop an unfortunate into a hell of nonsensical geometry. Rails and pipes haphazardly jutted throughout, useless as handholds but always a threat to unwary heads. It was rumored that the chaos was deliberate. Another form of training. Eventually, the squad reached the pockmarked armory shrine in the center of the complex.

Besides the exarch's tower, it was one of the most secure places in Argead territory, and for good reason. Behind a gargoyled stone facade were the accumulated arms and ammunition of the Temple. Swords and spears were common and available, but the shrine's true role was to safeguard and venerate the Dominion's stockpile of ancient guns, and the valuable ammunition that fed them. Far from the heavy and untrustworthy arquebuses in common use by peasant levies and mercenaries, Temple Guns were elegant, irreplaceable relics from a glorious age subsumed by fire. Inimitably fine engravings of archaic characters and symbols on unblemished steel spoke to their puissance in the hands of those worthy to wield them. The loss of a Temple Gun was always a calamitous occasion, and merited funeral rites more lavish than any given to its bearer.

The shrine was quiet that day, for most of the other fighting companies were out on assignment. War with the eastern horde was on everyone's mind, but so far there had been no battles of note. Taki took a moment to marvel at how spacious the nave seemed on the inside. Besides his squad, there was only a bow-legged old man scooting around on his hands and knees scraping candle drippings off the floor.

"In God's name, who let you idiots out of the kitchen?" asked a craggy-featured neokoros behind a templon of wrought and gilded iron. Draco sneered at him.

"We handle your food, you ass. Are you sure you should be giving us lip?"

"If I ever get the shits, I'm hunting you down. Make your withdrawal and get out."

"Here." Draco handed over a requisition Taki had drafted earlier. "And if you can't understand the funny-looking symbols, young Natalis here will help you out, so don't be afraid to ask questions, mmkay?"

"Blaspheming scum. Wait here and keep your filthy hands off my counter."

"He's on friggin' *fire* today," Hadassah whispered to Lotte, scrunching her brow in disdain.

"You were really concerned about him, weren't you?" Lotte winked back at her.

"Don't make me say it. That'll just pad his ego."

A few minutes later, the neokoros emerged from the vaults, carrying drab gray sacks. They clinked dully when he tossed them into a shallow trough underneath the templon so the squad could take them. Draco opened the sacks and showed their contents to Taki, whose nimble fingers sorted over the ammunition to make sure the squad wasn't being cheated.

The unfired military-grade surplus made before the Fall, or milligrad, was what really attracted everyone's attention. It was instantly recognizable by the gorgeous copper plating of the bullets, the seductively dusky brass of the casings, and the mysterious scripts and symbols stamped too finely for any workshop to duplicate. Fired from Temple Guns, they were unfailingly accurate and able to pierce most armor, even the plate worn by Imperial kataphracts. The very properties that made them so valuable in combat, however, fostered their use as currency. A nine millimeter round could buy a feast, and a rifle cartridge could pay for a month of lodging in the capital. Every round fired increased the value of the others. At the current rate of deflation, war seemed almost illogical.

Therefore, most people who shot at each other for a living used "dirty" reloaded ammunition instead. Reloading was the process of remaking cartridges by pouring powder into shell casings and seating a metal bullet on top with a press or mallet. Lethality was questionable as was accuracy, and any given round could simply blow a gun to pieces instead of fire. Worst of all, reloads produced a thick, acrid smoke that was the natural consequence of using black powder as their propellant. The most dangerous specimens were made of tin casings with rounded pebbles substituted for bullets. The best quality were brass-cased half-grad with lead projectiles and cordite propellant. Most reloads tended to fall in between, and producing these cartridges was mostly a cottage industry controlled by local ordinance exchange guilds. Good reloads tended to have high intrinsic value and could be easily traded for milligrad. In reality, they were the most widely used currency in the land.

"It looks like everything's in order," Taki said, satisfied that the actual counts matched with the list he had drawn up. "Since this is a dangerous patrol, everyone gets mostly 'grad."

"That's our boy!" Draco said happily. "I know your career's in the jacks right now, but we certainly appreciate the abacus in your head. These assholes will skim you blind if you're not careful," he said, gesturing to the sexton behind the bars, who glowered silently back. "You know, a Luger here, a double-deuce there…"

"Corporal…" Lotte warned him.

"But can't you read too, Emreis?" Taki said, putting the cartridges back into the sacks.

"I can read most things, but I never learned to write or factor," Draco said.

Taki rocked back and forth on his heels. "Do you…do you want me to teach you at some point?"

"Dassa and I would be obliged, so long as you don't try to do it like at the academy. I'm a bit tired of smacks on the head."

"I'm done with school," Hadassah said.

"Quiet, you," Draco huffed. "Education is important. If you become smarter, maybe you'll find the secret of smokeless powder, make a mountain of milligrad, and live in a castle."

"Don't make me laugh," Hadassah said. "Even little kids know that you'd need to find the azoth for that to happen."

"But the histories say that everyone and their mother had 'grad in abundance. Surely we'd have unearthed a friggin' azoth by now if it one was *truly* necessary. It can't be *that* hard to make powder smokeless!"

"Says you. You're not an alchemist."

Draco put his hands on his hips. "I'm a *historian.*"

"You and your delusions," Hadassah scoffed, crossing her arms. "You'd be luckier with women if you thought about something useful, like why it takes so many stupid bullets to buy feta."

"Maybe you'd be richer if you weren't a cheese-eating heretic."

"Break it up," Lotte said, separating the two. "We're wasting our precious liberty here. Emreis, you come with me to go get our guns from the sanctuary. Natalis, Mikkelsen, go buy meat and bread. You can also buy some cheese and herbs if you like. And...and eggs. It should go without saying, but *absolutely* no potatoes."

"Yes, Captain!" they said, dispersing.

"Come with me, I know where we can get a good deal," Hadassah said, grabbing Taki by the hand. As she did so, he could not help but blush. Like most fighters who'd survived their share of battle, Hadassah possessed a multitude of scars. Lotte had more, including one that went from her hairline to her jaw. But for Taki, the fact that they were women was more than enough to drive him to shyness. And then there was Hecaton Mezeta. She was old enough to be his grandmother, possibly his *great* grandmother, and yet it was her that had convinced him to take the plunge based on merely her *voice.*

He was convinced of it now: too much time spent studying had permanently scrambled his libido. If he survived the battle to come, he'd go to the nearest cathouse and relieve himself of a specific, shameful burden that he alone seemed to carry. For that, he would have to start saving his milligrad. Taki smiled to himself. If nothing else, he could solve his problems through budgeting.

They left the next morning, bellies still full from a feast devoid of hated tubers. The path leading down the mountain from the Temple wound long and treacherously, but all polaris who survived their training were virtually guaranteed to be sure of foot. Before long they had made it to the first neighboring hub of civilization in the foothills, a small blotch of a village that provided services the exarch would not allow within his walls.

Draco and Taki began to stare longingly at the wooden brothel signs until Lotte dragged them both away by the ear and forced them into the busy caravan line leaving town. The northern border of the Dominion was days away, and the time was spent alternating between the crushing boredom of safe travel on well-frequented roads and the unwelcome tension of keeping vigil while traversing hinterlands infested with altered beasts and bandits. Though the others did not seem to mind or care, Taki noticed that at no time was the major with them during the journey. When he asked Lotte about it, the captain merely shrugged.

"Keep your sword sharp for when we get there," she admonished him, leaving him to wonder about the old woman.

* * * *

The Vergina town armory overlooked a bend in the river of the same name, and was an otherwise unassuming-looking structure: a large conical keep topped with a red dome and surrounded by a thick stone shell. At night, its otherwise monotonous face was punctuated by pinpricks of torchlight emitted from arrow slits. The fortified main gate faced landward and overlooked an ancient paved road through which it could receive shipments. A small town had sprung up around its barbican, a free-standing cannon tower which could send concentrated fire up to a kilometer away. Assaulting from land was futile. However, the keep's riverward entrances were accessible by a short climb up some stairs from the docks. The weak defense was shored up by the Dominion navy in the form of heavy-hitting lorchas. One always trolled the river, ready to rain canister shot and scrap-metal bombs on any invasion force approaching from the Imperium-held shore.

Taki shifted uncomfortably in place as he maintained stiff-backed attention behind Lotte, who was having a shouting match with the castellan. Usually, a junior officer would serve as captain's adjutant, but the squad had no other officers besides the major, and Hecaton had gone and faffed off to the grog stores as soon as they had crossed the keep's threshold. Thus, Taki had accompanied his commander into the office while the others stood guard outside. He had thought it a good sign, until matters promptly deteriorated.

He could tell that Lotte was expending great effort to keep herself from dashing her chair against the wall and possibly someone's head. Underneath that cool, sisterly exterior, Taki had seen hints of a temper that rivaled any he had ever seen in his life. *She'd have actually killed us back there in the kitchen.* In front of the castellan, however, his captain was doing an admirable job of holding back her rage. Threatening to choke the man on his own entrails would only endanger whatever cooperation the squad could eke out from the garrison. If the locals all decided to turn their backs to the polaris, or even worse, sabotage their efforts, securing the place from assault would become much harder.

"Look, honey," the castellan fumed, "the thing is this place always gets a lot of threats. If it isn't the Imperium about to send a destroyer upriver or the entire Ursalan Crusade just over the hill, it's dire warnings about the plague or locusts or mutants or what have you."

You lazy, impious ass, Taki thought. *It's your job to be anxious about those things. Haven't you sworn an oath of fealty to your lord? I'd do a better job if I had your rank.*

"First, it's 'captain,' and second, we were warned by a prime intelligence dispatch," Lotte said. "Do I have to tell you how many of our brothers and sisters probably died for this information? This is different from all of the rumors and old wives' tales you deal with every day. After all, why in God's name would they call us out here?"

"Eh, you're not the first tainted ones to visit. Bottom line is, we have a budget and a way of doing things. I'm not going to make the entire garrison stay up without rest and shoot at every shadow and scurrying rat because of some dispatch. The men get pissed off, I have to shut them up by opening the grog stores, and the baron gets pissed when I ask him for reimbursement. I mean, look out there! There's nothing on the riverbank, and we've got sentries around and the navy trolling the waters. I'll sound the alarm if we see anything. You're free to skulk around if you wish, but don't agitate the men or I'll have you witches thrown out."

Lotte's right cheek twitched at the term. It was common among the populace and especially used by Dominion regulars. Polaris had originally been given the task of quelling twisted beasts roaming the countryside and extinguishing dangerous elemental phenomena that tended to arise wherever a battle of the Gotterdammerung had taken place. Though they had excelled at these tasks, nothing could erase the fact that they were still the legacy of the abominations that had plunged the world into holocaust. Using their talents against their fellow man only cemented their reputation as pariahs.

"We will fulfill our duty, *sirrah*. Thank you for your cooperation," she said, rising from her chair. She cocked her head at Taki. They were done here. As she turned, the castellan craned his head to try to glimpse the underside of her buttocks past her lamellar skirt. Taki shot him a warning look before exiting himself. Draco and Hadassah saluted as the pair emerged.

"Where's the major?" Lotte asked, returning their salutes.

"No sign. Probably drinking this place dry and shitting in the river," Draco said. "Don't get me wrong, though. Her absence is a good thing, when you think about it."

Lotte nodded. "We're getting scraps at best. Mostly that the garrison continues to sleep and those on night watch won't attack us for looking around. But perhaps that's for the best. Jumpy soldiers mean accidents. Everyone, have your full kit accessible at all times. Mikkelsen, you're up on the roof with Emreis. Natalis and I will do sweeps of the lower levels including the gates. No point in using a voice sutra here, it's too cloistered. If you see anything, just start shooting."

"Heh, race to the top, you big lump?" Hadassah prodded Draco, who grunted imperiously in response before bolting down the stairs in a head start. Miffed at his quickness, the redhead started after him and disappeared around a bend in the stone halls.

"Let's go," Lotte said.

"Of course...Captain," Taki said. He glumly readjusted the leather sling of his carbine to ease a growing ache in his shoulder.

"Something the matter, Corporal?" she asked, picking up the troubled expression he unsuccessfully tried to hide. For a moment, Taki considered lying to her with a simple denial, but squelched the thought.

"I... Captain, don't you actually rank on par with that castellan?"

Lotte shrugged. "We don't answer to the same lord, but I suppose I do. Why do you ask?"

"I was surprised by his...um, disrespect? If I'd addressed you or the Major like that, I know I'd be flogged or stuffed in the brig at least."

"Oh? Do you regret that you can't talk to us in the same fashion?"

"What? I... *No!*" Taki protested, his eyes widening.

Lotte chuckled. "Sorry, I shouldn't tease. I keep forgetting that this is your first mission. About the castellan, did you grow up around soldiers before you were taken?" she asked.

"No, I didn't."

"Did you notice, Corporal, how Mikkelsen and I are the only women you've seen here wearing any sort of combat kit?"

Taki frowned. What she said was true. They had seen many women in and around the garrison, but they had all been scullions or maids. He had also seen a knight's entourage in passing, and with them the man's wife on a palanquin, but the squires had all been men. He nodded to Lotte.

"Our kind are rare enough, so that's why we have boys and girls recruited into the academy. But the basileus and his vassals don't allow women to take up arms otherwise, so men like him aren't used to seeing someone like me with a captain's braid. If you hadn't been around many fighters beforehand, you wouldn't know that," she continued.

"But shouldn't they respect the rank?"

Lotte smiled sadly.

"You're very young, Natalis. I hope I get to see you grow up. Now, come along, we're wasting time here."

With one hand, she grasped the leather-wrapped hilt of the zweihander leaning against the wall and effortlessly hefted it to rest on her shoulder. Forged from the steel found in old-world leaf springs, it was as tall as she was from pommel to point. It also weighed enough to prevent Taki from lifting it off the ground, much less swinging it. The blade was as thick as a man's thumb and wide as a palm. A blow from such a weapon would crush as much as sever.

The other arm she slung into the loops of a round greatshield. Hers was constructed of split wood laminate embossed with a layer of precious ancient aramid and then sealed behind riveted steel plate. The metal was engraved with a sun wearing a confused expression that was probably meant to be haughtily serene. It weighed nearly as much as her sword, and was thick enough that she would die of old age before most weaponry could penetrate it.

Her load was impossibly heavy and virtually suicidal on the battlefield. But Lotte's prana had developed in a way that she could move and fight as freely with a hundred kilos on her back as she could in her smallclothes. Only a few others shared her particular talent, among them the exarch of the Cloud Temple. She briskly made her way to the stairs, the lightness of her steps contrasting with the creaking of wooden planks under strain. Taki was agog at the sight, and he decided that he would do his utmost to avoid being disciplined by her hand.

* * * *

Hecaton grinned as she slapped her cards down on the slate-cobbled floor to reveal a royal straight flush. In front of her, four men-at-arms in various stages of undress groaned and cursed under their breaths. A few flung their hands in the air to rain down pairs of eights and other useless combinations. The game had started out with wagers of steel-cased .32 caliber and fingers of grog, with a battered half-grad Luger thrown in to spice up the odds. Her goading and the men's desire to see her in the nude had turned the game to strip poker by the time Lotte and Taki found her squatting in the kitchens.

"Major, if I recall correctly, gambling while on duty is forbidden for Dominion soldiers, am I right?" Lotte asked cheerfully as she dug the point of her zweihander into the pile of winnings. It scratched a deep pit between the cobbles as if to accentuate her displeasure. Taki flinched at the sight, unable to shake the image of the massive sword going through his midsection. The keep guards started to make themselves scarce. Some attempted to surreptitiously reclaim their losses from the pile, but Hecaton shot them an imperious glare and they froze in fear. Satisfied that she again had a captive audience unlikely to make off with her winnings, Hecaton turned her attention back to Lotte, shrugged, and took a long drag of her cigarillo.

"That's your bonus pay you're skewering, Captain."

"We both know it's not, Major."

"You and the boy should join the game."

"Strip poker, is it? I'm afraid I can't really get out of my armor. Some of us need to be patrolling the citadel, you know, against the Imperium."

Hecaton hopped forward on the balls of her feet, reminding Taki of an overgrown frog. She thrust her cigarillo dramatically in the air and let out a throaty, masculine grunt.

"I ask you, my soldiers. What is best in life?" She pointed glowing embers at Taki.

"Um..." he began. *What the devil is she even asking me? Is this some sort of weird heathen enchantment?* He looked to Lotte for help, but she only responded with the same expectantly fearsome look as Hecaton. *Jesus, I have to say something or they'll think I'm totally witless!*

"The, uh, open sky over your head? The caress of a woman, or a man, I suppose. Riding a horse? Eating delicious things?"

Hecaton snorted derisively. "Wrong! Lotte, what is best in life?"

Lotte clasped the hilt of her sword and twisted, fracturing stone. "The greatest happiness is to crush your enemy. To drive her before you, to see her cities reduced to ashes. To see those who love her shrouded in tears, and to gather into your bosom her husbands and sons."

Sweet merciful God. Taki swallowed on a dry throat. Hecaton, however, pumped her fist in glee.

"A good answer! And one I used to agree with. But a wise woman showed me that in actuality, it is the simple pleasure of watching others work hard."

Lotte rolled her eyes. "You're not even doing that, Major."

"It's because I trust my soldiers fully."

"Then raise our pay."

Hecaton waggled a finger. "Professionals don't get overtime."

"You know that's a lie. The Code lays out what we get paid, and that includes overtime."

"Are you going to make a grievance?"

Lotte scowled. "Perhaps I will."

"Then I'll tell them I saw you plotting against the exarch."

"And I'll tell them I saw you jerking off the padishah."

Hecaton let out a throaty chuckle at that.

"You're getting better. Kid, you'll learn a lot from her," she said to Taki. He blinked in amazement and found not words to convey his horror.

"We're wasting time here," Lotte said in resignation. She slapped Taki on the shoulder. That was his cue to follow.

* * * *

With the barely audible hiss of steel burying itself into flesh, the blackened stiletto found its mark in the Argead sentry's upper back, twisted, and tore into his aorta. Although the unfortunate soldier's mouth was uncovered, he issued naught but a strangled gasp in response, as the pain was instant and overwhelmed even his training to cry for help. With viscera lacerated so savagely, he lost consciousness in seconds as his abdomen filled with blood. Death followed quickly.

Aslatiel von Halcon, oberleutnant commander of Alfa Gruppe, slowly—almost tenderly—eased his victim to the ground to rest unmarked in the tall grass growing on the east bank of the river. He wiped the crimson off his weapon on a cloth and replaced it in the sheath at his hip as he scanned the riverbank. The Dominion keep's sentries patrolled fifty meters apart on the shore. If his company eliminated even a handful of sentries, the result would be a massive blind spot through which the janissaries could slip through unopposed. The men would then take advantage of the thick fog over the river and stealthily paddle up to the low-decked carronade ship anchored in the depths. From there it was a simple matter to slip on board, kill the night watch, and take out the rest of the crew in their bunks. Meanwhile, the Alfa would swim the river, infiltrate the docks, and prepare the way for the meat of the invasion force.

"Lucatiel, report," he murmured. The wind carried his words over the distance and into Lucatiel's ears.

"I've got my man," she said. "And Mikhail and Elsa report success, too. It's been a long time since we swam together, dear brother."

"You haven't seen Ba'gshnar sneaking around, have you?"

"I haven't. But I can feel him watching us."

Aslatiel glanced over his shoulder, though he knew it a useless gesture. "The first boats will be here soon. We have a half-bell before the next watch comes on. Watch for any unexpected company in the meantime. Silent techniques only. Enjoy the fall weather."

"I'll expect you to warm me up later," Lucatiel whispered.

"That's a little difficult when you always steal the bedding."

She giggled. "What a tease you are, dear brother! I just wanted a cup of mulled cider."

"I'll give you a castle, instead," Aslatiel said. He scanned his surroundings one last time to make sure he wasn't being watched, waded into the water until the waves lapped at the top of his head, and vanished into the foggy depths.

4

"This godrotting fog…"

Draco cursed under his breath and attempted to scan the riverbank again through his spyglass. After a rowdy footrace through the claustrophobic passageways and winding staircases of the armory's outer ring, he and Hadassah had settled into overwatch within a spire that looked over the water. After what seemed like an eternity of fruitless searching, however, his frustration was overtaking his vigilance. The drafts blowing through the ancient tower also did not help.

"*I'm cold*," Hadassah said. She shivered against the parapets, miserably clutching her rifle. "I command you to warm me up. Anything will do. Even *your* body is fine at this point."

"Whatever," Draco snorted. "You'd kick a guy in the crotch and then die of blushing if he actually laid down beside you in anything but full plate."

"Bullshit. I've been with guys before, lots of 'em."

"The captain using you as a huggy-pillow doesn't count."

"She's manlier than you by far."

"I can't argue with that," Draco sighed. "Well, what's it like?"

"What's what like?"

He quickly looked around to make sure they weren't being eavesdropped upon. "You know, sleeping with her."

"Lady fluids everywhere."

"Really?" Draco steepled his fingertips.

Hadassah rolled her eyes. "Of course not, you nitwit. It's actually annoying most times. I'm always too warm and she's always too cold. If I toss and turn, she swats me. And sometimes she'll just start weeping for no reason."

Draco pouted. "When you fart, I also feel like crying."

"Oh, go sniff your own bung."

"If I could sniff my own bung, do you know what else I could do? I'd never want for company again…"

"And the world would be better for it," Hadassah said, smacking him on the chest. She yawned, flailed as if to fend off sleep, and poked Draco in the arm. "Actually, speaking of wanting for company, do you think Natalis has been with many girls before?"

"Oh, so you fancy the new boy?" Draco chuckled at the thought. "He's only a bit younger than you are, anyway…"

"N-no! I just, you know… All men are dangerous perverts, and virgins are even worse, so I just kind of wanted to know if he'd try to molest me in my sleep or something."

"If that happens, kick him in the dick."

"Were you serious about getting him to teach us about how to write and do numbers?" she asked, changing the subject. Another deep yawn escaped from within and she fanned at her face.

"I was. And I intend to make him follow through. If we can learn that, it means that our lives after our fighting years won't be so hard. You remember how hard the scrubbers worked, all scrabbling around the academy? How Maryam's hands are always aching and bound up and shaking? They were once fighters like us, and they were among the best. Basically heroes. Now their bodies are spent, but they still have to live, you know? Sometimes I see them picking through the midden for scraps. I don't want to end up like that. I don't want you to share that fate, either."

"That's assuming we don't die first."

"Compared to slowly grinding apart, dying would be a relief. The thing is, they don't tell you this stuff at the academy. We live to fight, yes, but what happens after that? It's not like we can go and start our own little farms, and it's too expensive to lease a storefront. We're stuck wasting away on our sacred rock."

"Maybe I'll just trick Natalis into marrying me. He'll probably end up working at the shrine or something. The neokoroi don't seem to have it that badly, with their fancy linens and pompous attitudes."

"Don't throw all your chances into some guy. What if he dies, or turns out to be a philanderer?"

"Then I guess I'm just *screwed!*" She spat. "Why are you lecturing me about this, anyway? Hell, why are you always *lecturing?*"

"Because you're the most disagreeable little twit I've ever known. So I want to set you straight."

"You can't tell me what to do, damned oppressor."

"Says you." Draco rolled his eyes and continued his attempts to scan the river. "God's droppings, it's got to be four bells by now. Even the Imperium needs to sleep. Let's give up on this and just pack it in up here…"

He almost missed a subtle flicker in his vision. Not really wanting to, he focused his lenses on a break in the fog and clenched his jaw.

"Wait, you don't think Natalis is queer, right? Then I'm really out of options…" Hadassah said, sleepily.

"Damn!" Draco said. "Put glass on the riverbank, *now!*"

"Okay, okay! Keep your leggings on." Hadassah balanced her rifle in the crook of her elbow and peered through the attached, fabric-wrapped scope. The Mosin-Nagant fired one of the most powerful types of ammunition they had, with a heavy bullet that could punch through brick on a direct hit. Built by an empire that had fallen long before the first prana users walked the old world, it was the ultimate in simplicity and ruggedness. A Nagant also performed equally well as a spear or a club.

She slowed her breathing and steadying her muscles. The Pritsel Ukorrochennij scope mounted on her rifle was vastly superior to the coarsely ground lenses of Draco's spyglass. It allowed her to focus with more clarity even though her field of view was much smaller.

"Imperials! Either janissaries or mamluks," she said. "A lot of them, too. Looks like they're pushing boats into the river and paddling across."

Methodically, she tracked the figures walking along the bank through the scope. It was clear from their heavy armor and weaponry that they were no mere scouting party.

Draco scowled. "Why isn't the fornicating *ship* doing anything? They've got enough cannon to wipe out a legion!"

"Maybe they don't know?" Hadassah shrugged.

"Or they've been taken."

"Do you suppose there are spetsnaz-types down there? I don't see any."

Draco patted the grip of his sidearm to reassure himself. "If the rumors are true, they're already here. We need to raise an alarm."

"A fat lot of good that'll do," Hadassah said. "We're like, the only ones on the wall right now. This garrison really likes to fap itself to sleep."

"Aye, and it rubs me wrong. The more I think about how undermanned this place is the less I like that castellan."

Hadassah frowned. "You think we're being set up?"

"I do. But I won't let assholes disgrace us that easily. Not from their side, and not from ours. Look, there's an officer near the large pile of fallen trees directing the boarding effort. Kill him, and it'll cause some confusion in their ranks. Make them slower."

"I have the bastard. Range two-hundred twenty. Elevation minus thirty. Wind speed six to the north. On target!" She emptied her lungs and licked her lips.

"Send... Wait! What's in your chamber?"

"Milligrad, of course."

"Fine, send it."

With a loud crack and a titanic amount of smoke, Hadassah's Nagant flashed and turned night into day for a millisecond. Its 200-grain lead projectile screamed through the air at five hundred meters per second and slammed into the janissary leutnant's chest on the opposite end of the river. Having lost minimal velocity, the bullet tore through his plate and brigandine, bored through an overlying rib, and sent pieces of lung out of the exit wound in his back. The rounded ogive of the projectile sheared away from the spitzer point and yawed to the side, entering a sergeant's throat. The men toppled over, dying. Soldiers surrounding the fallen cursed and dove to cover. They aimed their rifles at the citadel but preserved enough sense not to fire blindly back.

"Hit, right chest. Second hit, center of neck. And for fuck's sake, that was a reload!" Draco frothed in annoyance.

"I got a double-kill, didn't I?"

"I swear, I'm going to take that 'grad you just hoarded and toss it in the river next time you do that."

"Don't you dare, pervert!"

Movement down in the water caught Draco's attention. The Argead lorcha had been suspiciously quiet the entire time, but now it bustled with activity. Besides the four short-barreled carronade cannons lining the top deck, it also had a mortar that could lob massive shells over the horizon. A tiny glint and puff of smoke from a firing pan confirmed his suspicions, and his eyes widened with realization.

"Oh shit… We're being shelled!" Draco snarled. He wrenched Hadassah by the arm and tossed her down the nearby hatch. A high pitched whine grew in intensity just as he hopped in himself. The two rolled painfully down steep, circular stone steps and crashed ungracefully into each other at the bottom of a landing just as the bomb hit.

On instinct, Draco threw one arm over his companion's head and the other over his eyes as they were pelted with a sudden spray of fiery dust. Training and muscle memory kicked in for both and they invoked a quick protection mantra with sweeps of their fingers and whispered invocations. Protective energy enveloped their bodies just in time to mitigate the impact from chunks of stone and concrete bouncing down from above. Draco coughed and spat, looking up at the flames that sealed the path upward, and exhaled in relief.

"Hah! Stupid motherfuckers!" Hadassah cackled in satisfaction as the subtle shimmer of her prana dissipated back to nothingness. "Try to blow *me* up, will ya?" She stood up haughtily and slapped the dust out of her padded doublet. "Emmy, are you going to sit there all day?"

"Oh, if only I could be so blissfully dense…" Draco muttered, and rose painfully to his feet. One of the shoulder guards attached to his gambeson had bent and dug into his bicep when he moved, probably a result of the tumble. Annoyed at losing part of his armor, he drew his dirk from its sheath and pried the damaged segment loose. It fell to the floor with a clank. His partner topped off her rifle's magazine and he took the moment to inspect his sidearm.

A black-powder arm using a caplock action to fire, the LeMat revolver held nine shots of .44-caliber lead ball. The reason Draco favored it over a more advanced pistol, was because, with a flick of a lever, he could have it fire a 20-gauge lead-antimony slug from its massive secondary barrel. This feature was perfect for dispatching royal templars or Imperial guard, who wore such thick armor that killing one cost far too much milligrad. It also let him keep more milligrad in his pockets.

Satisfied that the gun seemed to be in working order and the selector switch moved the hammer easily from barrel to barrel, he holstered it back under his shoulder. It had been foolish to assume that his luck had changed. He'd merely traded death by potato peeling for death by Imperium. The same invaders he had seen from below would be infesting the fortress by now and looking to kill.

"Ah well, at least this way is more interesting," he sighed.

* * * *

As soon as the alarms started to ring, Lotte and Taki had rushed back to the galley in an effort to find their commander and regroup. They recognized the same men who had been gambling earlier. The dead guards slumped against the walls clutching their leggings and pooling blood on the cobbles. To no one's surprise, the winnings pile was completely absent and Hecaton nowhere to be seen. Lotte sighed and squatted to examine the ground for anything she could use to track the elusive major.

Behind her, a tankard clanked against the floor and her pupils dilated instantly. "Watch your back!"

Lotte's warning registered in Taki's consciousness just in time for him to sidestep a sword thrust to his ribs and counter with a jab of his yatagan. He slipped through a gap in the cuirass and managed to bury it a good hand's breadth into his attacker's side. With a sweep of his arm he cut away a swath of tissue before following with a whirling blow that cleft his enemy's tinpot helmet down the middle. Two more men with axes charged forward, one aiming for an overhead cut and the other going for a horizontal sweep. Taki opened his gates.

"*Plei Khala,*" he hissed. A rippling pocket of super-compressed air shot forward and hit the two attackers. The sudden release of pressure threw them against the far wall to shatter bones and fill their lungs with blood.

Taki realized, as he shook the frost off of his palm, that in the space of less than a minute he had made his first kills. His first human kills. Training at the monastery had involved fairly realistic targets. Never was he slashing or shooting at a mere bullseye, but always a man-shaped dummy. Yet there was still a difference. The dummies did not gurgle, nor did they have eyes that refused to close in death. His instructors had warned him of what would happen next. Euphoria, followed by near instant regret, and then rationalization. *Strange,* he mused. *Where's the guilt?* The men had charged him with intent to take his life, and he had killed them in return. It was part of his job, after all, to dispatch his enemies.

The thought that they were among the elite of the Imperium filled him with giddiness. He triumphantly charged his gates again and turned to see if his captain needed assistance. *When I bail her out, she'll see my worth for sure!*

Lotte brought her greatshield up and a janissary's double-headed axe smashed into it and bit wood. The blow would have shattered most other fighters' defenses, but Lotte shrugged it off as easily as one would flick a bug away. Before her opponent could recover, she burst forward and thrust with her greatsword. It punched through his cuirass and he retched gore through the slits of his facemask. Continuing the momentum of her attack, Lotte effortlessly wrenched the blade out and swung it in an arc to take the top off another enemy's head and cut a third man in twain under the armpits. A fourth janissary tried to harass her with the end of a pike. Unfazed, Lotte lopped the spearhead off, causing him to drop it and draw a thrusting sword. Before the blade cleared its sheath, her greatsword smashed into his neck and sent his head flying. While the body toppled, she firmly chopped the air to send the blood on her blade splattering on the ground.

Taki gulped at the sight. His captain had never needed his assistance in the first place. In fact, she had probably saved him from being completely overwhelmed while he had concentrated on casting. He clenched his teeth, feeling embarrassed. A staccato press of gunshots rang out and forced him to retreat behind a corner.

"Corporal, go back and round up the others and the major if possible. I'll finish them off here and meet up with you at the gatehouse." Lotte said as she brought out her pistol and started to fire back. A Temple Gun of the highest grade, hers was marked with a rearing Colt on its deeply blued slide. Brass casings pinged against the walls and settled into divots between the cobbles. "If the enemy opens the inner ring, the fortress is theirs for the taking. They probably have spetsnaz to make sure this happens. We need to face them together or we will fail!"

"But Captain, I can't just leave you here," Taki protested as he unslung his carbine. He leaned around the corner and fired twice. His eyes instantly watered from the smoke and he regretted not spending milligrad. The gun he carried barely qualified as a relic at all, and was colloquially referred to as a "Bastard" by those who used it. Assembled with a hodgepodge of parts from ancient arms deemed unworthy of salvage, no two Bastards were alike, save for their inherent unreliability. They even generated more smoke than the meanest conscript arquebus. Lotte angrily waved away the caustic billows that clouded her vision before pointing her Colt at Taki's face. He flinched in surprise and fear.

"Do *not* question my orders," she hissed. "I don't intend to stay here and get slaughtered. Just meet me at the gatehouse with the others. Trust me!"

She shifted her aim away and squeezed off another two rounds to fell an enemy, who slumped over into the hallway. In response, a hail of shot left deep gouges in the soft stone near where she crouched and forced her to duck. The fallen man's companions dragged him out of danger by his ankles, leaving streaks of crimson on the cobbles.

Taki grit his teeth, regretting that he had forgotten his place and hoping that she would not hold it against him. The realization that he was more worried about a blemish on his record than survival struck him as perverse, but he could not spare the time to reflect on it. More importantly, she was right that he would contribute little to stem the onslaught. With a final glance at his captain, he slung his smoking carbine across his back and raced down the hall to find his companions.

As he ran down nearly-deserted corridors, worry nagged at him. The Vergina citadel was the Dominion's most important bulwark against Imperial aggression from the north. So why had it allowed an army inside its walls without a fuss? Surely the castellan wasn't a traitor. Taki paused to chastise himself. Seditious thoughts opened the gates to heresy, and polaris were especially prone to committing that gravest of sins. They were locked away from good people for that very reason, after all.

The sound of fighting nearby diverted his attention. He inched forward and peeked his head around a corner.

"These shitlords coming out the walls or something?" Hadassah snarled as she parried a saber cut to her head. In exchange, she sank the chisel-point bayonet at the end of her Nagant into his gut. Seeing that her weapon was still stuck in his comrade, another tried to bash her head in with a mace. She whipped her own pistol out from her baldric and shot two rounds into her attacker's chest and one into his forehead. He fell, blood spurting from the fatal wounds. She turned on another man and punched the muzzle into his teeth to knock him back before shooting him in the throat. "Say hello to 'Esther!'" she cackled, blowing acrid smoke away from the thickly pitted barrel.

"If you're going to name your piece, you should feed her a better diet!" Draco countered as he swung his fighting iron in an arc. His swing connected with an unhelmeted enemy and knocked the man over with his brain exposed. He deftly avoided a sword thrust from another enemy and lashed out with the iron again. The janissary caught it with the aid of a heavy gauntlet and pulled. Draco drew a fighting dirk and stabbed it into his enemy's neck through a gap in the armor.

"I think I like weapons better than people. They don't bitch and complain over every little thing," Hadassah said. She twisted a commando's elbow into a joint lock and whirled him into a sword thrust meant for her. The body dropped and she planted two rounds in the swordsman's chest before executing her stricken quarry on the ground.

Her slide locked back on an empty magazine. She drew one of the wood-handled canister bombs from her baldric, lit the fuse cord, and made to throw it in Taki's direction.

"Hold!" Taki emerged from his cover.

Hadassah frowned. "Shit, I thought you were one of them! What're you doing skulking around there?"

"Your bomb!" Taki pointed. "You're still holding it!"

"Oh, this?" Hadassah pinched out the sparkling end and shoved it back in its place.

Taki stared, dumbfounded. "Are you insane? What if it lights back up again?"

She laughed. "It's a fake. I use it to flush out idiots. You know, like yourself."

"L-ludicrous." He clenched his jaw, angry at having been so easily fooled. "We need to regroup with the Captain. She mentioned a gatehouse. Head there with all haste."

Draco waved dismissively. "Aye, we will, but after taking care of necessities."

Taki grimaced. "*What* necessities?"

"Our spoils, of course." Draco took out a knife and crouched over one of the fallen. He started, methodically, to cut away the straps on the dead man's armor and rummage through his pockets. To Taki's horror, Hadassah was busy doing the same. "You're welcome to a share, by the way, so don't be shy."

"We're in the midst of battle, and all you can think of is *looting?* What of our orders?"

"If you're worried about the Captain, don't be," Draco said. "She'll take care of herself, and she's also entitled to plunder."

Taki balled his hands into fists. "This is unforgivable. Where's your valor?"

"Valor doesn't pay for food. It also ends up getting you killed. Relax. The place will hold up for a few minutes."

"I've never seen such cowardice!" Taki fumed and paced. "If you won't help fight, then *I* will!"

"Have it your way, man." Draco shoved a handful of milligrad into a pouch hanging from his belt and moved on to the next body. "Dassa, help me. This one's a *woman.*"

"So what?" Hadassah said. "She's dead."

Taki turned and ran. *Godrotting losers! Pieces of shit! I'll show them how a real patriot comports himself!*

✳ ✳ ✳ ✳

Aslatiel stepped into the citadel with his Alfa. The janissaries had been brutally efficient, and the armory's forces completely unprepared and undermanned. Dominion men lay strewn across the corridors of the outer fortifications in gruesome poses, with bodies studded by bullet wounds to complement their missing limbs and heads. Now he needed to make sure that the inner ring would fall with the same ease. He picked up the subtle essence of prana discharge wafting down from above. So there *were* polaris on the premises. He would have to find them and snuff them out before they could coordinate an effective defense.

Shots burst out and provoked the soldiers to instinctively duck. At the threshold of a metal doorway leading to the inner ring gatehouse, two janissaries rolled down the stairs bleeding and limp. The rest of the entry group froze, still stacked up outside and unsure of whether to keep going. With one hand resting on the hilt of his blade, Aslatiel sidled up the steps while avoiding exposing himself to fire and placed his other hand on the cool surface of the door. With his prana he could sense the enemy's location when sight, sound, and smell could not. To others, this sort of tactical prescience was tantamount to witchcraft. Usually, that earned his kind fear and resentment.

"Hold fast," Aslatiel commanded. "They've got at least a dozen in there behind concealment, all with crossbows and guns aimed at whoever comes in. It's a deathtrap."

Their leutnant seemed like he wanted to object, but caution won over bravado and he held up his fist to signal the men to freeze. Aslatiel nodded his thanks to the officer. Some would have simply ignored his assessment and ordered their troops to press on, and then blamed him anyway when the rest of the squad was inevitably shredded by a well-placed ambush.

"What do we do now?" the Leutnant asked.

"There's an officer in there leading them. Possibly polaris. I'll talk with him—see if he'll yield."

"I thought your kind were all about killing everything that moved."

"We do negotiate occasionally. Under no circumstances should your men enter the room before we give word. Zhukov, Rana," he said, turning to his group. "You're taking care of the light if things get loud. Lucatiel, you're with me."

"Yes, dear brother." She marched up to the door to join him. She slowly worked out the kinks in her neck, and made sure that the straps on her armor were fully tightened.

Fahnenjunker Mikhail Zhukov, the third member of Alfa, knelt nearby and murmured an incantation. His body started to fade and blend in with rough pattern of the walls, until he was but a subtle distortion against the stones. Fahnenjunker Elsa Rana, fourth and most junior, followed suit and disappeared too. The room grew oppressively silent as the preparations came to an end. Many of the men had still never seen true prana usage up close.

"Men and women of the Dominion, will you parlay?" Aslatiel shouted at the door.

"Fill your hands, you Imperial dicksuck!" replied someone from the inside. "Who wants to know?"

"The leader and second in command of Spettsgruppe Alfa."

There was a pause. Finally, the door opened a crack and suspicious eyes glared through the opening. Aslatiel shifted to avoid the muzzle of the firelock that also protruded through the gap.

"Disarm yourselves and step in. No funny movements or witchery or we splatter you on the walls."

Aslatiel nodded and unslung the gear that held his sword and submachine gun before handing them to a janissary nearby. Lucatiel passed her twin jian to another soldier. *I see fingerprints on the steel and you're dead*, she signaled with a playful wink. They entered the room.

A dozen Argead soldiers nervously rose from the safety of their cover and trained muskets on their new prisoners. At the head of the group was a man in his late twenties, clad in polished half-plate and heavily armed. He wore the brass sigil of a knight on a chain across his chest and on his pauldrons were engraved a pair of lions rearing on their hind legs. The knight confidently strode forth with a double-barreled howdah pistol leveled at the pair.

"I thought you'd be smarter than to actually take me up on the offer," the knight sneered. His eyes flicked between the two siblings and he licked his lips. "Now I've got two captives of some renown. Tell your slave-soldiers to retreat back across the river, or we'll cut the tendons in your ankles and show *her* what really happens to little girls who think they can fight alongside men."

Lucatiel rolled her eyes.

Aslatiel wanted to sigh with disappointment. These were not the Temple soldiers he sought, just braggarts.

"My offer is this, Peer of the Dominion," he began. "Surrender at once, and you and your men will be allowed to retreat with your weapons and banners intact. Your standing will be preserved in the eyes of your lord. You have my personal assurance of this."

The knight laughed, as did his men.

"You want me to run away like some sort of... *eunuch* making a back-room deal? You Imperials either have no sense of shame, or the rumors are true and all boys are castrated before they start making seed. Certainly explains all the sodomy in your armies. No, you demonspawn pigs, we men of the Dominion believe in honor and loyalty. Something *your* kind wouldn't understand."

Aslatiel shrugged. "Would you prefer to die in battle instead? That can be arranged."

"After we cut off your feet, we'll all bugger *you* as well. Since you have no manhood it doesn't make us queer."

"Dear brother, this is boring. May I kill them now?" Lucatiel drawled, tapping her foot impatiently.

The knight shook his gun at Aslatiel's face. "Silence your whore!"

"You keep shouting at *me* for some reason," Aslatiel sighed, wiping spittle off of his jaw. "But it's *her* you should be afraid of."

The torches blazing against the walls died without leaving embers. Panicked, the Dominion men reacted with a barrage of musket- and crossbow-fire that bathed the room in murky, dull orange and roiling smoke. The room sank into blackness again.

"Cease fire, you cockgobblers! You'll hit me!"

The men started to cough and gag from the fumes.

"Did we get him?" whispered a shaky voice.

"Shut up! They're still here!" hissed another.

"Light the torches…"

Rapid-fire thunder from dual pistols interrupted the last command while white novae flitted around a woman in the center of the room. In the last visions of dying Argead soldiers, Lucatiel moved with stuttering grace, with not a single wasted movement as she sent hollowpoint rounds into their bodies. As abruptly as it had begun the firing stopped, and the room was again plunged into acrid silence.

"Approach," Aslatiel said, smiling grimly in the darkness.

The janissaries rushed into the room with torches while Lucatiel slowly released herself from her end-stance. Her foot eased off Aslatiel's shoulder, allowing him to rise from kneeling. All of the Dominion men-at-arms had fallen, slumped in the indignity of death with perfect clover-leaf groups of bullet holes in their foreheads. The knight was bent backwards over a barrel, still clutching his expensive pistol as a death reflex.

"That's our Leutnant," said Elsa with an appreciative whistle as she emerged into visibility under an extinguished torch.

"Did I do well, Aslatych?" asked Lucatiel to her brother as she changed magazines and holstered her guns. Though tiny compared to the dead knight's hand-cannon, her pair of ancient pistols marked "26 Austria" were far better tools of destruction, and entirely worthy of her power.

Aslatiel scanned the interior more closely. It was a powder repository where the frigates' spare shells and bombs were stored. Naked explosives stacked on wooden shelving gleamed with cosmoline in the light of the Imperial torches.

"Yes… But I fucked up," he muttered, a sick feeling mounting in his gut. Using that tactic had been a mistake. One misplaced shot or ricochet and she might have blown the lower levels up. It would have meant an abrupt end to everyone's life, and most of all, failure in the eyes of his master. *Ba'gshnar* was right. Lucatiel could take care of herself, but he still had much to learn. A solid punch to his arm shook him out of his dreadful reverie.

"Aslatych, just how bad of a shot do you think I am?" Lucatiel said, crossing her arms in frustration. "I'm not going to get blown up by some stupid warhead. If I did, who would protect you then?"

Aslatiel had to smile, despite himself. He was foolish to have doubted her in the first place, and they were most definitely alive. Gently, he took her hand and touched his lips to it with as much chivalry as he could muster.

"Luca, my dear, you are the only woman I would fear to face in combat. If you weren't my sister I'd want you as my wife."

She beamed in pleasure before suddenly drawing him in and wrapping her arms around his waist with a grunt of effort. The bear hug was capable of crushing an enemy's spine, and Aslatiel struggled to breathe. He was embarrassed, but at the same time, flooded with an unreasonable sense of fulfillment.

"I'll hold you to that," she said, looking intently into his eyes.

* * * *

Taki panted as he reached the wooden doors to the winch house. Everything else could fall or burn but this one place. Below, the keep's innards were protected by two kilotons of solid steel gate that would never fall to even the most determined ram. If he protected it well, the Imperials would have to turn back. He didn't care that the squad wasn't there to back him up. With the exception of the captain, the others had shown their true nature as conniving layabouts. He angrily pushed against the doors, and they grudgingly swung open with much creaking and flying dust.

To his surprise, there were no soldiers tugging at the wheel, and no barrage of lead screaming his way. Merely a single woman wielding two straight swords, a demure smile, luxuriously straight midnight hair, and the sapphire eyes of a murderess. She gave Taki a coquettish wink and tilted her head from side to side. Though she was comelier than any other woman he'd seen in his life, the sight of her made his blood run cold for some reason.

"I-identify yourself!" Taki leveled his saber at her.

"You can call me Lucatiel," she said with a playful curtsey.

"I am Taki Na—"

She raised a hand to cut him off. "No need, dear boy. It's really not important."

Taki glared. "So be it, Imperial. Will you surrender or will I be forced to dispatch you?"

Lucatiel let out a chuckle. "Why don't you be good and sit in a corner until your fellows arrive?"

Taki flared his nostrils and tightened his hold on his weapon. No matter how comely this Lucatiel was, she'd have to die for such an insult. He let out a battle-cry and lunged at her with his blade raised high to cleave her neck. She raised one of her swords to counter, but her movement seemed too slow to counter his. He could almost taste her blood.

His vision flashed white and he instinctively pulled back before he'd have completed the downstroke. Everything he saw was doubled and spun around crazily. His ears rang with painful tinnitus and his sword-arm spasmed involuntarily. His yatagan had been reduced to a jagged stump and its fragments littered the ground before him. Something salty dripped into his mouth. He put a hand to his face, only to feel a deep cut on his cheek. He pulled the hand away and gazed at the blood with a mix of surprise and horror.

Lucatiel yawned. "Brother, kill him please. I don't want his stink on my blades."

Taki cast aside the useless weapon remnants and pointed an open palm at her. Even if the woman was a supreme fencer, no blade would protect her from a proper frying. His channeling ability had always been his strength, and the reason for his success in the academy. Now, the Imperial would pay, and painfully. He'd just opened the last gates when something hard crashed into the back of his neck. As if a torch had been snuffed, he lost feeling to his body and collapsed in a heap.

"No need. This one's just a novice. I want to know where his commander is."

Taki stared up at the ceiling, spread-eagled on his back and unable to do more than twitch. A new arrival stood over him wearing the same sigil Lucatiel had: a maroon cherry blossom motif over a white griffin. The mark of Sevastopol. *Spetsnaz,* Taki realized. *I have to stop them.* He strained and tried with all his might to get to his feet, or at least roll onto his side, but all for naught. Below his neck, everything felt blanketed by stifling fog. He'd heard of this happening before—a fall from great height or a careless blow to the back making a man a cripple—but only as a parable against recklessness during training. Realization hit him along with a wave of cold sweat.

"Imperial," Taki groaned. "Have you made me an invalid?"

The man looked down at him and sighed. "Most likely."

Taki swallowed back tears. "Then I beg you to kill me."

"And I beg you forgive my sister's rudeness. She sometimes lacks in the social graces. Pray tell me your name."

"Taki Natalis, a corporal."

"I am Aslatiel von Halcon, and I will honor your request. May you achieve enlightenment in your next life."

Aslatiel drew a curved sword and held it firmly for a downward thrust into Taki's chest. Taki trembled and tried to peer at his executioner, but the effort was too exhausting. Taki closed his eyes. He always knew he'd die in battle, but what irked him was that it had been so soon after graduating, and under such unheroic circumstances.

The brick wall of the gatehouse exploded as Lotte crashed through it and knocked Aslatiel aside like a ragdoll. She let out a triumphant roar and promptly turned to face Lucatiel with her weapons drawn. Draco barreled in after her and threw Taki over his shoulders. Hadassah squirted by and promptly tried to bayonet Aslatiel while he rolled away.

Two more figures, also wearing spetsnaz insignia, melted out of the darkened corners of the gatehouse to attack with thrown darts and flashing knives. Lucatiel became an inhumanly fast maelstrom of blades focused on Lotte. Sparks flew as the greatshield's engraved sun was obliterated by deep gouges and the zweihander's keen edge turned to fractured teeth. A spear-tip snuck under Draco's armor and he dropped Taki to the ground.

Taki groaned, vomited, and to his own surprise, shakily pulled himself to his knees. His lower half no longer felt leaden and insensate. His legs burned and now he could tell that he'd pissed himself. The sensation was mortifying, but more importantly he could feel again, and most importantly, move again. Slowly, painfully, he pulled himself to his feet. His sword was broken, his Bastard missing, and he was in no shape to channel sutras. To his great shame, there was nothing he could do to help.

"Who dares wake me from my slumber? I'll devour you all!" Hecaton cackled as she emerged through the hole in the wall. She sent an arc of blinding, violet current upward and instantly blew the gatehouse roof to smithereens. The Imperials quickly hopped back and pulled out their guns while the Tirefires did the same. For what seemed like an eternity, silence reigned save for the pattering of raindrops. Hecaton licked her lips.

"We meet again."

The Unified Imperial was grammatically perfect, but accented with something eastern and more remote than the diphthongs of the Chung Kuo. When Hecaton saw who had spoken, her expression soured and she turned pale, if only for a moment. Chronicler carried no visible weapons, not even the usual dagger or officer's pistol. His bare hands were sufficient to murder each and every single person in the gatehouse, the castle, and the town.

"Major! Let's wreck this sonofabitch!" Draco growled. He gripped his pistol assuredly and tensed on the trigger.

"No!" It was the first time Hecaton had raised her voice at them in a long while. "All of you retreat. The fortress is lost." Draco opened his mouth to object, but was silenced by the look on her face. "Do what I say or you will definitely die."

As Hecaton's charges started to slink back, the von Halcons attempted to step forward only to be halted by a casual wave of Chronicler's hand. He spoke, now in a foreign tongue that only the spettsgruppe had heard him speak before: *"It has been far too long since we parted ways. But I was not mistaken to come all this way to find you. For that I am relieved, Sirin. Now, come with me, away from this place. We have much explaining owed to the other Powers."*

Hecaton squinted, let out a resigned chuckle, and replied in the same tongue. *"You always were a dumbass."*

She joined her hands with a complex interlock of the fingers in front of her. Before Chronicler could react, the gatehouse was choked with billowing, blinding smoke.

A torrential ejaculation of lead shattered the wooden walls, dead bodies, and stone blocks facing Alfa Gruppe as they simultaneously magdumped into the space Hecaton and her cohort had occupied a half second before. Chronicler grimaced, drew in a breath, and violently exhaled. The smoke parted instantly and fled as if moving of its own accord.

* * * *

"Bitches and whores!" Lucatiel bellowed. Sullenly, she ejected the empty magazines from her pistols and shoved them into pouches.

"There there, my dear. You are a more respectable young lady than that," Chronicler admonished, switching back to Unified Imperial. "Spettsgruppe Alfa, you have done well. I will inform the padishah of your prowess and see that you are rewarded justly. That being said, you should open the gate to allow our commandos to penetrate the inner fortress."

Frustration leaving her face, Lucatiel nodded to Mikhail and they set to work turning a large wooden wheel on a pintle. Elsa joined in, speeding the process. The gatehouse rumbled, and triumphant roars erupted from below as the gate lifted and janissaries flooded the courtyard. Unlike other men-at-arms serving the Imperium, they were forbidden to sack the town or take liberties with the inhabitants, as they received a regular salary. Pacifying the surroundings would be easier once the Argead citizenry realized they had no reason to fear for their lives.

"Ba'gshnar," Aslatiel said, kneeling contritely. He swallowed back a wave of nausea provoked not by his brush with death, but by the fact that he'd almost died to some damnable old hag. "Once again, you lay bare my unworthiness. You have my limitless gratitude for saving my soldiers."

"Rise, Aslatiel," Chronicler said. "You have incurred no disgrace. The woman you faced is unlike any other in the world, and even a match for me. She and I are bound by an unfortunate string of fate."

"Who is she?"

Chronicler smiled wistfully. "I once thought her beautiful. But now that she is wizened and hateful, she is even more enticing."

A non-answer. Aslatiel bowed again to his master. The Alfa knew better than to ask more, though he craved to do so. Chronicler rarely changed his mind, especially when he chose to guard the details of his past. Trying to probe would only lead to blood and loss.

5

By the time of his capture, ulcers raked Taki's feet from constant rubbing against the insides of his boots and his heels wept where blisters had burst along the way. After a hasty descent down the walls of the keep, he and the rest of Tirefire the Lesser had sprinted, jogged, and then trudged for the rest of the night until light from burning towers no longer punctured the horizon. Every breath felt like a lungful of searing volcanic ash, and Taki wanted most of all to die, vomit, and rest, in that order.

He spent a good portion of his attention furtively looking around for any sign of a mount or wagon. Anything would suffice to rest his burning calves and soothe his chafing thighs, but the roadway was barren. He recalled a tale of some king who had offered to trade his domain for a horse under similar circumstances. At the time, he had thought the man foolish, but now the logic was flawlessly clear. Especially since the mere act of placing one foot in front of the other was becoming progressively difficult by the step. Draco slogged on ahead, arguing with Hadassah over something that involved tossing her rifle back and forth between them. Their words were gibberish. Taki felt himself falter and he sank to his knees.

"Natalis, have you the strength to walk?" Lotte asked as she crouched down next to him.

"I can. I'm fine," Taki said, though not believing it. He struggled to rise but found he couldn't. Staying in place and falling asleep, even forever, was becoming dangerously enticing.

Lotte clapped an ungloved hand over his forehead and frowned. "We're far enough from the enemy by now. Take respite."

"I'm sorry," Taki croaked. "I didn't mean to disappoint."

"It's okay, just rest. The Cross will be here for us any moment now."

At her words, Taki brightened. An escort home was the answer to all of his consternation. His instructors at the academy had never quite explained what happened to a unit on the retreat, but hearing her words gave him hope that he would not be discarded, after all. Something nagged him, however.

"Why them? Have we broken the Code?"

Lotte closed her eyes. "That's not up to me."

A few moments later, they were surrounded by riders. A midnight tabard with golden trim over mail was the uniform of the Black Cross, enforcers of Temple law. Taki blearily raised his head, only to find himself staring down the barrel of a gun. He felt someone wrench his Bastard away and glimpsed Lotte surrendering her pistol and dagger to a mailed lieutenant. Draco and Hadassah were already in chains, and gloomily tromped their way into the bed of a wagon penned by thick iron bars.

With the aid of a cursory shove, Taki collapsed onto the gritty floor of the prisoner carriage near Draco's feet. He closed his eyes and slept.

✳ ✳ ✳ ✳

Later, things only got worse.

"This court-martial shall come to order." The duty sergeant sharply rapped the steel-clad butt of his halberd on slate to create a sound not unlike that of gunfire. Despite his best effort to comport himself, Taki flinched at the noise. Fortunately, he was shivering so much that no one noticed.

His knees were sore from forced prostration on stone, and the tight-fitting manacles around his wrists caused them to ache. The worst source of his discomfort, however, was the itchy burlap prisoner's apron that was his only item of clothing. The air in the high-ceilinged, open-roofed court lanced his flesh with goosebumps, and his pitiful excuse for apparel covered little. Trying to shift around to avoid a chill only exposed more flesh. Two days in the brig had been a frosty hell that made years of spartan living at the Academy seem luxurious by comparison. Far worse, though, was the potential compounding of disgrace to come.

I haven't even been out of the academy for a month and I'm already being judged. Taki panicked. *It's not fair. It wasn't my fault we lost the keep! It was...* He glanced at his fellow accused. *It was theirs!*

"Natalis," Draco whispered. The rest of Tirefire the Lesser was similarly fettered and as wretchedly attired as Taki was. "Natalis, listen to me."

"About what?" Taki hissed.

"I know things look bad, but it's okay."

"It's *not* okay!" Taki squeezed his eyes shut and bit his lip.

"It is. Look, we've all been here before. Trust the captain," Draco said.

Taki blinked, incredulously. *But you're wrong!* When a squad committed an offense, it was the duty of the senior officer to administer the lashings, or hangings, or both. If someone like Lotte were to flog him, there would be no flesh left on Taki's back. Tears escaped from his eyes and dripped to the floor. He would die from a lashing, or they'd decide to hang him. If by some miracle he survived the inquest, he was absolutely sure to never be promoted or transferred. He'd die a mere corporal in the worst unit in the Cloud Temple.

"I said *order!*" the sergeant barked at Draco, who returned a derisive raspberry. The sergeant shook his halberd in warning. A door swung open within the chamber, and three figures emerged and sat in thrones on a wooden dais in front of where Taki knelt.

Taki's eyes widened in recognition of who the trio were. Of course, he knew from the academy who to expect, but they were still an impressive sight. Second in power and authority only to the exarch of the Cloud Temple, the three men and women of the Agia Triada judged all cases and decided all punishments. Only the exarch could judge them in turn, and since the man was practically never present, the triada had authority over nearly all affairs of the Temple.

In the foremost and largest throne, a blond man with widely-spaced eyes and a pious-looking bowl-cut sat at weary attention. He let out a perfunctory sigh and passed his gaze over the shackled squad before him. Taki lowered his head and tried to surreptitiously edge the hem of his tunic down to cover his loins. When he could not, his cheeks burned in shame. Thankfully, the archangel Michail either did not notice or did not care. He finally focused on Lotte.

"Satou, do you realize what you've done?" Michail asked. Lotte raised her head and met his eyes.

"No, milord," she said. "I only know Vergina has fallen, milord."

"Show some respect and avert your gaze, hussy," snapped the archangel on Michail's left. A woman with an oval face and an upturned nose, Yuriel was second after Michail in rank and could bend rivers and oceans to her will.

"Yes, milord," Lotte said, and bowed her head.

"Let it be," Michail said. "She's always been defiant. A character flaw even our love cannot diminish. The important thing here is the keep that you helped lose, Satou. Its fall has cost us not only men and milligrad, but also *face* in the eyes of our enemies. Now the Osterbrand scum will be emboldened, and as a result, more of us will die when the inevitable sieges begin in earnest. We had a fine détente going and you ruined it."

"My deepest regrets, milord."

"To think that you were once the exarch's protégé," sniffed Yuriel. "I'm glad he recognized you for the trash you are."

"Milord Yuriel," Lotte said, ignoring the latter statement, "how fares Lord Choniates?"

"He's in Athenaeum right now, answering to the basileus for your mistakes. Fortunately, Niketas Palaiologos is a man of infinite compassion and wisdom. Still, you should be ashamed of putting our exarch in this position."

Lotte locked her eyes with Yuriel's. "The loss of one castle does not mean we give up and show our bellies to our enemies. Did our captain not tell us this when I was your lieutenant, and you my cornet?"

"Temperance, Satou," Michail barked. "You know I will not brook disrespect to your betters." Lotte bowed her head. Yuriel looked as if she wished to speak, but merely flashed an indignant glare at Lotte instead. Michail continued. "Who put you up to the task, anyway? The defense of Vergina was supposed to go to Pantheon, not Tirefire the Lesser."

"Major Mezeta ordered us to the citadel."

"Is the old hag causing trouble yet again?" whined the third archangel, on Michail's right. Jibriil, the most junior of the triada, tugged at the spiked collar of his leather jerkin and scratched at his bristly neck. "Can we just kill her yet?"

"Hold your tongue," Michail snapped at him. "We will deal with Hecaton Mezeta at a later juncture. For now, these miscreants are to be judged." He turned his attention back to Lotte. "Regardless of the inherent malice of your flag officer assigning your squad to a task it could not possibly carry out, you must still be held accountable for your failure, Captain Satou. I bequeath you ninety-nine lashes of the cat to administer to your men."

"I beg of you, Archangel Michail, to increase the number threefold," Yuriel said. "Or, if you are inclined, make them all undergo a sound birching. Do not forget that this particular band is also under chastisement for blasphemy."

"I already gave them permanent potato duty for that," Jibriil chimed in, merrily.

"Self-congratulation is a *sin*, Archangel Jibriil," Michail said. "I wish that you would come up with a more appropriate punishment for their recalcitrance. For the loss of the fortress, my judgment stands."

Taki grew pale and started to tremble. Was Lotte not even going to argue in their defense? Why was she not demanding Hecaton's presence as their advocate? Why was there no mention of the spetsnaz and the one-eyed overlord who had cowed even the infamous Hundred Arms? Thirty-three lashes from his captain with a cat-o-nine tails was more agony than he would be able to stand. And even if he succumbed to unconsciousness, it only meant that Lotte would have to wait for him to wake up before continuing the flogging.

An idea raced through him at the speed of panic. Before the triada left, he would throw himself at their feet and beg for mercy before his honor and his back were forever scarred. There was little reason for them to decline, after all. He was one of the few initiates who could wield the elements on any appreciable scale. He had graduated near the top of his class. He knew how to read, write, and factor. Surely his future was worth more. Surely the compassionate, powerful archangels would lift him up from this hell if he could only make a sincere plea. He opened his mouth to speak.

"Then I invoke the Code and my privilege as commanding officer of my squad," Lotte said, and stood. "I will take all ninety-nine blows."

Michail frowned and opened his mouth to speak, but was beaten by Hadassah.

"Absolutely not! Draco and I will take our even share, and so will Newboy." She glanced over at Taki with an expression that did not brook dissent. *"Right, Newboy?"*

"Right," Taki yelped. His eyes widened in shock and he would have clapped his hands over his mouth if not for his manacles. *Did I just agree? What the hell is wrong with me? Speak now, damn you! This is your last chance!*

"Silence!" Michail bellowed, half-rising from his throne. "I wished to teach you an important lesson on accountability, Satou, but I see that you continue to defy my efforts. Very well. I sentence you all to twenty-five lashes each, administered by an executioner of the Cross. The punishment is to be carried out immediately. We are adjourned."

"See, Natalis?" Draco winked at him. "I promised you could trust the captain."

Taki slumped forward in anguished disbelief and let his forehead rest on the stones. The triada had already left, as quickly as they had arrived. There would be no more chances to save his future. Now that he had taken lashes with them, he would remain a Lesser Tirefire forever.

When the executioner arrived, Taki gave no resistance as he was hauled up and dragged away to the next chamber, where the punishments were carried out. The fearsome sights within—the glistening rack or the pile of irons glowing red-hot in the hearth—were nothing compared to the loss of his prospects. He'd die a corporal in Tirefire the Lesser, and now the only question was whether he would do so fast or slow. Taki let his head roll forward as his manacles were secured to a length of chain dangling from above, and he was hoisted upright by his wrists. *Everything's ruined. Everything's shit.*

The first cut of the cat-o-nine abruptly broke him out of his stupor, and he let out a pitiable cross between a squeal and a gasp. He had been given a taste of the whip once in the academy, but that was only because the instructors had wanted everyone to know what awaited disobedient students. That time didn't count, and thus the pain wasn't so bad. The next blow came before he could brace himself and he let out a shrill cry of terror. With the next kiss of tails he started to whimper. Surviving twenty-two more of these seemed like a fantasy. The pain was compounded by the shame of knowing that the rest of his squad hung nearby receiving their drubbings without complaint.

"Natalis, your attention!" Lotte commanded. She had been strung up to face him. Her rags left nothing to the imagination, and Taki tried to restrict his gaze to above her neck. It struck him as strange that he was worried about propriety when nothing about his situation was actually proper. "Listen," she began, "when I was a corporal, my captain taught me a trick to lessen the pain. Do you want to know it, too?"

Taki nodded, desperate.

"It may sound strange, but you need to remember your first time. Who the girl or boy was. Where you were. Was it in a bed, or in a pile of hay? Where did you touch each other? Just remember, and concentrate on reliving the memory."

"Captain…" Taki burbled, and shook his head. "I can't!"

"*Try*, Natalis. If it helps, you can look below my collar," Lotte offered.

"Don't you dare look in *my* direction," Hadassah growled, before sucking her teeth at the force of a lash.

"Captain, you don't understand," Taki said, now crying in earnest. "I haven't *had* a first time!"

Lotte's compassionate visage broke under disbelief. "Wait, you're really a virgin?"

Hadassah started to giggle uncontrollably, and Draco let out a chuckle that rebounded off the walls. Taki's cheeks burned freshly as he even heard his tormentor with the cat-o-nine snicker from behind.

"Hey, Executioner!" Draco chortled. "Try not to lash the kid so hard from now on, eh? He's in pain every day of his life!"

"A true paragon of self-abuse," Hadassah gasped.

"Onani-Master Natalis!"

"He'll be dancing with himself."

"Watch your tongues!" Lotte snapped. "Oh, Natalis, I'm so sorry!"

"Alright, alright, you lot shut up and stop giggling," growled the masked man wielding the cat-o-nine.

"What's the matter?" Hadassah asked. "You mad 'cause Newboy's better than you at *whippin' it?*"

"I said, silence!" the executioner roared.

"Yeah, why don't you help him beat something else?" Draco cackled.

"He doesn't have time for that! He's got bishops to choke and monkeys to spank!" Hadassah said.

"Executioner, give me that whip!" Lotte growled as she tried to kick at Draco. "I'll flay them myself!"

The executioner stomped his feet and buried his face in his palms.

"Everyone just *behave*, already!" he whined.

Hadassah's eyes narrowed and the ends of her lips curled with sudden recognition.

"I've got a better idea. Let us all down, or I'll tell your mother you're flogging virginal boys," she said.

"You're not telling her shit."

"Oh yes I am, *Herschel.* Don't think I don't know who's under that mask. My poor *tante!* Still thinks her innocent little son is a scribe. Instead, he's doing unspeakable things to helpless, pure young men, not to mention pelting *me* on my *bare ass!*"

"Screw off, Hadassah! You're the rottenest!"

"Are you going to let us go, or do I have to keep belittling you?"

"Fine, I give! I've got better things to do than whip your pimply rear! But don't tell the triada about this, and especially not mother."

Taki's feet hit the ground as his chains were lowered and he sunk to the floor on jellied knees. His back felt simultaneously soaked and on fire, and he had not strength to stand. Whether it was from shock or mortification, it didn't matter. He felt arms wrap under his shoulders and hoist him up, but this time with a gentler touch. The rush of blood from his head overwhelmed his senses, and he knew no more.

✳ ✳ ✳ ✳

When he woke up, Taki noticed that the cuts on his back had been bandaged, and even the aching gash on his face had been smeared with a coat of menthol-smelling liniment. He was still in the brig, though in a different and much warmer cell than he had previously occupied. Careful to avoid putting undue strain on his wounds, he gingerly sat up. From the top of his scalp to the bottoms of his feet, he felt a century old.

"You finally awake?" Hadassah said. She leaned against a nearby wall picking her teeth with a piece of scrap wire which looked suspiciously like a lockpick. Taki nodded and looked around the cell. It was a communal affair meant to hold a squad, rather than the oubliette he had festered in for two days before the trial. It was also warmer, much to his relief.

Draco sat nearby, reading a dog-eared, leather-bound text. His eyebrows arched delicately as he pored over the words, giving him an uncharacteristically academic appearance. On hearing Hadassah speak, Draco snapped the book shut and shuffled over on all fours.

"Hey, Natalis," he said contritely, but without looking Taki in the eyes. "About what happened in the stockade, I mean, it's a bit weird for a man to stay—how should I say this—pure at your age, but I didn't mean to insult you or anything-"

"Where's the captain?" Taki snapped, cutting Draco off.

"She's with the archangel Jibriil," Hadassah said. "He summoned her shortly before you came to."

Taki frowned. "For what?"

"Dunno," Hadassah said with a shake of her head. "Creepy bastard's always had a thing for her, though, so I hope she's doing alright. But you know what they say. 'Never force yourself on a woman who can crush your skull with her thighs.'"

"That sounds like something you made up," Draco said.

"Doesn't make it any less true."

Taki rubbed at his eyes and tried not to smear ointment into them. The captain was in a private audience with one of the triada? If the trial had shown anything, it was that Lotte knew how to negotiate her way out of a bad situation. Draco had been right about one thing, at least. *Perhaps she's trying to get me transferred?* He shook his head. That was just ludicrous, unwarranted optimism. With a courts-martial verdict now on his record, no other unit would accept him and he was forever stuck as a Tirefire.

He regarded the others. They were good fighters both, but still small-minded dead-enders. They had no chance of advancement in the Temple hierarchy, and would be drummed into menial servant labor the moment they lost their fighting edge, or a limb. Dying in battle would be a mercy. *But if I play my cards right, and impress my captain, I might at least get promoted. Make officer-candidate and then perhaps one of the better units will overlook my early mistakes.* Taki clenched his jaw. Whatever came next, he'd come out on top. All he needed to do was work hard, distinguish himself, and please Lotte. And he also needed to fix the problem of his virginity.

Taki patted his cheeks and rose to his feet. It was time to play to his strengths. As usual, Draco and Hadassah were bickering again. When an opportunity came, he snatched the book from Draco's hand.

"Oy, what're you doing?" Draco asked.

"Remember that I said I'd teach you how to write, and Mikkelsen how to read? I intend to keep my word. So, no more leisure until you've learned your letters."

Hadassah twirled a lock of hair around a finger. "*I said* I didn't wanna learn."

"So you like it when the major insults you?" Taki scoffed.

"No, but…"

"How sweet are Thy words unto my palate! Yea, sweeter than honey to my mouth," Taki intoned. "A psalm of the most renowned king of the Israelites. A command to his people to be literate so they could know the word of the Lord for themselves. If you won't do that then you're not one of them."

"T-that's really underhanded, Newboy."

"Dassa, you should let him teach you," Draco said. "It's your only chance to learn. Else, you'll spend your old age scrubbing floors and whelping kids for the only nice Jewish boy in the Temple. And *he* lies to his own mother."

Hadassah crossed her arms, rolled her eyes, and let out a fitful sigh. "Oh, fine!"

"Oh, hush. I can tell you're actually excited about it."

"Shut your gob, schoolboy."

Draco clapped his hands. "Then it's decided! Natalis, you'll teach Dassa to read and me to write."

Taki nodded. "I'll teach both to each of you. We'll start now by scratching in the dirt, but ideally you should have a quill, ink, and parchment."

"Oh, I can get those now," Hadassah said.

"In here?" Taki scrunched his brow. "In the brig?"

"Yeah. Our pudgy little gaoler needs 'em to fool his mother into thinking he's a respectable academic." She slunk up to the cell door, grasped two of the rusty iron bars, and started to shake them with her prana gates fully opened. A deeply unsettling rattle echoed off dripping stones and forced Taki to clap his hands over his ears. Before long, the masked executioner stomped up to where Hadassah was and slammed his cudgel against the bars.

"Enough! You've giving me indigestion," Herschel whined. "Why can't you just be *good?*"

Hadassah stuck her hand out and poked him in the belly. "I want to use your scribe set. Give it up, fatty."

"No."

"I promise to return it, and return it looking used. You *know* how valuable that is for you, right?"

Herschel crossed his arms. "But you can't write. How do I know you won't just draw cocks all over the parchment?"

"You don't. But there's also a kid in here who wants to teach letters, so maybe I'll just draw a few and make you look like you actually scribble for a living."

Herschel pouted, but then shrugged in defeat. "If that's the case, I suppose I can lend you the set. If I see more than one dong on it, though…"

"Yeah, yeah. You'll shove the pear of anguish up my hoo-hah and turn the needle to eleven."

Herschel seemed taken aback, even through his mask. "What? No, that's horrible! I really wouldn't do that to you! Not even if the Archangels ordered it."

"Aw, you're a sweet boy," Hadassah said with a smile, and patted Herschel's cheek. "That is, when you're not being a leather fetishist."

"Oh, just shut up and take the set," Herschel said, and grumpily tromped away. A few beats later, he returned and shoved a goatskin roll through the bars. Hadassah let out a melodic giggle and flitted back to Taki.

"Here, all the stuff we need," she said.

Taki accepted the roll and opened it on the floor. Within were pristine wooden quills with sharpened metal nibs, fresh bottles of inks in black and blue, a flat-bladed ruler that doubled as a scraper, sealing wax, and several sheets of unmarred vellum. A far finer array of tools than any he had used back at the academy. He pressed one of the velvety sheets to his nose and inhaled its musky fragrance.

"This is great, Mikkelsen!" Taki gushed.

"It's really nothing," Hadassah said, suddenly looking embarrassed. "I just know a guy, that's all."

"She knows everyone in the Temple, practically," Draco said, patting her on the back. "Despite her disagreeable personality."

"I'll show you disagreeable, goatfucker."

"Now that's just rude."

Taki cleared his throat. "If you don't mind using the floor as a desk, we can start now." He took the largest of the precious leaves of calfskin and a quill, uncorked a bottle, and inked the nib before starting to scrawl away. Before long, he finished and laid out the sheet before his would-be students.

"This will be your master reference. I'll write numbers in later, since they're another subject entirely and I don't want to confuse things. Here," he said, pointing to the top-left of the page. "This is Aelph, also called Alpha. Next is Ve, once known as Bet: Hence, 'Alpha-Bet' as the name for this chart. Combine the letters of the alphabet and you form words. Combine words and you can make sentences. Combine sentences and you have stories and books."

"So I could be an author one day?" Hadassah asked, her eyes widening.

"Yes," Taki said. "Anyone who can write can make books to be read later. You can tell truths, you can lie, you can go in between. It doesn't matter what your sex is or if you're a demonspawn or a human. As long as words are written, most readers will assume them true. But before you compose histories, let's have you both start simple and write your given names. That way, you'll have a signature that no one can duplicate. Prepare your quills and get a sheet of vellum each. Don't worry about writing small or in straight lines for now, because we'll just scrape the ink away later. Use the alphabet in front of you as a guide to how to form your letters."

"Let's see," Draco said, and dipped his nib in ink. "Probably for me it's a Delta, then Rho, then Aelph, and then Gammad?"

"I'd use Chi, with or without an Omicron. Otherwise, you made good choices," Taki said. He turned to Hadassah. "Your name is longer, but still doable. What do you think you'd use as the first character?"

"That thing that looks like crosshairs, except with an 'X' through it," Hadassah said, triumphantly.

"That's Zhe, so it won't work. But you have some options, even though our Alphabet doesn't have the same 'chha' sound as the original Hebrew. You can use Ghe or Khe. Notice how the overall pronunciation ends up the same."

"But it doesn't look as cool," she pouted.

"Not spelling like a bumpkin is much cooler," Taki said.

"Oh, fine. Is there a character for 'ahh?'"

"Use Aelph. Then Delta, Aelph, Sigma once or twice, then another Aelph."

"Wait, which one is Sigma?"

"This," Taki said, and pointed to a spot on the chart. "It looks like a snake, doesn't it? Think 'sss' like a hissing serpent."

"I guess that makes up for the lameness of the first character. I can have double snakes."

"Yes, you can. So, write it down."

After a few minutes of tense concentration and a chorus of scratching, Draco proudly presented his efforts.

"What's this?" Taki asked with a frown.

"My name. Right?"

"No, this is gibberish. It's full of hesitation marks and stray ink, and I can tell your hand trembled like a leaf. Also, you used Omega instead of Omicron. Failure." With that, Taki whipped his hand out and rapped Draco atop his head with the flat of the ruler.

"Ow! Damn you, Natalis, I thought you said you wouldn't go at this like they did at the Academy," Draco said while rubbing at his aggrieved scalp.

"It's the only way you'll learn as an adult," Taki said with a shrug. "*Children* get sweets and coddling. *Men* get whacked."

"In that case, I quit."

"You should quit being a pansy," Hadassah said to Draco, and swatted at his rump. "Didn't you tell me you wanted to be a historian, and write lies and blasphemy for saps like you to read thousands of years later?"

"I did, but—"

"This is the only way you'll ever get to do that. So harden the hell up and *write gooder!*"

"Godrotting heretic," Draco whined and writhed. "Okay, fine! I won't quit. Do your worst, Natalis. I'm a man. I can take it."

"Thank you, Mikkelsen," Taki said. "Now, show me yours."

"Ta-da!" Hadassah shoved her vellum forward. Taki looked at it and then looked blankly at her.

"This is a picture of a cock. Failure!" Before she could hop away he swatted her shoulders with the ruler.

"But I'm a woman! I thought you said only men get whacked!"

"No man desires a woman who doesn't take her education seriously. Do this right or don't do this at all."

"How'd you suddenly turn into such a hardass, anyway?" she complained. "Weren't you just bawling your damn eyes out at a little paddling?"

Taki glowered. "My letters are my strength, and without them I'm a worthless virgin. I can at least do *something* right with my life. Now, write your names again. We won't stop until you've got it correct. Then, we'll start making basic words."

"How do we write 'virgin,' anyway?" Draco chortled. "Ve then Upsilon?"

Taki swung his ruler and whacked Draco again.

* * * *

An hour later, Draco's scalp was red with welts and Hadassah's shoulders looked as if she had spent days harvesting deuterium salt on the beach. However, their hands were steadier and their letters more legible, and now, each could write his or her name without looking at the Alphabet as a guide. So engrossed were the trio in their studies that when the door to their cell bloc finally opened from afar, they almost didn't notice it.

"I hear the Captain talking!" Hadassah whispered and bounded excitedly to the door. Unbidden, Draco also sidled up next to her and strained to peer out between the bars. Taki set his vellum down and carefully cleaned the nib of his quill before joining them.

"You have my answer, milord," Lotte said to someone they couldn't see.

"No. You can't continue like this. Mezeta will only lead you to ruin." Taki's eyes widened with recognition. The voice belonged to the archangel Jibriil.

"The major owns me. I owe her a debt, and am bound to pay it."

"She forces you to accept humiliation, and me to punish you and your men. Be my wife, instead. I'll treat you well. I'll protect you from Yuriel and Michail."

"I can watch out for myself."

"Damn you, Lieselotte! I grant you salvation and you repay me with indifference. What must I do to gain your affection?"

"Nothing. I have none to give you."

"But I love you!"

"And I lie back, open my legs, and think of the Dominion."

The unmistakable sound of a slap rang out through the cell bloc and Taki flinched to hear it.

"One day," Jibriil growled. "One day, you'll learn to be grateful. I'm giving you a chance to restore your honor in Kosovo, and I expect you to have a better attitude when you get back."

"I will carry out my mission as ordered," Lotte said. "Jailor, escort me to my squad."

Hadassah signaled to her compatriots to step back and try not to look as if they had been eavesdropping. A few moments later, the cell door swung open and Herschel gently prodded Lotte to step in. After she did so, he left without locking the door again.

"Officer present!" Draco bellowed to the others. He straightened his back, clunked his bare heels together, and saluted. Taki and Hadassah did the same. Lotte smiled and returned the salute.

"At ease." She looked around the room at the sheets of vellum and bottles of ink, as well as the welts on scalps and shoulders. "I see you've been studying while I've been gone. Do I have Natalis to thank for this?"

Taki blushed. "Yes, Captain."

"Try not to smack them too hard, 'Confessor Natalis,'" she said blithely. "I appreciate your efforts, though."

Taki swelled with pride and relief to hear this. *Good, she's noticing me.* "Just doing my duty, Captain."

"Now hear this, Tirefire the Lesser," she continued. "The Agia Triada has deigned to release us from bondage, that we may go fight again for the glory of His Grace the basileus."

"To the Duchy of Kosovo?" Almost immediately, Taki knew he had made a mistake. Hadassah shot him a toxic glare. *Shit.*

Lotte chuckled. "I see you're an eavesdropper, too. You're fitting in quickly."

"Sorry, Captain. I overstepped my bounds."

"No, it's fine. Our kind must think more independently than other soldiers. As you must have heard, we're going to the duchy. I'll fill you all in on the details later, but for now, get your gear and weapons back from impound. We depart immediately."

"The triada didn't give us much time to recover, did they?" Draco frowned.

Lotte shook her head. "No rest for the condemned, I'm afraid."

"I'd rather they'd waited, with all of us injured…"

"We'll manage. Don't misjudge my strength," Lotte said, patting him gently on the cheek. "Oh, Mikkelsen, shouldn't you return those supplies to Executioner Cohen?"

"Hold on, I've gotta draw more dicks on it, first," Hadassah said.

Taki bowed his head in silence. He was starting to wish he hadn't heard her earlier words. What had Lotte endured to get them released back into duty instead of spending the next year peeling in the kitchens? *Surely an Archangel, a paragon of justice, isn't…* The thought turned his stomach. *Remember what they told you at the academy, damn you.* He closed his eyes and rocked back and forth in place. *See no evil. Hear no evil. Speak no evil. That's how you survive. That's how you prosper. That's how you get out of this pathetic excuse for a unit and get your life back.*

6

Hadassah grumpily uncrossed her arms and leapt off the back of the wagon. Mud splashed from her landing and spattered on her boots as well as on Taki's legs. The roads were simply too boggy for their teamster and his oxen to continue, so they would have to make it on foot to the city and the palace.

"Welcome to the swinging ballsack of the Dominion!" she announced aloud to the grumpy sky. "Woo!"

"What's so bad about it?" Taki asked, adjusting the hood of his poncho. Wads of rain spat from the clouds above smacked on his head. Against stiff waxed canvas the drops made popping sounds that reminded him of treats from his childhood. His swollen cheek throbbed angrily, as if he were already an old man with a wound that predicted the weather. The thought crossed his mind that he might bear a hideous scar from Lucatiel's attack, but he was glad to have simply saved his eye.

"Yeah, technically, since this is north of Athenaeum, it's more like the sweaty armpit, not the hairy ballsack," Draco said.

"What's bad about it? Let's see…everything?" Hadassah said, rolling her eyes. "It's completely ass-backward, the food sucks, and the people are schmucks. If it were me in charge, I'd pay the Imps to take this place off my hands."

"What she wants to say but can't because of her underdeveloped brain, is that this entire area has been a clusterfuck of hatred and warfare since the beginning of time," Draco began to lecture before narrowly avoiding a punch between his legs. "And it's only gotten worse since the Hero took over."

"You mean the duke?" Taki said, interested now.

"Yeah, Gul Hekmatyar, seventh of his line. Or was that sixth? Anyway, you know who I'm talking about."

"How are things getting worse? He's the biggest hero in the land. Didn't he save us all ten years ago at New Istanbul?"

"Not out of the goodness of his heart," Draco sniffed. "Look, the guy was a minor Khazari prince who fled from an Osterbrand Liberation Army with his tail between his legs. Word was that the Imperium really wanted his head on a pike. So he makes an arrangement with the basileus and they stop the Imperial advance. His Grace gets a powerful ally and the duke gets this chunk of land as his personal fiefdom. It was just a business transaction, but they make it out to be this epic tale about the power of friendship and honor and such."

"Draco, how do you know about this stuff?" Taki could not help but feel impressed.

"I *liked* the history classes at the academy. It's always good to know who wants to kill who, because then you can make sure it's not you."

"Emmy will believe anything he reads," Hadassah said. "Like how once we all traveled to the moon and some place called Mars or something, on board ships set on fire. Such bullshit, isn't it?" She snickered.

"It's not bullshit, we *did* travel to the moon and even beyond Mars!" he insisted.

"Draco, the friggin' thing is too far away." she said, gesturing to the silvery orb cresting the horizon. "You can't even hit it with bullets!"

"You tried to shoot the *moon?*" Taki asked, furrowing his brow.

"You haven't?"

"Look, I'll show you when we get back," Draco insisted. "There's a picture of someone in white armor planting a flag on its surface. 'Astromen,' they were called, and they fought against chimerae in the stars."

"But even if that was true, our kind brought an end to it all," Taki said. "That's why we're compelled to serve the basileus and donate to the priests."

"Maybe our ancestors did go out of control at one point, but it doesn't mean we're at fault. That's why I don't give to those damned beggars."

"You don't?" Taki crossed himself, aghast.

"Of course not!" Draco crossed his arms and laughed. "They're all fakers, anyway. They spend your 'grad in the cathouses."

"That's heresy."

"No, that's just Emmy being jealous," Hadassah said. "The real problem is that the priests all claim they're praying for the restoration of the old world, but look around you. All that's survived is rubbish, plastic, and crumbly ruins that smell like rotten eggs. For every good relic there's a whole mountain of shit. Was that really all the golden age was? If that's the case, I don't want it back. I'd rather live my life in the now."

"As long as you only fight easy enemies and have unlimited time to loot the dead," Draco said.

Hadassah flared her nostrils. "You think this is a game?"

"Alright, enough bitching! You three, fall in!" Lotte ordered.

"Captain, how're your wounds in this rain?" Draco asked.

"A bit sore, but I've had worse. I'm angrier about what the blue-eyed girl did to my shield and armor."

"The look on her face was priceless when we stormed the place. I've never had a woman look at me with such malice. She was poetry come to life! 'All that's best of dark and bright met in her aspect and her eyes,'" he sighed, wistfully.

Lotte shook her head. "No, the bitch was just crazy. I hope we won't be encountering her again."

"Captain," Taki began. He almost raised his hand but remembered not to. "Speaking of those Imperials, who was that old, asiatic man? He didn't seem like the rest of them."

"Oh yeah, that guy! The way he and the major talked to each other, you'd think they were a married couple," Hadassah said with a snide chuckle.

"I can't say, Natalis. I've never seen him before," Lotte said.

"Mikkelsen, did you understand what they were saying?" Taki asked.

"Of course not," Hadassah said. "But a lover's spat sounds the same no matter the tongue."

"You've never had a lover," Draco said.

"I've also never gotten the pox, unlike a certain someone," Hadassah sneered.

Syphilis? Taki grimaced. Draco didn't seem quite so pretty anymore.

"That's a…a nasty rumor," Draco huffed. "I've never had the sores."

Hadassah snickered. "They say it settles in your brain and drives you mad!"

"Enough!"

"Venereal disease aside, she has a point," Taki said. "The old man and the major definitely know each other from before. They also had similar facial features, and spoke the same language." He frowned, scratching his chin in thought. "Captain, you have the major's ear. Have you asked her about what happened back there?"

Lotte shook her head.

"After we got back home, she went off to the capital with the exarch. I know nothing that the rest of you don't. The best we can do right now is to concentrate on our mission."

Taki nodded. Lotte had to know more than she was letting on, but he decided to drop that line of inquiry for now. Appearing too persistent would make him lose esteem. "We're to meet up with this Duke Gul and help him quash rebellion, right?"

"Yes. We're to aid him in driving out insurgents. Mainly Imperialists, I'm told."

"Captain," Draco began. "You have to wonder. Why are all the rebels trying to go over to the Osterbrands, anyway? The Ursalans also love to incite the rabble, and their lands are practically next door. So what are the Imperials offering that's so enticing to your average peasant?"

"I know not, Emreis," Lotte said. "But it's better for you not to persist with that line of thought. Trying to understand the enemy is an easy trap to fall prey to. They'll entice you with sweet lies and then slaughter you when you're drunk on their poppycock. But you will always find the truth in war and blood. Split someone open and you will see her true character: the shit in her guts and the pus in her womb."

"Aye, Captain," Draco said.

Taki swallowed in awe. Lotte hadn't simply been performing for Hecaton, earlier. His captain was an unyielding warrior and a born killer, and he very much wanted to be like her in that moment.

Lotte continued. "Also, we're to investigate the fate of one of our own. One of the Archangel Jibriil's men, a certain lance corporal Gillette who disappeared recently. If he's dead, we're to recover his remains. If he's alive, he's going to have to explain why he hasn't sent a single report to the Temple for months."

"You don't suppose he's turned traitor?"

"It's always a possibility. If that really is the case, we're to execute him and await further instructions."

"Ugh, if he's dead, why can't we just leave him for the crows?" Hadassah asked. "I don't want to lug a body around. They always smell like poo and ooze juices on you."

Taki wanted to ask her how she knew that, but decided against it. He had seen dead bodies being readied for final rites at the Temple, but had never touched one himself. There had been little time to remember the recent battle, and the three he had killed. When the enemy attacked, he had countered without needing to think, and this pleased him. The academy instructors always told scornful tales of new graduates who upon seeing an enemy for the first time froze with indecision and were struck down. He had avoided that disgrace, but now had blood on his hands. It was important to not feel guilty, though. If he started to imagine the men's faces in an idle moment, he simply repeated to himself what the instructors had taught him: *They died gladly for their masters. You will one day do the same.* For now, it worked. Still, the thought of hauling a corpse across hundreds of kilometers...

"Even in death, we're still the exarch's property," Lotte replied. "You wouldn't just leave a brass casing out on the field after battle, right? That's valuable stuff—it can be melted down or reloaded."

"But we all just get cremated anyway," Hadassah said.

"That's just because there's no space for a graveyard. But more importantly, it's so that the impurities in our flesh aren't used for evil purposes. There are creatures out there that'll mutate into even more dangerous forms if they consume one of us. Plus, well, the Ursalans."

"Aye," Draco said. "The templars literally sew things like severed hands and feet onto their own bodies if they think the part is better than their own, and will hunt you down until they get what they want." He stuck his tongue out with disgusted, boyish glee. "If one of them ever sees my manhood, I'm in trouble!"

Taki resisted the urge to gag.

"No one wants to see that," Hadassah admonished. Draco casually flipped her off.

"That's probably a myth, but it does go to show that we need to be careful, even in death," Lotte said. "Anyway, unless this Gillette has turned into soup, we're to take him back."

Hadassah shook her head and sighed.

"Yeah, I get it, but still, it's kind of depressing to know you're kinda like a piece of market meat. Can't even get left for the rats."

"I'd buy you for a bent reload," Draco said, pretending to weigh her. She lazily kicked at him and missed.

"Actually, Natalis, I should probably know this already, but where did you come from before you joined the academy?" Lotte asked as they continued to trudge along the dirt road to Pristina.

"I don't really remember much, actually. I think I grew up on an island, maybe, but after that it's all hazy until the orphanage," Taki said.

"Good lord, an orphan?" Hadassah sighed. "How much more cliché can you get? Next thing you know he'll pull Emmy's manhood out of a sheep's bung and become the basileus!"

"You should be so lucky to witness it!" Draco countered. "Besides, that means my member is a legendary sword. Go ahead and tug it, Natalis! Become the Chosen One!"

"Er, Emreis," Taki cringed. "Can you not *thrust* in my direction?"

"Emmy, that's illegal," Hadassah countered half-heartedly. Sensing her waning enthusiasm for bickering, Draco smiled and left it at that.

Lotte looked to the sky, displeased with what she saw. "We should get a move on, or it'll be dark before we get to the walls."

* * * *

The dreary sky had turned to diluted ink by the time Tirefire the Lesser entered the duchy fortress. From the headless icons dotting exposed brick, the building had likely been a cathedral in a more peaceful era. Over the years, it had slowly accumulated more militant features. An outer palisade of poured concrete over twisted metal rebar was studded with embedded broken glass. Access was only granted by a drawbridge over a dry moat lined on the bottom with rusting, lacerating husks of trashed relics from the Fall. Footmen patrolled the walls and parapets, sweeping their crossbows and rifles over the rest of the city with callous disregard.

The farmlands of the region were fertile enough and the ancient asphalt roads mainly intact. The city of Pristina had the benefit of an underground river passing through, which allowed an easier time during a siege. Whoever occupied the capital controlled a swath of land of over ten thousand square kilometers in area. Control of the duchy was a prize worth clutching no matter how much it cut the hands.

"So you're the guys Niketas sent to fuck shit up?"

Duke Gul Hekmatyar, Hero of the Dominion, reclined on a leopard skin-pattern throw draped over a sagging throne in the middle of what Taki could only describe to himself as a perversely appointed dungeon. Tapestries of naked prisoners being beheaded hung from sweating walls tinted garish crimson. Mounted swords and arquebuses cluttered the rest of the space without any thought to proper arrangement, and flickering torchlight cast everyone within the chamber in an infernal rather than regal light. A waifish girl barely past puberty leaned up against the duke on one side holding a cigar and clad only in a pink loincloth. Her twin propped up the other side holding an ashtray. Taki started to go agog at the sight, until he saw the healing bruises on their faces under makeup and the thin skin over jutting ribs.

The duke himself was younger than expected—mid-forties, with dyed-black hair and a camouflage-pattern tabard adorned with golden chains and medals for valor. Most notably, his long cloak was trimmed with ermine, a privilege only the basileus enjoyed. In a shoulder holster sat a large and heavy old world revolver done in gold tiger stripes and engraved with the crest of the Duchy on mother-of-pearl grips. There were four other guards of his at the corners, all wearing thick boiled leather and carrying Simonov rifles with bayonets extended. Lotte motioned for her squad to kneel.

"I am Captain Satou of the Cloud Temple," she said. "We have been ordered to carry out your will against Imperial sympathizers in your demesne."

"God bless the Dominion." The duke grinned. "Five witches to command—that's as good as an entire army. Hey babe, why don't you have your guys join up with me and we'll go and knock the basileus off and screw on his throne?"

"Your pardon, milord?"

"What are you, deaf? Let's go fuck Niketas up. We'll rule the land together."

Is he asking us to commit treason? Taki felt his guts churn in anxiety. *What the hell is going on here? Isn't he the greatest hero of the lands?* He raced through the Hoplite's Code in his mind, trying to figure out what to do. Polaris were employed by the lords of the realm and beholden to their orders while lawfully engaged, but if a lord spoke openly of revolt, then...

Lotte answered his question by drawing her flamberge in a single, fluid motion. Her decisiveness cut through Taki's panic and he warmed with gratitude. Now, all he had to think about was the simplicity of combat. He chopped the edge of his hand against the charging handle on his Bastard to rack the bolt and shouldered the carbine. A heartbeat later, he aligned sights on one of the dumbfounded guardsmen and started to put pressure on the trigger. Something flashed in the corner of his vision.

"Not so fast, Christmas Cake," a polaris said as he phased into view in front of Lotte and pressed a stiletto to her throat.

Draco cursed and jammed the muzzle of his LeMat against the new arrival's scalp.

Lotte peered at the man who had put her in check, and cracked a half-smile. "Lance Corporal Karma Gillette, the penalty for assaulting a superior officer with a weapon is death."

"Nice to meet you, too," Karma said, wincing at the steel pressing against his temple hard enough to dent bone. "Mind telling Biggie there to drop his iron?"

"Emreis, kill hi-"

"This is fucking great!" the duke cackled as he applauded. "Man, you witches are the real deal. Hey, if you train my guys to do those fancy tricks, I promise you I'll give you each a *belt* of 'grad for your time. Seriously, I know how to pay people well, that's why I'm in charge here. Anyway, what I said earlier, it's a joke! I love Niketas like a brother, and he loves me too. I mean, why'd he send all you guys to me when he just lost that castle of his?"

"Belay the order...for now," Lotte said, and slowly sheathed her flamberge. Draco's annoyance was unmistakable as he slowly eased down the hammer of his LeMat, pausing after each click of its resetting action. Karma's knife edged away and disappeared into a sheath hidden in the folds of his buff coat.

Taki eased his finger off the trigger of the Bastard. He had beaten his target to the draw with ease, and he relished that fact. Compared to the humans, he was like a demigod. And if this was how the triada, or the exarch was compared to novices like Taki, then truly their ancestors had been the scourge of the old earth. The guardsman grimaced. Taki winked in condescension but quickly realized he was straying. Making the less powerful feel like ants was wrong, he had always been told. The lords of the Temple did not stoop to this level. *And yet archangel Jibriil is forcing my captain to share his bed...* Taki realized where his thoughts were heading and quickly chided himself for blasphemy. *Foolish bastard! The archangel is your lord and your better. Never forget that if you want to get out of this shitty unit.*

"Shit, you guys need to learn to relax," the duke scoffed with malice barely contained under a cocky grin. "Normally I'd spit you all from ass to mouth for threatening me like that, but I know you did so out of loyalty to Niketas. I'd expect you to kill any of my men who talked about going against me, too. So, let's forget about this and begin again." He waved over a servant. "Sasha! Fucking get these guys drinks. Put on some music! What the fuck else do I let you live for?"

Scratchy accordion chords erupted from an array of angrily sparking relics hung from scaffolding above. One of the guards hurried to a nearby bar and started to pour spirits into mismatched, lopsided glass tumblers.

"Your Grace, we need to discuss-" Lotte began. The duke seemed to look through her as he rose from his couch, turned, and approached one of the rifle-wielding guards. The man attempted a bow only to be answered by a savage punch to the face which toppled him where he stood. Almost methodically, the duke started to kick at the guard's exposed back with his pointed and gilded metal boots. Sasha continued to slosh murky fluid into glasses, and the other guards looked onward, stony-faced. Lotte's expression soured, and she started to move toward the pair.

"I'd let it go for now, Cake. Anger the duke more and he'll send those girls back to their parents in a bag and demand payment for his trouble," Karma interjected softly, tilting his head toward the two slaves. "Of course, they're dead anyway so it really doesn't change a lot."

Lotte exhaled slowly, and faced Karma.

"Lance Corporal Gillette, you heard me announce my name and rank. So why are you calling me 'Christmas Cake?'"

"Oh, it's a saying from the far eastern lands. 'No one wants a Christmas Cake after twenty-five.'"

His chuckle died in his throat as one of Lotte's hands closed around it and the other shoved her Colt down the front of his trousers.

"If I was *really* angry with you I'd just let you mouth off to the major, but you're kind of cute, so I'll simply blow your left nut off to teach you a lesson." Her smile was positively saintly.

"No more lip from me, Captain," he gasped. Lotte slowly let go of him. He rubbed at the reddened marks on his neck.

"Why have you stopped correspondence with the Temple? That could be construed as desertion."

"I'm no deserter, and the situation here is a lot more complicated than it looks. We should discuss this at a more opportune time. Please." Karma's hand strayed unconsciously over his manhood as if it would actually protect him from a dum-dum bullet.

"Very well, Gillette, I'll let you off the hook for now, but I'm keeping you under watch. Effective immediately, you're my man, not the Duke's, and you will follow my orders without question. If you have cause to object, you may roust the archangel Jibriil from his chambers. Understood?"

"Yes, madam."

"I'm not an old lady," she warned. "Calling me 'captain' is fine."

A few seconds later, the squad found themselves with shotglasses of rotgut in their hands being encouraged to toast to the basileus, the Dominion, the Trinity, and to the padishah taking it up the ass with a red-hot poker. Liquor seemed to smother whatever resentment still remained in the duke for the earlier show of force, so they drank and drank and drank.

Later, Taki half-slumped against the back cushion of one of the smelly couches and peered at his squad mates and also at the duke. A shot of the fiery booze burned his stomach and filled his eyes with tears, so he had feigned intoxication in order to avoid having to partake of more. The duke had laughed and derided him as a lightweight, but Karma had managed to steer the man's attention away. This was the first time Taki had been in such close proximity to an actual noble of the Dominion, much less an epic hero. Perhaps foolishly, he had expected the man to look and act like the exarch, who Taki had heard speak soon after he had sworn his vows and entered the academy. Constantin Choniates was gravely dignified, powerful and purposeful, and of course incontestably righteous. Even a neophyte could see that. One day Taki would die for the exarch in the line of duty and if he were lucky, his name would be remembered fondly by the man. At first, he privately doubted the truth of this oft-repeated phrase. After seeing the man, he had lent it more credence than he thought possible.

Gul Hekmatyar, however, seemed like no more than a petty thug who had inherited both a lot of milligrad as well as a chance friendship with the basileus. He was being generous with his liquor and his praise, but there was a sense of underlying malice to it all that gave Taki pause. He was filled with the desire to leave, but quickly extinguished it. Who has he to question the virtue of a man who had saved his entire people and paid the iron price a thousandfold for it? The duke was the greatest hero in recent history and Taki was but a mere fledgling in comparison. The histories always said that martial men were rough around the edges, even impolite, but that was because they lacked duplicity. Duplicity gave rise to softness and invited evil in. No, the duke's mannerisms were signs of honor and bravery, and Taki would have to learn from them to succeed. He had a career to consider, after all, and earning the Duke's favor now would be valuable later.

By chance, he glanced at one of the girls sitting at the duke's pleasure. For a moment, his eyes met hers. She looked at him and smiled unhappily. He could see small, scabbed-over blotches riding up the insides of her arms, and knew she was here for life. He looked away and forced a nagging feeling back into the depths of his consciousness. "They died gladly for their masters," he repeated under his breath.

* * * *

"Balls, this is totally excessive!"

Draco gawked as the countryside rolled by and the wind whipped stands of hair into his face. At the head of a column of the Hekmatyar legion, Tirefire the Lesser all sat on the roof of a hulking, box-like contraption that gouged the road as it trundled toward the village of New Petrovic. It resembled a carriage from far away but moved without a team of horses or oxen, and belched thick smoke into the sky. If the priests were to be believed, the squad rode on a holy rolling temple eight centuries old which ran on pure diesel. And if there was anything more valuable than milligrad, it was that ancient, heady, liquid fire.

"It's a waste, when any war-wagon would do the job with less noise and complaint," Lotte said, tugging at the harness holding her flamberge to her back. "Then again, if the Hero wants to squander his funds, so be it. At least we don't have to walk."

"I'm not sure it's a waste." Taki shrugged. "I think burning a hundred liters of fuel may seem like colossally stupid excess to us, but to a man like the duke, it's a good investment."

"More like it'll leave him bankrupt before long. Heroes can't run on goodwill alone. And I think he has a certain lack of goodwill," Draco said.

"It looks like it does the trick for him, though," Taki said. "You can either rule through fear or love, right?"

"Maybe, but I wonder where he gets all of his ammunition. Feelings don't get you 'grad."

"Oh! I heard a rumor," Hadassah said. "He promised his liver to the Murdercube, and the spirit rewarded him in turn. I mean, do you see what we're carrying? All clean and smokeless, even the bombs," she said, fondling a faded green fragmentation grenade. "I'm getting hot and bothered just thinking about it! It wouldn't surprise me if he found this awesome thing in the same place."

"Still, never thought I'd be actually riding one of these for real. It's smaller than the one back at the Temple," Draco said.

"This is different than the one we have. I believe this is more of an 'armored personnel carrier' and the one we have is a 'main battle tank.' That's what the ancients called them." Hadassah said, brightly.

"I didn't know you were interested in this sort of thing, Mikkelsen," Taki said.

"Of course I am," Hadassah said. "This is the coolest shit the Golden Age ever produced. They go 'bang!' and growl at you. How could you not want to hump something so powerful?"

Draco snickered. "Now you'll be able to. The Duke's little monstrance can actually get it up unlike the one back home."

"Hey, shut the hell up, Lumpy! Noel tries her best, but she can't do anything if the exarch won't let her get fuel for it!"

"Noel needs to get more sun."

"Are you talking about High Neokoros Graz?" Karma asked. He had been silent until now, lazing against a waterskin while staring up at the sky.

"Yeah, she's a good friend of mine! You know her too, Gillette?" Hadassah replied.

"I do, actually. I once helped her acquire a heart for an analytical engine. On the sly, of course. Got my arse kicked for it when the archangel found out," he whispered, causing her to giggle.

"You know, I don't think she's ever mentioned you."

"Then I need to complain to Lady Graz, for never telling me about her lovely friend." Karma smiled softly, and Hadassah's usual retort died in her throat when she met his eyes.

"Hey man…" Draco started to say, his expression darkening.

"Everyone, check your powder," Lotte said. "The village approaches with haste."

"Yes, Captain!" they replied in unison.

"Remember, these are mainly unskilled rebels, but don't let your guard down. There may be Imperial agents or even Forsworn among them, so don't do anything vainglorious."

"Great. Forsworn," Draco muttered as he inspected the wax-slathered spare LeMat cylinders kept in pouches on his belt. Reloading his sidearm was a simple matter of swapping cylinders, though preparing the under-barrel slug launcher was a tedious affair.

"Are there a lot of traitors in these parts?" Taki asked. He drew the charging handle back on his Bastard and let go. The bolt cycled forward, slamming a gleaming brass round into the chamber. Carefully, he closed the dust cover on the ejection port and flipped the safety on.

"Actually," Karma said, "I've encountered a few men here I thought were actually Forsworn or well-disguised Imperial spies. Untrained, but powerful. Sadly, I was unable to capture them."

Draco huffed and sneered. "Oh? Undeveloped mooks too much to handle, Gillette?"

"I said I couldn't capture them. I was forced to kill them," he said with a thin-lipped smile.

"Seriously?" Hadassah asked with a poke to Karma's arm. "When did you see those guys? What were they like? I've never actually fought one."

Karma shot her back a wink. "I'll tell you all about it over dinner. In fact, I know a nice place in the city that serves Ursalan wine from Bordeaux. Let's say tonight after the mission?"

Hadassah gave him a sideways pout. "How do I know you won't try to off me like you did the captain?"

"Because you're witty and beautiful, and I want to know you better."

"I'll think about it," she said, and turned away blushing.

"On your order," Draco muttered to Lotte, "He'll disappear."

Lotte shook her head.

"We're here but we're taking fire!" shouted one of the Duke's footmen, who rode alongside them on an armored destrier. Like the rest of the Khazari forces, he was expensively equipped with good half-plate, a metal helm, and a bolt-action kalash, and flanged mace. "Someone tipped off the fucking partisans that we're coming!"

The village's corrugated steel walls were in full view ahead, and so were the makeshift barricades blocking off the main gate to the town. Tiny shapes of men scurried around, accompanied by flashes and smoke of rifle and musket-fire. Lotte regarded the scene with a hard stare. Sieges were undesirable in general and meant boredom and casualties. A ball whizzed by her head and she paid it no mind.

"Keep going, driver! Nothing they shoot will penetrate," she yelled down the hatch of the relic. "When you're within fifty meters, go at full speed and ram the gate."

"You'll fly off!" the driver objected.

"That's the point!"

"Nothing quite like fighting in the shade of Persian arrows, is there?" Karma quipped before mouthing the Thureos sutra. A shimmering veil of blue surrounded him to provide a temporary shield against fast-moving projectiles. The rest of the team followed suit and tightly gripped the handholds around them. The rolling temple lurched as it accelerated. Bolts and bullets pinged against the armor like hailstones, and Taki grunted as a musket ball grazed his shoulder. Due to the protection of his prana and the low power of the projectile the blow felt no worse than being punched. He could not help but smile at the thought of what awaited. He glanced down at his Bastard and felt warm from the anticipation. Virgin Newboy though he was, he was still a titan compared to the ants in New Petrovic. Battle was most exciting when one was sure to win.

Metal squealed and crunched as they plowed through a pile of molding plastic, broken furniture, and banded barrels that blocked the village's entrance. Bolstered by their momentum, the squad leapt off the roof and started their attack. Ruddy-faced peasants charged them, carrying stolen muskets and crudely-fashioned spears whose heads were smeared with excrement. Lotte swung bloody arcs in the air as she hacked off limbs, gunbarrels, and heads with her massive sword. Draco pushed up the center firing and leaving great clouds of smoke in his wake before switching to his fighting iron. Hadassah's Nagant thundered as she sent rounds downrange to blow off helmets and splatter the brains of crossbowmen firing from windows. Karma unsheathed twin spatha and lunged into a group of bannermen. With expertly done spins and leaps, he cut throats and chests before finishing his ballet with a snap-kick and a beheading.

Taki whipped his gaze around wildly, looking for a target. A splinter of resentment burrowed through his thoughts. His companions were too efficient. He could not distinguish himself if there was no one for him to kill! *No, that's wrong thought,* he chastised himself. He forced himself to smile. After all, a battle won without bloodshed was equally honorable.

Bricks exploded in front of him from minie balls fired from the right flank. Muscle memory took over and he rolled to face his opponents. He could see two heads bobbing up and down behind a junked wagon. They had hoped to score lucky potshots, but had missed. Such an attack would have usually provoked anger from the intended target, but Taki felt glee instead. He knelt and invoked the Pyr sutra. Gouts of flame belched from his hands and enveloped the wagon's carcass. It was not a sutra he usually deployed, since it tended to singe the hairs on his arms, but he wasn't sure if Khala would be enough in this instance.

As predicted, the two rebels panicked and ran from their disintegrating cover, discarding their muskets in their haste. Without pause, Taki switched to his Bastard, took aim, and pulled the trigger two times for each rebel. The duke had provided milligrad, and the weapon sang joyfully in turn. Rounds punched into the fleeing men's backs and they skidded on the street as if they'd tripped over their own feet. Neither, however, got back up. That they had been unarmed and fleeing briefly registered in Taki's consciousness. *They're the ones who threw their guns down. They made themselves defenseless and acted in error. Now they've paid the price.*

Within minutes, the battle was over. Lotte held up a fist to signal her squad to rally and be ready. They crouched and waited, but the gunshots had stopped coming toward them. Amidst the wreckage of the barricade, the duke's men started to stream in on horse and foot. At first they cautiously moved in cover while sweeping the area with their kalashes, but quickly found their progress unimpeded. Triumphantly, they let out a shout and shot their guns in the air.

"We didn't expect that last move on your guys' part. Very ballsy, very cool," a Hekmatyar sergeant said to Lotte as he offered her a moldering cigarette. She declined with a polite wave.

"For us, this is minimal resistance. The relic helped things as well."

"Your orders are to be rearguard and make sure none of these scum escape now. We'll go and take care of the rest. Teach them a lesson for sucking the padishah's tiny cock."

Lotte nodded and motioned for her men to remain on guard. Taki again glanced at his kills. They lay sprawled out on the street. Contrary to his expectations, there was little blood that pooled around them. It mattered not. The corpses were his tribute to the glory of his country.

The next hour passed by uneventfully, save for the occasional gunshot from the distance – nothing that indicated a firefight had broken out. The squad was getting bored.

"I'm glad we won, but I wanted to do something cooler. Maybe kill some Imperials or save a room full of naked wenches," Hadassah finally remarked. "Those rebels were total amateurs."

"Watch your tongue, lest you get what you wish for," Lotte said.

"Naked wenches?"

Lotte leaned over and pulled at one of Hadassah's ears until the girl started to whimper.

"The rebels don't seem very good at fighting, even for humans," Taki said. "Are we really needed here or is this all an expensive farce?"

"You're a smart guy, Natalis," Karma said. "You see, this kind of gig is the ultimate easy job and it pays well. Far better than fighting real enemies for a few measly bullets a month."

"And so that's why you neglected to send your superiors any status reports for the last two months?" Lotte asked, smirking in annoyance.

"Touché, Cake-, er, Captain."

"Have a care for your balls, Gillette."

"Sorry, Milady," he said, and unconsciously crossed his legs.

"How many little places like this are there around the province?" Taki asked. "It seems like we're going to be doing this type of thing for a long while yet."

"You'd be right," Karma replied. "The countryside is dotted with these little hamlets. Most of them are occupied by Arben and Szerbek, while their overlords, the Khazari, occupy the cities. To me they all look like the same hairy bastard, but the way they blather on you'd think we were dealing with harpies versus skiapods. The hamlets tend to band together over these divides and start raising a stink over how the minority in Pristina are oppressing them and then it's only a matter of time until some tax collector gets defenestrated. The men dust off their old muskets in the attics and then you have a peasant revolt."

"So it's all about the money in the end?"

"Oh, everything is. You see, if you succeed in establishing a settlement then you can charge tolls on the roads and tariffs on trade, and thus make yourself very rich. If the guy you're supposed to send nearly all of your bullets to is over a hundred leagues away, then it's very tempting to just stop doing so. That leads to thinking you have the right to make your own rules and perhaps even tell the basileus to go fuck himself because what has he done for you lately?"

"But then Hero Hekmatyar squashes you like a bug."

"Another reason these pezzies are total amateurs," Hadassah said. "Instead of chucking the tax collector out the window, you should just make a big show of apologizing and weeping and kissing his hand, and then you give him a small sack of ammo saying that it's all you have right now because you're poor, but not to worry, you're honest and you pay your debts eventually."

"Just don't let him find your real hoard, right?" Karma asked.

"Exactly. You deserve what you get in that case."

Karma chuckled. "You're spiteful. I like that"

"And you're a poxy rake yourself, Mister Gillette."

"Can the flirting already, we're on duty," Lotte said. "Has anyone seen Draco?"

"He needed to go rub one out, Captain," Hadassah said.

"Enough slander, you crappy reformist," Draco said as he emerged from around the corner of an alley. "I was just pissing. And I also brought a friend." Held by the back of his collar was a dirt-smeared boy in his early teens.

"You were pissing on a little boy? You cock-monster!"

"Oh, give it a rest! I can't believe that's the first thing that crossed your filthy little mind!"

"Quiet, Mikkelsen! Emreis, where did you find him?" Lotte demanded.

"He was trying to sneak out over the wall," Draco said. "I saw him just as I finished up. Almost cut myself on my britches, too."

"Y-you people are witches, right?" the prisoner gasped, wide-eyed at the sight of the group.

"That's 'polaris regiment of foot' to you, kid," Draco snapped.

"Corporal, shackle his wrists and administer any necessary first aid. We'll hand the prisoner over to the duke's men when they come around," Lotte said.

The boy started to flail in panic. "W-w-wait! Please! If you hand me over, I'll die!"

"No one's going to kill you. Maybe rough you up or make you shovel shit for a while, but that's all," Draco scoffed.

"Y-you don't u-understand! It's not like that. It's-" The boy began with a stammer and ended with a sob.

"A jeni shqip?" Karma asked, crouching. The boy shook his head. "Kako se zoveš?" he tried again.

"Marko. Marko Princip."

"Žao mi je. I mean it," Karma said, patting the boy on the shoulder before turning away.

"Gillette, what's going on here? What did you say?" Lotte asked, her eyes narrowing in suspicion. Karma looked stricken for a moment, but shook his head with a dismissive smile.

"It's fine. Kid's got nothing useful, so we should let him go. No one will care about it."

"Step aside," she said, brushing past him. "You, prisoner, tell us exactly what's going on."

"They're killing everyone, even the ones who didn't fight you. Even the ones who didn't do anything. They do it to any village where people want to rebel against the Duke. I heard about it from my cousin who escaped Derthona. They come and round everyone up in a forest outside the village and shoot them in the back of the head, and anyone still alive afterwards they stab with their swords. Even the elderly and the babies! They take the girls and…"

"That's not possible!" Taki blurted out. *A hero doesn't do that! A hero punishes justly!*

"Comport yourself," Lotte snapped, and clapped a hand on Taki's shoulder.

Taki nodded, feeling chastened. If he was to impress his captain, he needed to be more coolheaded than this. "In that case," he asked, "should we retreat now and warn the duke?"

Lotte shook her head. "We still don't know whether the accusation is true or not. I will not slander our fellows without cause."

"You seem like you know something," Draco said to Karma. His eyelids narrowed.

"I can't say. I don't mix with the grunts," Karma huffed, and turned away.

Lotte bit her bottom lip in thought, and turned back to the prisoner. "Marko, was it? Do you have any proof?"

"If…if I show you, will you let me go?"

"No. But as long as you are bound, you fall under our protection," Lotte replied.

"Do you promise? Do you promise you won't hand me over?"

"We serve the exarch Constantin Choniates. You will have to trust in that."

"How can I trust in a man I've never met?"

Hadassah punched Marko lightly on the arm. "Don't be so stubborn, you little bastard. We'll protect you. The captain's a hardass but she's a just person. We're not the bad guys, you know."

Marko hung his head, before shaking it hopelessly.

"I'll take you there. It's going on right now," he said glumly.

"Very well," Lotte said. "I'm warning you though, if you try to escape, or if you're lying to set some plan into action, you will die first. Do you understand?"

Marko nodded.

"Emreis and Mikkelsen, stay behind on guard. Myself, Gillette, and Natalis will go with the prisoner. If we're not back in a half-bell, flee to the Cloud Temple. Do not wait for us, but make sure the exarch knows that we perished."

Taki swallowed hard. Being chosen to accompany the captain like that was a sign of her favor, and yet anxiety welled in his chest all the same. Draco's words from earlier had called to mind a drily-written passage about the wars that ravaged the region before the Fall, and about something called "ethnic cleansing." It sounded like a wholesome pursuit on its surface, for reducing mutation was always commendable. But to cleanse could also mean to destroy. He looked at Marko. *Is it possible to destroy an entire people?*

When he passed through the town square, Taki could not contain the increasing dread lapping at his mind as he gazed on the utter desolation mixed with fresh signs of life. Overturned carts had spilled vegetables onto the street that had been crushed by hobnailed boots. Half-eaten food cooled on metal plates on tables near an eatery. More perceptive eyes saw fresh bullet holes studding stucco walls and bloodstains spattered on cobblestones. *Something is wrong. Something is terribly wrong.*

"Where are the bodies?" Taki asked, frowning at a pool of crimson that slowly spread along mortared crevices.

"If I were trying to purge a place and yet remain discreet, I'd simply have bodies carried away and dumped somewhere," Karma said. "And I'd use the people who were still alive to do the work."

"Why not just set it all alight if you wanted to drive everyone away?" Taki asked.

"Because the people have little value, whereas the buildings and farmlands are the important stuff. That way, you can quickly resettle a place with the people you want, and offer your supporters and friends a nice bunch of houses in the process."

"Where did everyone go?" Lotte asked the prisoner. Marko pointed his bound wrists ahead to the rear gates. Splintered posts hung from wooden hinges and swayed pathetically in silence. The ground below was well-worn, but the dust and dark stains were fresh at the precipice. Further on, the grassy fields were trampled and broken, as if dozens of people had trudged their way along the path to the woods nearby. Karma's gaze flicked over streaks of blood dappling the leaves, but he kept quiet. After the acrid stink of smoke and lingering sweat, the piney smell of the woods was a relief.

Gunshots rang out in violent overture, causing them to dive to the ground with weapons drawn and curses flung. After a few minutes, however, it was apparent that there was no more danger to be had. Taki briefly indulged in the fantasy that perhaps Lotte would permit them all to lay low in the grass for a time. Nothing good would come of advancing. Here, under cover, it was safe and secure. They could simply remain there for a good long time before slowly retreating from harm. *It's not our fight. This has little to do with the Imperium. I don't want to go on.* Taki shoved his words back down his throat before they could erupt and unman him. Lotte was signaling for them to rise and advance.

They penetrated the treeline, quickly following the trail of trampled shrubs and torn branches. No special skill or training was needed now but following one's nose. The humid, acrid air bit like burning gunpowder shoved up a nostril and left to smolder. Finally, as Taki crested a low ridge, he saw the killing field.

A twenty-meter-long trench was crudely dug in the loamy topsoil of a clearing, within which were bodies wreathed by settling gunsmoke. The sight spurred a regression into calculation. Numbers were safe. Numbers did not cause him to feel overcome with terror and nausea. How many bodies were there? If he went with five corpses per meter, that meant at least a hundred; some large and developed, some small, some hunchbacked with old age. Some still writhed, whether out of pain or as the last reflexes of a dying brain. How many were women? How many had died clutching their children? Taki bit the webbing between his thumb and index finger to stifle further speculation.

Standing over the corpses near the trench were the Khazari Hekmatyar legion, kalash rifles still smoking from the barrels. A few men dressed in village clothes still knelt in front of the pit, hands tied and blindfolded. They bobbed their heads in confusion, as if indignant to not receive a bullet like the rest. Their would-be executioners had probably used reloaded rounds with bad powder or just the wrong caliber altogether, Taki realized. One of the bound men tried to flee, only to have his head caved in by a mace. The rest of the survivors were quickly set upon with axes before being pushed into the trench. Another detail spread quicklime over the bodies. It was a common belief that the white, caustic powder would dissolve flesh faster and dissuade scavengers from spreading the remains. The footmen looked up now, muttering to each other and pointing at the new arrivals.

"I told you we should've just let the kid go," Karma muttered.

One of the Khazari, with an ensign's stripes, charged up to Lotte.

"Didn't we tell you to stay at the entrance?" he shouted at her, his rifle sweeping her face.

"Watch where you point that," she growled, gesturing at his muzzle.

He swept you with it, Captain, Taki thought with oddly fierce anger. *He could have shot you. Kill him, now!* He gasped softly when he realized what had passed through his mind. To think like this was unlike him, but something within was starting to scream louder and louder as the seconds passed. Fortunately, the ensign lowered his rifle a small bit.

Lotte continued. "My men stand guard as we speak, and if we do not return, you may expect a legion of our Black Cross to come wipe you off the map!"

That's not true, but the man doesn't know any better, Taki realized. The bluff seemed to work, as the ensign's eyes went wide and he finally lowered his gun all the way.

"Explain this!" Lotte demanded.

The Khazari was silent for a moment before he let out a contemptuous laugh. White mist rose from the trench as shovelfuls of lime landed on bloody backs. Small, dusty mushroom clouds sprouted to mark the end of individual lives. A thousand deaths would probably make a much larger cloud, Taki figured. The other paramilitaries turned their attention back to smoking and taking sips of local moonshine from their flasks. From within the trench, someone's moans were smothered by a shovel smashed into brain.

"You witches are good fighters but you're kind of stupid. What the fuck does this look like to you? It's a purge, plain and simple. We had the scum dig their own graves and then we plugged them in the heads."

"My squad took care of all the resistance at the gates. None of these people were the ones shooting at you!"

"Look, wench, these are subhuman scum and rebels. They're all plotting to kill us anyway."

"That's 'captain' to you. You could have arrested or exiled them. To execute the entire village is boorish excess, and no honorable man could recommend this," she snarled, glancing at the boy prisoner. Strangely, he did not weep or flail or attempt to run. He simply stood there with a look of resignation on his face.

"Do you think you can talk to me about honor, witch?" The ensign scoffed.

Lotte leaned in to stare the man in the face. "Who ordered this?"

The ensign let out a quizzical frown. "Do you have the pox? This is a mandate of the greatest hero in the lands. He gives us law. He gives us justice. Who the hell are you? Just a grunt like us. Forget it and go back before you end up dead."

"This isn't justice. This is just murder, whether willed by a hero or not."

"Whatever you want to call it, I really don't give a shit. It's either them or us."

"I will be sending a full report to the exarch of the Temple. This will not go unnoticed. Your lord will be censured and it will be your fault."

"Go ahead. Also, hand over that prisoner of yours. Then fuck off. *Captain.*"

"By the Hoplite's Code, this prisoner is ours," Taki blurted out. *Shit. Again I've spoken out of turn, and to an officer, no less.* But even this thought seemed tiny in comparison to the increasing indignation he felt. There was no possible way the Hero of the Dominion was really ordering these men. The only logical explanation was that the squad had been duped. Yes, these men were the actual Imperial agents, sent to discredit the Hero by committing dishonorable acts in his name. Taki could not help the people in the trench, but if he saved Marko's life, the boy's testimony would help inform the Hero of pervasive treason among the rank-and-file.

"Fine, keep him." The ensign raised his kalash and shot Marko in the chest. The boy's eyes widened in shock before he crumpled to the ground and bled out.

Taki felt his own insides twist hard enough to wring out his lungs and let out a soundless scream. It was all wrong. Everything about this was wrong. He had to make it right. It was time to listen to what raged inside. He thrust his arm forward, braced the elbow with his free hand, and opened the gates to call forth raging fire. These traitors would burn. For killing Marko, for discrediting the Hero, *for... for...*

A hand clamped around Taki's wrist before the swirling energy within achieved fiery coalescence and Taki felt the prana charge leave his body as Karma siphoned it away. Taki's face contorted in anguish: it felt as if his insides had been ripped out through his chest and then replaced with dry cotton. He wheeled on Karma. *What the hell are you doing?* he wanted to scream at the man, but before he could open his mouth, he felt a gauntleted fist smash into his cheek. His wound opened back up and sprayed blood on his eyes. The world went into a maddening spin. Angry shouts and curses in Khazari pinpricked the edges of his perception.

"Stay your hand, maggot," Lotte snarled, and righted him. She grabbed Taki roughly by the hair and forced him to one knee with her dagger pressed against his throat. He blinked at looked back at her. Her eyes flashed with anger, but to his horror, also smoldered with disappointment. The truth of his actions now hit him with merciless clarity. *Oh God, no. What have I done?* Taki hung his head and tried not to cry. That would be the ultimate dishonor on top of disgrace.

Karma seemed to have defused the tension in the meantime. Slowly the rest of the men dispersed, followed by their commander. Before he stepped away the ensign spat brown-streaked phlegm on Lotte's boots. Such a slight would have merited a duel under any other circumstance, but she had little to back her position. Disregarding the insult, she instead helped Taki to his feet and perfunctorily pressed a kerchief to his bleeding wound. He opened his mouth to speak. To explain himself, or at least to apologize.

"We'll talk about this later," she said.

Taki wanted to claw his wound open till his face peeled from his head. He had always, always, hated those words.

7

The evening air around the fortress of Sevastopol smelled like fish suffocating in a latrine—like almost any other coastline in the world—but for Aslatiel, it had a homey quality that he missed while on assignment. The cool stone of the parapets soothed his palms, which burned for reasons unknown to him as he stared over the illuminated skyline of the city below. The avenues bustled with the activity of twilight and the smoke of cooking fires bathed the half-lit streets in a dusky haze. Periodically, the cries of the water merchants filtered up to his level. Fresh and clean! No gutrot here! and other familiar sales pitches. Most of the groundwater was either rotten with pestilence or tainted with deuterium, and so became a commodity just like everything else. The fortress had not only its own purification system but also working pumping, which he sorely missed while on assignment.

As Alfa Gruppe commander, Aslatiel was afforded his own expansive private chambers with a balcony view of the city. Even higher ranking officers got the views of the Black Sea, where the pink auroras of beta decay danced above the waters at night. Most importantly, he had space and silence to collect his thoughts. Once, he had been one of the dozens of shaved-headed children cloistered in cells many floors below. Barely human, and incredibly dangerous. If left alone, the children typically went insane under the burden of their own uncontrollable abilities, and after they killed their own parents the entire town was typically next to go. Thankfully, prana manifestation was ordinarily unsubtle, and only by virtue of this fact did the Imperium avoid being overrun by predatory gangs of feral bush mages. Through the wisdom of individuals like Ba'gshnar, they instead became a precious resource to be molded into the fine warriors for the Imperium's defense. It had been individuals like him who had apparently caused the Gotterdammerung, so this was a just penance, Aslatiel reasoned.

"Luca," he said as he sensed her approach from behind, though her footfalls were typically muffled out of habit. Their master had always impressed upon them the value of silence in all things.

"Aslatych."

She sidled up next to him, inhaling deeply as she beheld the cityscape, as if she had missed the smell of the coastline too. Her hair was slick with water from a drawn bath, and she smelled ever so slightly of roses. Thin white terrycloth was wrapped tightly under her arms, and ended just above her thighs. He disliked it when she did this. There was no reason she couldn't have changed into something else before approaching him. It was hard to tell if she was being deliberately provocative or whether she was simply oblivious. But he was the one who suffered for it. It was hard to avert his gaze, as mortified as his enjoyment of seeing her curves made him.

Lucatiel was truly in the prime of her youth and turned heads wherever she went. He remembered how in the southern desert outskirts, an amir had once demanded to buy her in exchange for a working chaingun and a thousand rounds of explosive ammunition. Only his sister's gentle humor had prevented Aslatiel from stabbing the corpulent old man in the throat. Such things never happened in the civilized, central parts near the capital. In the Imperium, women were equal to men, and individuals were judged on their merit, not their skin color or the shapes of their noses. He again noticed his gaze tracing the enticing concavity of her lower back and he felt dirty for it, like a lecherous old tribesman in sweaty silks. His eyes focused on a jagged white line on her back which went from under her shoulder to just below the base of her neck. He had a similar mark from a sparring accident as a basang, and he always wondered if she had permitted herself to be struck in the same way so she could mimic him more closely.

"How are you holding up?" he asked, finally forcing himself to look away. Perhaps there was some merit in getting promoted, after all. Then he would at least have the radioactive sea to occupy his vision.

She slammed a fist down on the stone railing. "My body is fine. But I let those damned buffoons surprise us, and I should've seen it coming.

The novice was nothing more than bait, and I nearly let you be hurt! I still have much to learn, it seems."

Aslatiel shushed her with a finger to her lips. "But we survived and triumphed all the same. You didn't endanger me, but rather saved me."

Lucatiel turned her face away from him and unclenched her fist. Where it had landed, the granite bore a new crack. "I am grateful to you, Aslatych, though I do not completely believe you."

Aslatiel chuckled. "I inquired about who those polaris were. A poorly-manned company, really only half of a squad, that calls themselves 'Tirefire the Lesser,' of all things."

"Why would they insult their own lords so flagrantly?"

"I don't know, but I am most fascinated with that older woman who appeared to control them. I think she may be a contemporary of our master. They both spoke the same tongue, and she seemed abnormally powerful. Similar to Ba'gshnar. Although in a very different way."

"Have you asked him more about her?"

"I dare not. You know how secretive he is about his past. We two probably know the most about him out of all citizens."

"Then you should avoid prying. He has never betrayed us."

"Of course, Luca. I trust the man with my life and also with yours. Still, I would like to know more about this new threat to our nation. She almost bested us. That must never happen again."

"You can rely on me, Aslatych. And also on Elsa and Mikhail. We're all here for you."

For me, and not the Imperium or even our master. He knew her too well by this point. Knew that this what she would have actually said had she less restraint. Such passions, however, quickly gave way to treason. It was a possibility he could not permit.

"Remember, you and I serve the padishah," he cautioned her.

"Only because I like you very much, dear brother," she replied, rolling the curling edge of her towel between thumb and forefinger like one would handle a round of milligrad.

It was Aslatiel's turn to avert his reddening face from his sister's inquisitive gaze. "Are you looking forward to our new mission?" he asked, bringing her back to more mundane matters.

"Of course! We've waited for a very, very long time to see Irulan again."

Aslatiel nodded. "Our efforts will hasten the end of the Dominion."

Lucatiel rolled her eyes. "I thought you'd be more excited to see your woman again."

"We haven't been together since our time at the bihara. Surely she's moved on by now. Perhaps forgotten me."

"I'll wager my pistols that she hasn't." Lucatiel's palm came to rest on his knuckles and her fingers curled their way in between his.

For a moment, Aslatiel savored the sensation, but quickly moved his hand away. "What's important now is the war. Go back to your quarters and get dressed, sister. I must meditate. I must be stronger."

* * * *

Days later, they had arrived in Pristina, the Duchy capital, and deep behind enemy lines. Aslatiel finished his mug of mint tea cut with teeth-shattering amounts of sugar, and gazed casually at his surroundings to make sure they were not being eavesdropped on. Around him, Pristina bourgeoisie went about their business of eating, cutting deals, and planning their days. Most of the men and some of the women puffed on clay pipes packed thick with resin-flavored tobacco leaves, permeating the streets and alleyways with sweet-smelling smoke.

Spirits were high in town, at least among the Khazari. Though fall was approaching, the harvest had been decent, and the worst of the seasonal plagues had already moved on. Dyscrasias, fluxes, and distempers claimed a certain number of lives every year and maimed forever many more. The dead were buried and the living endured these trials that they believed were sent from on high to test their faith. When the specter of disease began to wane, it was time for celebration.

Aslatiel, like other spetsnaz, was party to the forgotten knowledge that miasmas and fevers were not in fact the will of the Lord, but rather a result of infestations by creatures too small to be seen by the naked eye. Bathing regularly, washing one's clothes, and rinsing the hands after defecating were all ways to avoid coming into contact with these creatures. In his troop, hygiene was taken one step further in that they were not allowed to drink water, but only hot or cold tea like Ba'gshnar did. Gutrot was thus unheard of in Alfa Gruppe, and the practice had since spread to other units in the padishah's service.

Aslatiel glanced at his men, or rather, two women and another man. His squad, he thought to himself with a swell of pride. Only in the Imperium would such disparate individuals be brought together so willingly and with such dedication. Elsa, a woman from Gujrat, should have been mortal enemies with Mikhail, a Mohammedan from the Caliphate. And the von Halcons should have been enemies with both. Not under the padishah, however. The king of kings had united the broken peoples of the old world and given them singular purpose under the guidance of The Way. Here, in this blighted, corrupt place, Alfa would make a difference and bring light to the wastes.

After a final check with his enhanced senses to make sure that no one was spying, Aslatiel spoke to his squad in a lowered voice. "It took a while, but the papers we passed on to the resistance have been vetted and we can finally meet their organizer."

"You mean Irulan, don't you?" Lucatiel asked.

Aslatiel nodded.

"I hate having to wait to see her," Lucatiel said. "It's irksome that we had to go through such a long process with the locals to even meet with her. A paranoid bunch, they are."

"This region is now considered highly probable for auto-annexation," Aslatiel replied. "The majority of the population is Arben and Szerbek while the Dominion-backed ruling minority is Khazari, and their leader, the Duke Gul, is a notorious enemy of ours. The brutality he practiced in his original lands is magnified tenfold on his current subjects. The majority, if given the chance, will likely want to join the Imperium, which will destabilize the Dominion and likely set off a chain reaction of similar defections."

"But, dear brother, that still doesn't answer *what* we're supposed to accomplish here."

"I suppose that's up to Irulan." He shrugged. "Ah, there's our contact," he said, turning his head to someone approaching the table behind him a tawny-faced older Arben clad in a simple linen caftan. Deeply tanned and rutted skin and a lean but powerful figure told them that he was probably a farmer. His eyes told them he likely knew how to handle a weapon as well.

"*Mirëdita,* honored guests," the farmer said. "I am to take you to Suren's daughter."

"*Ni hao*," nodded Aslatiel. "I trust you remember the terms of our agreement?"

The old man nodded.

"Then we place ourselves in your care."

"In ten minutes, meet me at the stables. We have a wagon prepared for you."

* * * *

Aslatiel's pupils constricted with the sudden influx of light as his blindfold was removed. After the initial discomfort, he took in his surroundings with veiled interest. As promised, Lucatiel, Elsa, and Mikhail stood nearby and appeared unhurt. They were underground, he could tell by the musky and mossy smell. Whatever structure they were in had probably either been a wine cellar, as evidenced by the wooden shelves lining the walls, some of which still had long-empty bottles placed on their racks. Around the Alfa were Arben and Szerbek rebels with stolen straight-pull kalash rifles in their hands, staring at the newcomers with trepidation, but not being impolite as to muzzle-sweep them.

"Aslatiel! Is it really you?" asked an excited female voice as someone squeezed through the ring of armed guards to face the group. "It *is* you! You finally came!" Irulan said. Of medium height and build, her most memorable features were dirty golden hair and heavily-lidded eyes that gave her a look of childish innocence.

"Fahnrich Surenovna," Aslatiel replied, a bit stiffly. "Alfa Gruppe stands ready to render assistance."

"I accept your offer on behalf of the Resistance," she said with a bow. "You came just in time, too. There's been another massacre and even the sideline villages are starting to come around."

"Can you start by giving us a briefing on the military strength of your group?"

Irulan waggled a finger. "I'll be sure to bring you all up to speed, but first, the custom here is to share a meal. It makes you guests and thus grants protection. It just so happens you're in time for supper, too."

As promised, Alfa Gruppe supped well that night. Steaming plates of lamb hot from the tagine shared table space with bowls of lentils and greens, minced cabbages with beets, and a copious amount of scented rice.

The air was sweet with tobacco, and an ancient record player scratchily piped frenetic notes into smoky currents. Aslatiel, however, spent the majority of the time not eating, but exchanging pleasantries with the rebel leaders who'd been convinced to pledge their loyalty to the padishah once the duke was no more. Irulan was an operative from Vympel Gruppe, which excelled at fomenting local insurgencies for the benefit of the Imperium, and enjoyed a far more insidious reach than Aslatiel's Alfa ever could. She'd been hard at work in Kosovo, he could see.

When he'd gotten past the formalities, Aslatiel excused himself from the dinner. He was a fighter, not a diplomat. He also ached to see Irulan in private, which he hadn't done since their last days at the bihara under Ba'gshnar. She intercepted his silent signal to rendezvous and also departed the feasthall.

"I would like you to fight alongside me once more," Aslatiel said once they were alone.

"I was afraid you'd never ask," Irulan said, and slid fiercely into his embrace. "The duke's hired from the Cloud Temple. 'Tirefire the Lesser' is the company name."

Aslatiel's eyes narrowed at the mention. "We've had dealings before. I can assure you, they will not be an impediment this time. Are your preparations ready? For the parade?"

"Yes, my darling. We're going to start a revolution."

8

Taki moved without thought, his only impulse being Lotte's hand clamped around his wrist as she tugged at him. He bowed his head and focused his vision on nothing. He was too nauseous to vomit, and too breathless to pass out. The squad had ridden back from the village in silence, and had entered the barracks with nary a word to each other. It quickly became apparent that Hadassah and Draco had violated their orders and followed from a distance, and they too had witnessed the events in the woods. Lotte had chosen not to discipline them, at least not harshly enough to leave visible marks. Taki, however, was a different case.

"Sit," Lotte commanded, and pointed to a nearby wooden bench in front of a grease-stained table. She had dragged him to a now-deserted mess hall in their barracks. The Hekmatyar legionnaires were elsewhere celebrating their victory with gunfire and spirits. More than one of them would likely die of falling bullets or old vendettas that flared up with the aid of vodka and knives. In the distance, Taki could already hear faint popping sounds and cheers.

"Captain-"

"No. I talk, you listen," Lotte said. "But first, drink. You're wired to shit and I need you to remember what happens from now on."

She set a pair of tumblers on the table, sloshed yellow-hazed rotgut into both, and sat down. Without waiting for Taki, she took one of the tumblers and downed it. She poured another measure in and also downed that. She looked at Taki expectantly. With shaky hands, he clutched his glass and deposited its contents into his stomach.

The astringent burn shook Taki out of his hazy stupor. Now he remembered another tip the instructors had taught him. In combat, it always paid to take a swig from one's canteen. He had given the words little thought, but now he noticed his heart slowing and his thoughts coming back to a semblance of clarity.

"What you did was stupid and could have gotten everyone killed," Lotte said, to which Taki nodded, glumly. She sighed. "I'm not saying I'm better than you. What I did when we first met the duke was also incredibly dumb. I shouldn't have drawn my blade, even if I wasn't going to actually swing it. You and I both have a problem controlling our impulses. But I've learned, though incompletely, to keep them in check. If you can't master that skill, you'll die quick."

"I'm sorry." Taki looked into the bottom of his glass, unable to meet her eyes. "I'll accept any discipline you see fit to give me."

"Attacking a friendly officer means death."

"Then give me death."

Lotte reached out and slapped him across the unwounded side of his face. "Look at me."

Taki raised his head and tried to stare at the space between the top of her mouth and the bottom of her nose. In response, Lotte slipped a finger under his chin to bring his gaze to meet hers.

"I like you, Natalis," she said. "So does Emreis and even Mikkelsen. You're uptight and kind of a suckup, but you've got a soft heart like any decent human being. You really want to serve a righteous cause and be rewarded justly for it. You also really want to ditch us and get into a *good* unit."

Taki nodded, sheepishly.

Lotte smirked. "Don't worry, I take no offense. I'm a captain in command of a whole two corporals and a foul-mouthed lance. Meanwhile, Pantheon has a hundred and twenty of the deadliest fighters in the Dominion. Ours isn't a real company. It's the Temple's midden, where all of the unwanted people go to disappear. You shouldn't have ended up here. You were duped by the major, and I can't say why. She's always been inscrutable."

"It wasn't because I can write?"

Lotte chuckled. "Let me tell you something. That woman regards us as little more than smelly, hairy savages. She once told me that she could smell my cleft from thirty meters away and that I was forbidden to raise my arms in her presence lest I cause her to retch. Our only good attribute is our predisposition to kill with great brutality, and that amuses and benefits her. She doesn't care if you can write. It's all a joke to her."

Taki frowned, not so much from the major's purported view of the Argead race, but from what she had said to Lotte. "Captain, why are you so loyal to that horrible major, then? Why, when she's so godrotting cruel and…"

"I won't have you defame her, Natalis, and it's not just because of the Code."

Taki bit his tongue. "Beg pardon, Captain."

"She owns my life," Lotte said. "Mind you, I didn't say she saved my life. She owns it."

"I don't follow."

Lotte sighed. "A while ago, I commanded a much larger regiment. Guilty Throne, we were called. A stupid name, as the major would say."

"What happened?" Taki asked. He brought the edge of a thumb to his mouth and started to nibble.

"I killed them all."

"How? I don't…"

"It was before the armistice with the Ursalans. I led a hundred and fifty souls—*my company*—to take out the border fortress guarding the Sankt Gotthard pass. Locals call it the *Teufelsbrücke*. It was strangling our trade with the Cantons. Or maybe it was executing too many Argead citizens trying to cross. I forget exactly why it was so rotting important. I thought we could assault it from the front and overwhelm them with our strength. The Ursalans tore us apart. I'd like to tell myself it was because of an informant in our ranks, or because they had ancient Teutonic weaponry but the bottom line is that I was arrogant and didn't listen to wiser counsel.

"Everyone died horribly except for me, my major Enishi, and a lance corporal Sion. We were gravely wounded and then captured. The castellan wanted to send two of us back to the Cloud Temple to tell the exarch what had happened. If there was just one, they could question the truth of what happened, but with two, they'd believe us. But there were three of us, so one had to die." She took another swig of vodka.

Taki winced, both from her words and the fact that his cuticle now bled freely. "Captain, you don't have to…"

"He made me pick. It couldn't be me. Said he didn't have all day and that if I didn't choose he'd just throw us all from the peak. Enishi looked at me with those clear blue eyes of his and said if I didn't spare Sion then he'd never forgive me. I chose. I chose wrong."

"I'm sorry."

"For what? You didn't throw their lives away."

Taki could only nod, stricken.

"After I returned, I tried to rejoin my unit. Mezeta invaded my chambers, called me a coward, and started to beat me with a cat-o-nine, so I had no choice but to duel her right then and there. Sometimes I think I only lost because I'd already damned near bled out before the fight even started. In the end, she forced me into debtorship."

Taki grit his teeth. "That's horrid! Dishonorable to the extreme!" *And so like the godrotting major!*

Lotte laughed and squeezed his forearm with her hand. "You remind me of a cornet I once had. She was about your age and knew her figures like none other. She most wanted everyone to get along and be happy, and was a total pain about keeping us from overspending. Once, I ordered her to authorize us some extra grog, and she refused right to my face. The girl had some nerve, but she stuck to her principles, whereas I was dissolute and intemperate. Now, she's a paragon of success. So I don't blame you at all for wanting to move on with your life. I'm a broken-down disgrace, and I deserve everything I get. But you still have potential. I'll help you develop it, but you have to grow up, first."

"How can I do that?"

"Come with me," Lotte said, and rose from the table. She set her glass down and extended a hand. "I'll show you what a real Hero looks like."

When he was sober and not surrounded by armed men, Gul Hekmatyar seemed almost warm. Strangely devoid of pretense and that overbearing bravado that he had greeted them with on their arrival. Taki and Lotte found him with his wife, a kindly-looking woman, and his two daughters of ten and eleven. They seemed well-fed, well-dressed, and well-adjusted. Lotte knelt before him and Taki did the same. *"I'll do the talking,"* she had told him beforehand.

"Captain, to what do I owe the pleasure of a sudden visit?" Gul asked gaily. Casually, he waved a hand and two of his guardsmen nodded before herding the wife and children away.

"Milord, are you aware that your men carried out a massacre of unarmed innocents from the village of New Petrovic?" Lotte asked him, skipping pretense and greeting. Gul seemed to ignore her for a few seconds to peer down at the indoor garden in one of the palace courtyards. His wife now played with the children below.

"My daughters are named Alexia and Marija," he said, smiling broadly at their tiny forms below. "My fondest dream is to make them a world in which they do not have to worry about the things that I had to worry about all my life. Starving to death, fighting for your life, being a slave, getting eaten by the mutated things out there. I want them to live never having had to fire a gun to kill someone. Never having had to feel hunger or cold of their own blood coming out of a wound."

"An admirable goal, milord, but that does not answer my question."

"But it does. Because the only way I am going to accomplish this dream of mine, for my daughters, is to give them a better world than the one I was born into. A world without criminals or strife, where everyone knows their place and is happy for it. A Khazari world."

"You stand to dishonor your good name, milord. Your peers may punish sedition, but they do not murder."

"We are cleansing the region of filth and mutation. It is slow-going, because like vermin, the subhumans are constantly breeding and spreading. I can tolerate them for a while when they obey their masters, but otherwise I gladly put them to the sword. One day I will be able to exterminate the plague of inferior beings once and for all."

Taki brought his hand to his mouth to stifle a horrified gasp. *Ethnic cleansing.* But this man was a hero, was he not? Heroes and kings were the guardians of their subjects, no matter what. When Gul had accepted the dukedom, had he not sworn to abide by that sacred responsibility?

Lotte lifted her chin, so that she now faced the Duke with unambiguous eyes.

"The Ursalans shout 'inferior beings!' when they rush into battle. But this is the *Dominion.* I will *not* have my unit take part in these activities again. While you are within your rights to do whatever you wish within your province, we of the Temple are bound by higher law and greater purpose. We are compelled to fight *foreign enemies,* not subjects of the basileus. If you have a problem with this, you may address it to Exarch Choniates."

Gul looked taken aback, initially, but quickly assumed an indignant scowl.

"You think you are the only ones fighting a war? I fight *daily* for my daughters and my people. If you witches act against me, I will take you out!"

The corners of Lotte's mouth curled upwards.

"Oh? And what if the Imperium forgives you and offers that Khazari world you dream about?"

"Never question my loyalty again, or I will run you through, fuck the wound, and make you beg for more. Niketas and I are bound by fate, and it is because of me that he is your basileus. Friend though he is, he is soft in the head and short on honor, and thus tolerates nonhuman filth like you among our numbers. I dislike having you witches here but at least your kind know your place. Most of the time."

"I think I preferred it when you were drunk, Your Grace. Remember that we are feared for a very good reason."

"I will have you whipped and shamed in front of your soldiers, I swear it. Now out of my sight, wench."

Lotte rose, backed up three steps, and then turned. Taki felt shaky as he mimicked her, but managed not to fall. The ensign at New Petrovic had not lied, after all. The man was not a traitor to his lord. He was just following orders. Taki closed his eyes to try and calm his heart but found himself staring back into the trench where more than a hundred bodies lay sprawled in the mud. The irises of their eyes were black with hemorrhage, like those ancient black ivory balls marked only with the number eight. They looked back at him with those bloody orbs and remained silent. *I'm sorry,* Taki started to say, but his mouth was filled with sand. In turn, their pale lips began to move. *Why? You serve a hero,* they said. Taki buckled and fell to his knees.

"Natalis," Lotte said. Taki opened his eyes and found himself half-slumped against the stone corridor leading away from the duke's chambers. His captain's hand rested on his face. It felt ice cold, but he realized that was only because his skin burned. He blinked, and righted himself.

"Sorry, Captain. I just..."

"Remember, Natalis," she said. "Remember who you serve."

* * * *

Several days later, the squad received a letter by courier.

"Captain Satou:

Know that your correspondence has been received and your concerns noted. The Cloud Temple does not interfere with local affairs or challenge the rule of a member of the Council of Nobles unless explicitly authorized by His Grace the basileus. You and your squad are to carry out your tasks as ordered. I expect you to do your duty.

Long Live The Ethnomartyr.

C. Choniates, Exarch."

Lotte looked up from the paper, folded it neatly, and stuffed it into a belt satchel. Draco and Hadassah looked at her expectantly. Karma idly dug under his fingernails with the tip of a push dagger, and Taki sat listlessly nearby.

Draco broke the oppressive silence. "So, what news? When do we act?"

"And exactly *what* do you think the exarch wrote?" Lotte asked.

Draco smacked a fist into his palm. "He wants us to immediately arrest the duke and his commanders, hold courts-martial, and take them all out back and shoot them in their fucking heads."

"You know better than that."

"Right." Draco's expression darkened. "Good ol' Constantin, *always* a paragon of righteousness."

"Lest you forget, he is our liege lord," Lotte warned. "I will not tolerate the defamation of his name."

Draco wiped at his eyes in frustration. "It's just that I didn't expect him to permit this sort of travesty," he sighed.

"I think Lord Choniates," Taki began, "is a righteous man who must sometimes say one thing but desire another." He looked warily at the others, trying to gauge their response. Lotte raised an eyebrow but did not overtly shush him.

Draco smiled broadly. "Aye, he is! There have been many great leaders in the histories who've been muzzled in public, but had lesser men act behind the scenes for right. *We* are those men, Captain. That is, men and women."

Taki continued, bolstered by Draco's response. Though he was now resolved to temper his speech and his actions, as Lotte had told him to, his wrath still simmered. His captain hadn't told him to quell his feelings, just to express them in a more acceptable fashion. Now, he would use the full range of his faculties and his knowledge, as opposed to brute force. "Aye, so a righteous man exacts his desire through deeds, not words. And perhaps the Duke should learn to fear that righteousness."

"I could poison his wine." Hadassah volunteered. "Or push him out a window."

"But how can we deal with his footmen?" Draco started to pace frenetically.

"Maybe," she said, "those two slave wenches will want some revenge. I could talk with them. They could come back to the Temple with us."

"*Stop,*" Lotte commanded. "No more of this talk. And Natalis, I thought you knew better than to wag a serpent's tongue. If you pour treason in the ears of my men I *will* bend you over my knee and give you a caning you won't forget."

Taki felt his cheeks redden and he bit the inside of his cheek to stifle a retort.

"Captain," Draco pleaded. "Whip me if you must, but you *must* also realize that something rots in Kosovo."

"You're being overdramatic," Karma said with a long sigh. "We're supposed to do stuff that the levy peasants can't and the respectable soldiers won't. Massacres are part of the job, or were you asleep for that part of the academy?"

"Silence, Gillette," Draco said. "I've shanked more men in the exarch's name than you ever will, but they were trained killers, not old ladies and kids. We may be witches but we're not murderers of the innocent."

Karma's lips thinned into a smirk. "Oh? And who's to say that the villagers didn't deserve it? The truth is that practically the entire countryside is itching to go over to the padishah. They're all traitors, and if you're talking about killing Gul Hekmatyar then you're traitors too."

"When did you go native, you godrotting *deserter?*" Draco asked, balling his hand into a fist for a strike.

"Yeah, scumbag, it's obvious you knew this was happening," Hadassah demanded. "How long have you sat idle while all those people died? Why didn't you do *anything* about it?"

"Emreis, Mikkelsen, this is your final warning." Lotte snapped. "As much as I hate to say it, Gillette is right. Have you two forgotten the *first* article of the Code?"

"No, ma'am," Draco said, through grit teeth.

"I know what the godrotting code says!" Hadassah protested. "But they can't just cut little kids' throats in front of us and expect us to scratch our balls and enjoy the show like it's the annual passion play! At least *we* know the guy who always plays Jesus actually gets off on being hit and the blood comes from chickens. But these are real people getting murdered. Why are we even needed in this shithole? Why, when the real war is a thousand leagues to the east and the Imps are busy kicking our asses? We're polaris! We're supposed to be—to be fighting *evil!*"

Lotte stood and approached Hadassah, who flinched reflexively. Taki held his breath and closed his eyes, knowing what would come next. As abrasive as the redhead could be, he did not want to see her receive a beating. *Damn you, captain. I thought you were a good person, not some godrotting...officer!*

When the thudding of boot heels and fists against flesh failed to arrive as promised, Taki cracked his eyes open. Lotte was in a crouch, gently holding Hadassah in an embrace.

"I know. I share your rage," Lotte said. "I also want to kill the duke and everyone who serves him. But the fate of those above our station is simply not for us to decide. Our purpose as soldiers is to defend the lives and property of the lords of the Argead Dominion. Nothing more, and nothing less. So I forgive you this transgression, but I don't want to hear any more talk from any of you about killing our betters. This is a trial we must endure, and though it is an unfair and heavy one, we must do so with grace and dignity."

"Y-y-es, s-sorry Captain," Hadassah whimpered.

"All of you, back to your quarters and rest," Lotte said. "Get your wits back, or else."

"Captain," Taki began, "I mean no insubordination, but..."

"Spit it out, Natalis."

He cringed. There was little to be done to please her, he lamented. *And does it even matter anymore?* He had just taken part in murder—mass-murder—after all.

"Yes, Captain. What will happen should we go to another village? Last time, we were just the rear-guard, but what if we're ordered to take part in the killing? There is nothing forbidding it in the Code, as you pointed out."

"If that happens…" Lotte closed her eyes for a moment and then opened them. "I alone will take responsibility for whatever happens. Live or die, we follow the code and do our duty as the exarch expects. But I won't have my soldiers dishonored. If necessary, I'll have you all sent back to the Temple."

"Captain, we can't just let you just stay here alone," Draco said.

"Are you going to follow my orders or not?" She fixed a glare at him, from which he promptly averted his gaze.

"Lucky for you, that's a ways off," Karma said with a shrug. "Next job is to run guard duty for the duke while he goes on one of his victory parades through the city. Pristina's packed with his retainers, and security's tight with his troops all bunkered here. There's little chance we'll actually see any action."

"You mean he's throwing parade over what just happened?" Taki asked, aghast.

"No, nothing so stupidly malicious. It's a tribute to how he single-handedly won the battle of New Istanbul. You know, he's a hero of the lands."

"But the basileus was there, too."

"You think he doesn't know that? Or that his men are going to really object? Anyway, it's a tawdry affair. Mainly him riding around in a gaudy old relic blaring his personal anthem and his troops wasting 'grad firing into the air in celebration. There's flower wreaths and singing children and a tiger cub, and that's not even the start of the true idiocy. If it were me, I'd have a judging instead of a parade. A good hanging is what *really* riles up the public."

"You're twisted, you know that?" Draco said, jabbing a finger into Karma's chest.

"Oh, spare me the self-righteousness, Emreis."

"You know what you are, Gillette? A psychopath. I've met a few assholes like you in the past, and they all bled the same color."

"I love it when you start monologuing like a protagonist. Especially when you see me talking with *her*."

"Leave Dassa out of this. And don't *ever* talk to her again if you know what's good for you."

"What's wrong, neckbeard? I'm not allowed to flirt with *your property?*"

"Defend yourself, you little shit!" Draco roared as his fist smashed into Karma's cheek and knocked him to the ground.

"Draco! No!" Taki latched onto his comrade from behind, struggling to restrain a hundred kilograms of muscle. Meanwhile, Hadassah held Karma back from landing a retaliatory strike.

"Oh, you're so friggin' *cool*," Karma sneered, blood streaming from his nostrils. "A *real* white knight. Do it again, asshole! Right here!"

Lotte's closed fist smacked into his other cheek and he crumpled to the floor with white floaters streaking across his vision like hail.

"*Enough,*" she hissed, her voice barely rising above a whisper. "Any further talk from either of you earns a hundred blows with a *knout*. Do I make myself clear?"

Draco seemed as if he wanted to thank her, but her eyes warned him not to. Karma rubbed his jaw, silently avoiding her gaze. Eventually, both men nodded resentfully to signal their understanding. Taki swallowed against a dry throat as Draco shuffled out of his grasp and stormed away. At least he could be grateful that his captain had not demanded they shake hands.

9

The day had gone from low to rock-bottom. Taki reasoned that with his particular luck, someone was bound to throw him a shovel. The victory celebration had placed him in a parade column consisting of yet more armored reliquaries, among them a real horseless carriage with tires that served as the duke's personal conveyance. The interior was adorned with faux-fur upholstery and even a working icebox stocked with bottles of Ursalan wine. Periodically, Gul Hekmatyar would stand up inside the carriage through a porthole on its roof and toss fistfuls of milligrad to the crowds lining the streets. In his wake, the desperate crushed each other for the chance to grab a spare round. A white tiger cub was resentfully draped on his shoulder, kept from tearing out the duke's throat by a leather muzzle and mitts over its paws. Music was provided by accordion-wielding soldiers and amateur singing.

"If I hear another verse of 'Gul is next to God' again, I might actually vomit," Draco said, shaking his head. The squad had initially ridden around on top of the same metal beast that they had ridden into New Petrovic, but gradually had managed to slip inside. The most immediate threat to the duke's health came from the angry carnivore held on his shoulder, not rebels.

"I feel bad for the tiger," Taki said, mashing his hands over his ears.

"Buncha slack-jawed catamites," Hadassah spat. "That's why I use this!" She pointed to a small, ancient contraption tucked into the hem of her skirt, from which a pair of yellowed cords ran and seemed to dive into her ears.

"What are those?" Taki asked.

"Take a listen. It'll turn you into a godrotting sexual tyrannosaurus," she said, and pulled one of the cords away from her ear. At the end of it was a small, bud-like protrusion that she clumsily jammed in Taki's ear. The deafening rush of noise and singing dropped his jaw and he instinctively ripped the device out of his canal.

"What is this witchcraft? Where the hell did you find this, anyway?"

She smiled at him, this time without being sardonic.

"It's not unholy. When I was in Ursala, we stopped at this deserted old village with some ruins nearby. I was digging around and found this buried under a silly-looking plastic emblem. I tell you, they had no creativity in those days. Looked like a white fruit someone had bitten already."

"What kind of fruit?"

"How the hell would I know? Maybe a napple or something?"

"Oy, aren't you supposed to be vigilant on duty? Suffer with the rest of us!" Draco said, tugging at her still-budded ear.

"Ow! I *am* being vigilant! Good music cancels out crap music, right?'

"No, it does *not*. Anyway, you should—"

His words were torn from his mouth as a blast front hit the head of the motor column. The concussive pressure was enough to flip the thirty-three ton mass of the rolling temple over onto its roof, cave in its front end, and liquefy the insides of its driver inside his armor.

Lotte flew to the rear of the hull and hit it with enough force to dent in her cuirass. Had she been unprotected, the blow would have been fatal. Reflexively, she extended her palms to dull the oncoming crush of bodies. Hadassah was the first to hit, and smacked Lotte with enough force to bruise limbs. The napple-crested device flew away and shattered into thousands of glassy slivers. Draco was next. His muscle mass was slightly harder to handle, but he was a convenient cushion for Taki and most of all Karma, who tumbled ingloriously in midair like the world's most terrible acrobat.

Draco was the first to recover. He inhaled ferociously and roughly pushed bodies away from him. Karma groaned as he rolled on the ceiling-turned-floor, gasping in pain and gripping his chest. Taki was on his knees, spitting bile. In the distance, two more large explosions sounded but did not seem to be as forceful as the first ones.

"D-Draco!" Hadassah shouted as she pulled herself up to her knees by the bulkhead. "Lotte! She's…"

"Captain!" Draco bellowed as he stepped over Karma and knelt next to Lotte. He cradled her head in his arms and tears flashed in his eyes. "No! This can't be happening! Goddammit!"

Her eyes opened and she fixed an incredulous glance at her corporal.

"Emreis, quit screaming. I'm *fine*," she said, sitting up stiffly with a cough. "Start patching each other up. We don't have much time."

"Y-yes ma'am!" he cried in relief.

"Fucking plastic," Hadassah snarled as she regarded her broken toy. "Okay, I can move around. Draco, go take care of Newboy next. I'll get the Shmuck!" she said before crawling through the cabin. It was bathed in subdued red lighting and Karma was barely visible. Deftly, she slid her palm under the cuirass on his chest to infuse her energy against his bare skin. Prana transfer could not repair broken limbs or knit together severed vessels. Those fixes required surgeons. What her technique did was promote clotting and dull pain enough for severely wounded soldiers to take to the battlefield.

"I thought you didn't want to take it too fast," Karma whispered coyly.

She blushed and scowled at the same time. "Do you want to die?"

"Point taken."

"Is everyone intact?" Lotte asked. More importantly, the squad's weapons had also survived. "Regardless of our sentiments, we must protect the duke from harm. Find him and remove him from this place, no matter what. And do not separate from the group."

With that, she kicked the dented rear door open and leapt outside with her flamberge drawn. The cityscape around Tirefire was a smoking, flaming vision of Armageddon. Heat from the burning corpses of diesel-rich relics was enough to scorch skin from ten meters away. Charred bodies of guardsmen and civilians lay sprawled on the rubble-strewn street. Smoking, liquefied fat spread out from the bodies like scorched butter and leaked between the cobbles. Popping of ammunition cooking off in the fires prompted reflexive ducking and furtive glances for cover. The rear of the column was also aflame, and whoever had survived the explosions was in no condition to fight. Gunfire rang out from the roofs as well as down a nearby alley that was unblocked. Streaks of rubber and shards of glass on the road told the tale of a rapid, but ultimately fruitless escape.

"There," Lotte shouted as she looked down the alley at a cluster of Arben men carrying kalashes and spears. "There's where the d—" She stopped, mid-sentence.

No one heard her but Taki. As he glanced at the rebels and then back at Lotte, he realized why she'd stopped. It would be easy to pretend to have lost the duke in the chaos. To let the rebels take care of the problem. Lotte mouthed something to him.

"Your call, Natalis," he could have sworn she had said.

He clenched his jaw. He wanted to remain silent, and desperately so. Gul Hekmatyar had violated his oath to his people. *But then,* Taki thought, *what happens to us?* What mattered was now survival. Not just his, but everyone's. If the duke died, it meant they would all go back to the brig, and he had the sneaking suspicion that their punishment wouldn't be limited to a simple lashing. Again, he thought of Lotte, and what she had endured to get them here. He had disgraced her enough. Now, he would prove himself worthy of being her corporal.

He spat in disgust and tapped Lotte on her arm. "Do it," he said with a shake of his head and his mouth full of the taste of ash.

Lotte nodded gravely and pointed her sword. "The duke is there! Go save his worthless ass! Charge!"

* * * *

Duke Gul Hekmatyar sat on the ground with his finery marred with soot and blood and rent by broken glass. He stared, cow-like, as the rebels wrapped a loop of twisted cloth around his neck and dragged him along the cobblestones. The gaudy revolver was no longer in its holster. The rebels' faces were ecstatic with fury.

"*Te qifsha, Kurve!*" spat one as he gave the noose a final yank and then started to turn a windlass at the other end. The duke grasped at the constricting tourniquet but could find no purchase for his fingertips. Piss leaked form his britches and pooled on the cobbles.

At the edge of the crowd, screams and cries of surprise erupted as bodies started to go flying. Gunfire crackled amidst the whooshing noise of blades cutting the air. The executioners abandoned the windlass and unslung their kalashes to meet the new enemy, but it was too late.

Karma whirled and plunged his swords into another man's chest before disemboweling his target with a downward swipe. Draco's fighting iron took off the top of a rebel's skull and wrapped around another's neck, breaking it. Lotte's flamberge plunged into another rebel and she hoisted her blade in the air, allowing his body to slip down its scalloped edges to shred his insides completely. Taki knelt beside the duke and threw one of the man's hairy arms across his shoulders to support him. Karma joined in quickly.

"Where the fuck were you bitches? What the fuck do I pay you for? Niketas will skin you alive!" the duke shouted in Karma's ear. Taki recoiled, stung at the man's response to being saved from certain death.

"More of them coming!" Hadassah shouted, uncharacteristically spending milligrad as she furiously worked the bolt of her Nagant. "And shit! *Out of nowhere is fucking spetsnaz!*"

With her words, Taki felt a wave of anxiety course through him again. He gulped air and had to brace himself against a nearby stone wall for support. His eyelids flickered shut. Aslatiel stood over him, ready to give the killing blow.

"No!" he bellowed, and swallowed the image back. He brought the sleeve of his padded jack to his mouth and bit down hard as if to chew his fear up and swallow it. He wouldn't be able to save his squad if he drowned in flashbacks and terror. It was time to fight.

"Get back! Get back!" Lotte shouted as she faltered under a hail of bullets she barely intercepted with her shield. The barrage rasped through wood and metal and turned the Dominion sun into a smoking crater. Taki immediately replied with a *Khala* burst at the direction of the attack, only to see a blonde woman leap out of the way and let off another burst of fire at him. Taki ducked behind crumbling stairs and let off a salvo with his Bastard to allow Lotte to pick herself up and retreat. Imperials flitted in and out of sight in pairs, with one taking shots and another trying to close the gap and melee up close. Draco's fighting iron whipped singing death through the air and clanged off blades and shields, while Hadassah covered him with her rifle and prevented any enterprising enemies from getting a clear shot at him. Karma tried to force a wrought-iron gate open, frantically bashing its padlock with the pommels of his swords.

This is just like before, Taki realized. *They're trying to pen us in, but this time there's no escape to the rear. And no Hundred Arms, either!* Space behind was shrinking. He noticed that Hadassah had run out of ammunition. The Bastard had jammed on a stuck casing and torn off the cartridge's rim. It would not fire again without a trip to the shrine. Taki diverted his prana again to cast sutra. It would kill his mobility, but there was nowhere left to run, anyway. He let out a growl and prepared to go out casting.

"*Spettsgruppe,* hold your fire!" a man's voice boomed down through the alley. Taki paused. Was this some sort of trick? To get his squad to cease their efforts and thus become an easier kill? To his surprise, no more rounds zipped his way. Taki held his palms out, nervously waiting to channel.

The Imperials began to show themselves one by one. There was no way for Taki to forget Aslatiel, who strode forward with the restrained confidence of a man who knew he was the imminent victor. A lump formed in Taki's throat, but he held firm. It was the same group who had trounced them at Vergina, but with one more addition: a blonde woman he had never seen before. It was clear that the Alfa had ammunition and prana to spare. Any way he figured it, Taki knew he was dead.

"What is the meaning of this?" Lotte snarled, pointing her flamberge at Aslatiel. "Why do you not finish us off?"

"I want to talk for a minute."

"We have little to talk about, Imperial. Slay us or get thee hence!"

"That is regrettable, Archangel Yuriel."

Taki's jaw dropped. *What did he just call her?*

Lotte spat and glared daggers at Aslatiel. "I am not of the triada anymore. I am simply Captain Satou."

"So be it," Aslatiel said. "Did you slaughter innocents and children at New Petrovic?"

"Trying to satisfy your conscience before you kill us? Yes, I *did.*"

Taki opened his mouth to protest. It wasn't right. She didn't need to take on the guilt by herself.

"You're a poor liar," Aslatiel said with a sad smile. "I would have liked to have faced you in your prime. Now, while it's not too late, tell your soldiers to surrender. I will make sure they are treated with dignity and repatriated to their homes once the war ends. Otherwise, they will not survive this. *You* will not survive this. Have pity on your mothers."

Lotte scowled and adjusted her grip on her weapon. "*Sirrah,* you seem to have mistaken us for limp-dicked mercenaries scooting around on our knees to fellate the first invader we come across. In truth, we all want nothing more than to rip open your throats and piss on the Imperial flag. Also, my mother's a raging bitch."

She reached down and pulled a ring attached to her torso. A daisy-chain all of the hand-held explosives she could carry fell from her waist, attached to a length of braided paracord. She swept the deadly charm necklace forward and then snapped it like a whip, sending its bangles flying at Alfa Gruppe. A catastrophe of pull-pins, striker levers, and live grenades clinked on the ground around their feet. Aslatiel glowered when realized what had happened, and he instantly whirled to make his escape.

"*Now!*" Lotte screamed as she yanked Taki and Draco by their scruffs and hurled them with all her might. They hit the locked gate and the padlock broke against the strain. The doors fell open and they tumbled through. Karma dragged the bloody duke through with Hadassah's help. A second later, the alleyway was enveloped in blinding firelight.

✳ ✳ ✳ ✳

Taki cuffed the side of his own head again to drive back mounting tinnitus. A migraine made him feel as if one of the Alfa had driven a spike from the top of his head all the way to his groin. Although he knew that wasn't really the case, he was beginning to wish for the lethal side-effects of an actual impalement. He counted his blessings, though. Draco had gotten the worst of the pressure wave from the blasts and leaked eschar from his right ear. The man could barely walk and streaks of vomit stained the rubble wherever he trod.

Hadassah had volunteered to watch over Draco, and secure one end of the maze-like complex they found themselves in. As far as anyone could tell, they occupied what had once been an expensive private dwelling, virtually a castle. Centuries of conflict had shaved off all but the bottom three floors of the place. Fortunately, it had good chokepoints and narrow hallways that would make getting to the duke a deadly ordeal. Their only chance to hold out against their attackers was to turn everything around them into a horrific maze of traps and ambush points. Hadassah's guns were out of ammunition, so Taki had lent her his Bastard in exchange for Draco's sidearm.

Taki looked down at the antiquated revolver and realized he had not the faintest clue how to reload the thing. There were five shots left, including the slug in the secondary barrel. He considered saving the big one for himself. Ursalans usually tortured prisoners to death unless promised a sizable ransom. Taki had no land, servants, or even spare milligrad to his name, so there was no telling what the Imperium would do to him. Especially after what his captain had said to the spetsnaz commander. Remembering her words made him tingly and brought a smile to his face.

Lotte and Karma were up on a higher floor guarding the duke. Gul's men had been scattered by the attack on the parade, but given enough time, they would be able to repel a poorly-armed rebel force and recover their master. Tirefire the Lesser was there to buy time until that happened, but with the Imperials stalking the premises, Taki wasn't sure the strategy would work.

At the edge of his vision, a shadow flitted past a crumbling doorway. Taki was savvy enough to not believe he was merely seeing things. He gripped the revolver, squatted against a broken concrete partition, and tried to calm himself. The fact that he was still alive meant that the enemy didn't know where he was. Concealment was the most important factor in survival now. The enemy could not kill what he or she could not see. *Now we dance, Spetsnaz.*

The top of the crumbling barrier exploded above his head and showered him with gritty, gray dust. Taki clamped his mouth shut to stifle a shout of surprise and willed himself with all his might to stay still. The enemy was trying to provoke him into moving or firing back. Such a course of action would only serve to expose him to concentrated fire, but if he could stay still and focus on where the shots originated from, he would know where his attacker was. *Set guard, O Lord, over my mouth; keep watch over mine lips.*

The next shot punched a jagged exit wound in the concrete, mere millimeters from Taki's shoulder. He trembled. Did the enemy know where he was hiding? If so, the next round would hit him for sure. He closed his eyes and started to bite his nails. His armor would hopefully stop the round if it lost enough velocity from boring through stone. Though the thought of getting hit filled him with wretched anxiety, it was essential not to move. The shots were coming from the northeast corner of the crumbling floor, and if the bullets weren't ricocheting, that meant there was a direct line of sight.

Another gunshot rang out, but this time the bullet hit more laterally than the one which had almost maimed him. Taki's eyes widened. Now he knew where the spetsnaz was. Trying to slowly flank his attacker was one option, but a smart enemy might already be on the move. What was needed was a direct, devastating attack. Taki inhaled, opened his gates, and collected power again. When he was almost at the breaking point, he whirled into the open with his palms outstretched. *"Plei Khala!"* he rasped.

The energy wave exploded forward and punched into Lucatiel at almost point-blank range as she rounded a corner with her pistols raised to blow his head off. The impact lifted her off her feet and flung her back through rotting drywall before punching her mass through the crumbling brick exterior. The last Taki saw of her were sapphire eyes flaring with vengeful indignation before gravity reasserted itself and she disappeared from sight.

When he realized what had transpired, Taki pumped his fist in victory. He was avenged now. Despite the triumph he felt, however, something nagged at him. Lucatiel wouldn't have been able to traverse that much broken flooring in so little time after the last shot. That meant...

He heard the kiai shout a millisecond before he felt Aslatiel's heel slam into his torso from a flying kick. As Taki hurtled through the air and crashed through termite-eaten studs, he retched a stream of yellow bile. His vision blurred when his back hit the front of a chest of drawers, but the softness of millions of accumulated moth and beetle cocoons within cushioned the blow and prevented him from losing consciousness. Through the man-shaped hole he'd made, Taki saw Aslatiel reach into a holster and draw a pistol. Fueled by adrenaline, Taki dove away from the shattered armoire before three rounds crashed into the spot where he'd been. He whipped around and tried to send another Khala burst at where he thought Aslatiel was. The sutra went wide and hit a solid pylon, causing the entire ceiling to buckle wildly. This sent a blinding plume of dust everywhere and plunged the entire floor into a haze of white.

Taki tried to breathe through the thick fabric of his neckerchief to avoid coughing and giving his location up. While the result of his spellcasting wasn't quite what he had intended, it had at least bought him some time to recover and think. He was out of usable prana for the moment, so he readied his revolver and drew back its hammer. The damned antique clicked and clacked far too loudly, in his opinion.

"Well-done, Corporal Natalis," Aslatiel said. "I am glad to see your injury wasn't permanent."

Taki tried to aim at the voice but saw nothing. He remained silent.

"Worry not about betraying your position," Aslatiel said. "I'm as blind as you are in this mess, and even if I were drawn to the sound of your voice, I'd just get tripped up along the way. Why don't we chat for a bit while this clears?"

"Why are you even here?" Taki demanded. "The front's elsewhere."

"We're here because the people of this land need our help."

Taki spat. "You're here because you want territory for your padishah."

"Wrong. We are the only Imperial force in the duchy. You seriously think we could occupy this place by force?"

"Don't tell me you're opposing the duke out of the goodness of your hearts," Taki scoffed. He pricked his ears up and tried to locate his opponent. Aslatiel's voice sounded reassuringly distant. Still safe.

"I saw the aftermath of New Petrovic. And if I'm not mistaken, you were there, too."

"And if I was?"

"Then you know exactly why the people of this land asked for our assistance," Aslatiel said. "Thus, I have a question for you. Why do you fight to protect the duke, and the men above him who foster such conditions? You don't seem like an evil person."

"You're assuming a lot! I just pitched your sister off a building, you know."

"Lucatiel is a plum blossom. Beautiful and impossible to kill. But you're dodging my question, Corporal."

"I was ordered to protect and serve the duke. That's all there is to it."

"So if you had been ordered to kill each and every one of those villagers at New Petrovic, would you have done so?"

"I'm a soldier of the Cloud Temple! I don't have a choice!"

"So you're just a tool?"

Taki grit his teeth. "Exactly."

"Guns and swords are tools," Aslatiel said. "They have no conscience or agency of their own. But you, Sir Taki, are a human being with ample measures of both. You cannot escape accountability for your actions. If you ignore your moral duty and just say 'I was following orders,' then it falls to people like me to dispose of people like you."

"Then what would you do, Sir Aslatiel, if your padishah ordered you to kill a thousand innocents? Are you not beholden to his will as well?"

"Two shots to his chest followed by one to the head."

"Isn't he your better?"

"Maybe he is, maybe he isn't. What matters, is you. Your willingness to speak up in the face of what you believe to be a grievous wrong."

"But I can't! I'm just not powerful enough!"

"Again, you're wrong. We all have the power to change things, especially from within," Aslatiel said. "I've studied the Dominion and its ways. And I think you and I both know that there's something very wrong at its core."

"It's still my country. My kingdom! I know nothing else."

"You can love your nation while acknowledging its faults."

Taki's eyes watered. *Just the dust.* "Look, damn you. I just want to help my friends live another day. It's all I can do."

"Then try to make theirs a home worth returning to."

"Why are you even saying this stuff to me? Aren't you trying to put a round in my head?"

"I was, but you're worth saving, I think."

"That's presumptuous. Why the hell are you allowed to determine my worth?" Taki demanded.

"Because I've got the drop on you."

Taki felt the unmistakable imprint of a muzzle resting against the back of his head. The LeMat was wrenched from his grasp in the same breath. His heart sank. He had fallen into Aslatiel's trap. The speech about not being able to find him in all of the dust, about conscience and agency, all of it had been an elaborate deception. Lotte had been right. *Never talk philosophy with the enemy, you dimwit.* Now he would die a corporal in Tirefire the Lesser. Taki closed his eyes and prepared for ignominious eternity.

"It's good to see you again," Aslatiel said, and stepped back. Taki turned, his hands raised. It was the first time he had truly seen Aslatiel up close, and realized he was a Chung-Kuo. *At least my destroyer looks better than me,* he thought.

"Aren't you going to kill me?" Taki asked.

"There's no need at the moment. Next time we meet, though, I might have to. Use your remaining time wisely, Sir Taki. I will remember you."

Aslatiel slowly slipped back into the haze of dust and vanished.

* * * *

"Am I safe now?" the duke bellowed at Karma as the polaris set him down on a tattered mattress to examine him.

"Yeah, I think so," Karma said. "You're losing a lot of blood from your scalp, so hold still while I heal you." He moved and spoke off-kilter, and his skin had an ashen look to it. Nevertheless, he placed his palms over the duke's head wounds and concentrated. Within a few minutes, the bleeding cuts had turned into angry-looking mounds topped with scabs.

"Good. I feel better now," the duke said. He rose from his seat and promptly sucker-punched Karma in the jaw. Unprepared for the assault, Karma went sprawling on the ground in a heap. "You stupid fuck! It is your fault they nearly killed me. I'm going to fucking kill *you!*" he screamed, stomping his iron-shod heels on Karma's back and head.

"Milord! Stop this at once!" Lotte commanded, advancing on the pair. The duke merely slapped her across the face with his palm. She did not try to block it or strike back. Better he struck her with his palm then Karma with his metal boots. Were he anything else but a lord of the realm and a hero of the Dominion, his head would have been freed from his body. Lotte still followed the rules, fraying as they were in this instant.

"Shut up, stupid cunt! I am ennobled by the basileus! If you lay a fucking hand on me, you're dead!"

"You have no authority to punish my men. Corporal Gillette is mine alone to discipline!" Lotte shouted back, her face turning an angry red where Gul had struck her.

"Yeah? And what the fuck will you do about it?" the duke sneered. "Give me that fucking sword right now, you bitch! That's an order!"

"It's too heavy for you."

"Then give me the gun!"

"I refuse."

"Then I'll fucking take it from you." He reached for the leather holster at her waist.

A closet door burst open nearby and a brown-haired Arben girl of no more than fifteen stepped out. In her hands was a double-barreled shotgun of indigenous manufacture, which she leveled at the Duke. Training kicked in and Lotte raised her flamberge, but it was too late and the girl pulled both triggers at once.

Reloaded buckshot smashed into Lotte's chest and tore a jagged hole in her plate mail. Because of the padding and silk top she wore underneath, the lead balls did not penetrate her skin. The impact was still enough to knock her back and break a slew of ribs. She collapsed against the opposite wall, her world fuzzy from pain. Her prana was virtually drained from the earlier fight, and she could do naught but slowly sink to the ground.

"Holy shit! God loves me and wants me to be happy," the duke gasped. He quickly snatched the shotgun away before the girl could fumble another brace of shells into the weapon's chambers. Plastic hulls clattered against the floor as he took her by the throat and lifted her to her tiptoes. She choked and sputtered, her fingernails digging at his forearms to no avail. Right as she passed out, the Duke released his grip and let her fall onto the tattered mattress. He stood over her and a look of particular menace darkened his features. Before he could go further, she woke up and started to scream and kick. He punched her face in response and she fell back onto the mattress. With a savage grin, he dug his boot-heel into her midsection and she vomited and choked.

"You see that? I cannot be killed! I am blessed by God Himself! You shitty witches, I didn't even need you assholes in the first place. But I am merciful, you see? Rather than execute your worthless asses right here, I'll have some fun instead! If that stupid fuck Gillette is alive, I'll even let him hump the body."

Stop, Lotte wanted to say, but found she could only hack up gooey clumps of red from her throat. Her chest was on fire, her breathing labored, and it was getting harder and harder to move or even breathe. Her eyelids grew heavy. She was back at the Teufelsbrücke again, with a templar's armored boot grinding between her shoulder blades to press her naked torso against the freezing steel floor. The blade of an axe cut the skin on the back of her neck. The castellan was telling her to choose a man to die. No, she could not choose herself. Her fiancé gazed at her with his serene blue eyes.

A sudden twinge of pain was enough to make her blink the vision back. No, this time was different. This time she wasn't helpless. And if she was to die anyway, she would make sure it was for a reason she could be satisfied to take to the afterlife. *Should have done this long ago,* she thought. Moaning in agony, she reached to her waist and slowly drew her pearl-handled Colt.

In a flash, Karma was upright and he caught the duke in a headlock from behind to tear him away from the bed. But, spent as he was, Karma was quickly on the floor with the duke aiming blow after blow at his face. Blood spattered, bones crunched, and Karma's resistance diminished. Lotte tried to align the sights on the duke, but found she had not the strength to lift her weapon.

In the end I failed again. Is it really fine this way? Enishi, I'll see you soon, Lotte thought as she prepared to succumb to a heady, painful death by suffocation. A movement in the periphery attracted a last bit of attention. The bloodied Arben girl was crawling toward her so as not to be noticed, hand outstretched and gesturing at the gun. With a final effort, Lotte pushed the gun forward and blacked out. It skidded across the rough hardwood and into the girl's hands.

Karma was both ashen and purple from strangulation when the girl pulled her trigger. The massive, hollow-pointed round entered the back of the duke's shoulder, mushroomed violently against his lung tissue, and erupted out the front of his chest along with chunks of purplish gore. With a cross between a whine and a shriek, Gul rolled to the floor clutching his new, bleeding orifice. The girl smiled and smashed her foot into his testicles, causing his eyes to roll into the back of his head.

"This is for my brother," she said, before pulling the trigger once more. The round entered Gul's mouth and exited out the back of his skull. Bloody brain and bone fragments painted a pink halo around his head, and he did not move again. She spat on his corpse and gave it a final kick in the ribs. Cracks of distant gunfire punctuated the acrid stillness of the air, though she remained silent. After a pause, she approached the unconscious pair of Temple witches, gun in hand. Idly, she raised it and pointed at the armored woman's head, finger tensing on the trigger. She clenched her teeth, lowered the gun, and squatted, hugging her knees for a while.

Lotte snapped back into the painful clarity of consciousness when she felt the sensation of something warm and comforting on her chest. She stared at the girl, who was crouched next to her with a hand placed on the shotgun wound. The shattered chest armor lay on the ground a short way away. Her gaze strayed briefly to Gul, and then came back to the girl. She really was a small thing, Lotte decided. A small thing with aged eyes, like so many children raised with war as their mother.

"Hold still, Big Sis."

"You... know how to use the healing sutra?" Lotte asked, finally able to cough and free the last of the clotted phlegm from her lungs. Fresh air burned painfully in her air passages, for which she was grateful. The girl nodded. "Then you are..."

"I'm what you would call a 'forsworn', right? Because I never went to the mountain like I was supposed to? I never made a promise to do that. I just wanted to stay with my family."

"I'm a polaris. An officer," Lotte said. "Surely you know we are bound to hunt your kind down. Had we met elsewhere, I'd have executed you without a second thought."

"Why do you tell me this?"

"Because you also have the right to kill me. It's only fair that you know."

"Can I tell you something honestly?"

"Yes."

"I thought about it. I pointed the gun at you afterwards. I was ready to shoot. But you seemed very sad." She shook her head, struggling with her words. "No, not that. Not sad, but, more like I thought we were feeling the same things? Like missing people? Is that strange?"

Lotte shook her head and smiled.

"No, not at all. When you were fighting, I was thinking of someone I still miss very much."

"So I was right!"

"What will you do now?"

"I need to tell Irulan what happened. Now, my people will join with the Osterbrand, and we will have a good future. And *I* will go to Sevastopol, if they will still have me. Irulan says I could become a special warrior like her, and bring hope to girls all over the world."

Lotte's chest felt heavy.

"Didn't you want to stay with your family?"

"They got killed."

"I'm sorry."

"For what? It was all his doing," the girl said, looking at the duke's body. "I need to go now. Your friends are coming." She carefully set the Colt down. "Thank you for letting me use it."

"Wait. Please, take it." Lotte handed the gun back to the girl. "You'll have to find your own ammo, but consider this a gift. From your Big Sis."

The girl smiled, finally showing a row of white teeth. Without preamble, she darted away carrying the precious artifact. A few moments later, Taki burst in with Hadassah and Draco in tow.

"Mother of God," Taki swore as he raced over to Lotte.

"Little help over here?" Karma groaned, feebly waving his hand.

Hadassah crouched next to him, gently channeling prana into his swollen face. "This is the second time in one day. Next time I'll just finish you off."

"Did you see a girl leave the room?" Lotte asked. The others shook their heads quizzically. "Never mind, it must have been my imagination," she said with relief. It was a violation of the Code to suffer a Forsworn to live. Just one more sin she would bear, though lightly.

Draco looked over to the duke's body and sucked his teeth. They had all seen enough heads blown apart that they knew they were irrevocably, completely fucked.

"Good riddance to that sack of shit, even if we failed. The triada's going to flog our bare asses for years but right now I don't give a damn," he said.

"We'd better make ourselves scarce. The duke's men aren't going to believe we didn't kill him," Taki said. He chewed his thumbnail. "That is, if we in fact didn't."

"As soon as everyone's healed enough to walk unsupported, we'll leave," Lotte said. "And no, I didn't kill him. Neither did Gillette. The Hero had it a long time coming, though." She shook her head slowly. "Are those Imperials still in the area?"

"For some reason, they retreated," Draco said. "Cheeky bastards. I can't believe so many cute girls tried to gut me in so many ways. Who the hell were they?"

"Spettsgruppe Alfa," Karma said, rising painfully to one knee by pulling Hadassah's arm. "The silly cherry blossom gives it away. I heard a rumor they'd been sent to Kosovo but I always thought it was just tavern bullshit. Guess I was wrong."

"*Alfa?* But that unit's a myth," Draco said.

"No, they're quite real. The batshit blue-eyed one is Lucatiel von Halcon."

Taki seemed to go pale and shudder to himself.

"The Prince of Maladies," Lotte said. She sucked her teeth in realization, and the old wound on her scalp started to throb again.

"Shouldn't that be 'Princess of Maladies?'" Taki asked, raising an eyebrow.

"No, it's definitely 'Prince,'" Draco said. "The Ursalans don't believe women have souls, so anyone who kills a lot of their men must obviously have a cock."

"So if I waste a ton of them, will I get a cool nickname, too?" Hadassah asked.

"Probably. They love that mythic warrior shit."

"Then I wanna be called 'the Reaper of Souls!'"

"They'll probably call you 'the Gleaner' or 'the Picker' instead."

"Shut up. You're not in charge of that. I'm gonna be the Reaper."

"You ignoramuses don't realize how close we all came to death," Karma said with a sigh. "How we managed to survive a fight with them is actually a total mystery to me. This is the unit that single-handedly took Krak des Chevaliers during the succession war in the Levant. Next to them we're fishbait."

"Show some respect, numbnuts!" Hadassah said, elbowing Karma in the ribs. "It doesn't matter if those dickbags can come lightning and shit fire. We all survived because of *Lotte*, er, the captain."

"Damn straight it was her doing. We trusted her and we lived. Don't ever forget it, Gillette," Draco said. Taki nodded, clasping a fist to his chest.

Lotte swallowed back a lump forming in her throat as she wiped at burning in her eyes. She had failed in her mission, and the province would fall into turmoil. If the little girl's words held truth, then Kosovo would be in Imperial hands by a fortnight. Jibriil would show no mercy unless she begged him on her knees. But at least they were all alive. For a brief moment, she was tempted to think that perhaps there was some inherent fairness in the order of things. Then she dismissed the thought as foolish.

* * * *

Several blocks away on a corpse-strewn rooftop, Lucatiel rested her finger on the trigger of an ancient steel deathbringer as long as she was tall, and lined Taki's head up in her crosshairs. Only a little more pressure and she'd send a .50-caliber jacketed slug to turn his brain into mist before the report even reached his ears. Her body ached from the prana burst he'd hit her with, but more wounded was her pride. The Imperial Ace was not to be bested by some random, pimply-faced virgin. Lucatiel knew her priority was to kill the officer, but having a semiautomatic anti-materiel rifle allowed her to deviate from protocol.

"Aslatych, I have them," she muttered.

"And Gul Hekmatyar?" Aslatiel asked.

"He's dead. May I shoot now?"

"No. Our mission is complete. We will withdraw for now and let rebellion take its course."

Lucatiel bristled, and made no effort to hide it. "Our enemies still *live!*"

Aslatiel slid a hand over the end of Lucatiel's scope, causing her to look up in consternation. He leaned over and planted a kiss on her cheek, to which she flushed.

"*Nyet!* We will be able to kill them in the future. For now, I want to see what happens with the boy. Out of all of them, he is the most vulnerable, and yet at the same time, has the strongest potential for change. So we will wait and see what he does."

"You sound like you want to make love to him," Lucatiel sneered.

"He's pretty cute," Aslatiel said, and winked at her.

"Asshole!" she snarled, and smacked him.

10

Karma's knowledge of Pristina's winding corridors allowed the squad to silently slip away from the burning city center before the Khazari or rebels managed to swarm Gul's body. Unlike their ignominious retreat from the Vergina armory, their ignominious retreat from Kosovo was made bearable by a mass efflux of merchant caravans. Unwilling to have their wares subjected to a sacking, experienced traders fled with practiced swiftness, and Tirefire the Lesser was able to hitch a ride by promising to serve as bodyguards.

Taki kept a nervous eye on the horizon for the next few days, expecting the gold and midnight banners of the Cross to crest over at any given moment, but they never came. When he wasn't scanning the roads and wheat fields for signs of trouble, he taught Draco and Hadassah more letters to keep himself from dwelling on what awaited them back home. They had failed another mission, and could likely expect another lashing, or even some time on the rack followed by a branding. This knowledge, however, seemed to make Taki's companions paradoxically more carefree. The night before the caravan deposited them at the entrance of the mountain trail leading up to the Temple, they shared Karma's last, small bottle of fine Ursalan wine.

When Tirefire the Lesser reached the gates of the Temple, however, there was no Black Cross escort to greet them with rifles and spears. The palisade seemed poorly manned, complementing a sudden sense of desolation that chilled Taki more thoroughly than his previous stint in the brig. Was the campaign against the Imperium really going that badly to require the services of nearly all able-bodied fighters in the Temple? He did not want to conjecture, for conjecture led to loosened lips and loose lips led to whippings. Perhaps their failure in Kosovo had already been forgiven in the name of expediency. His heart sank, however, when he saw who waited for them instead. He knelt and expected the worst.

"Lieselotte," Jibriil said as he wiped a runny nose with the hem of his gold-embroidered sleeve, "Get to my quarters and get changed into something more presentable. Your armor is unsightly enough without holes all over it."

"Yes, milord," Lotte said. She rose and turned to the others. "Squad, turn your guns in at the shrine and report to the kitchens for regular duty."

"Yes, captain," they said in unison. Though Lotte tried to flash him a reassuring smile as she left, Taki still trembled. Jibriil didn't seem like he wanted to kill her, and for now, it looked like they'd be allowed to skip the brig. *But he summoned her to his quarters, not to the exarch's tower or even before the rest of the triada.* He realized what it meant and tried to suppress a grimace. *Keep your head down. Trust her and do what she says. Don't lose your wits like you did at the village.*

"And you, Gillette! Get over here," Jibriil snapped. An uncertain expression washed over Karma's face and he walked over to where Jibriil was. Before Karma could kneel, Jibriil grabbed him by the collar of his doublet and drew a dagger. "I should slit your throat, you cowardly, mercenary fuck. Did you seriously think you could leave me and become the duke's lapdog?"

Karma shrugged. "I came back, didn't I?"

Jibriil sheathed the dagger and slapped Karma across the face. "I sent you to collect. Where's the 'grad?"

"In heaven, with the Hero," Karma quipped. Jibriil drew back his free hand and slapped twice. Rings on the Archangel's fingers raked across Karma's cheeks and tore skin away.

"The only reason you still have your manhood or your life is because your mother is in the diacheiristes," Jibriil snarled. "Once she falls out of favor, I'm going to feed your balls to my hounds. Now report to the barracks, on the double."

Wait a second, Gillette is in the archangel's regiment? Taki realized. *That means he's in the...*

Karma flashed a blood-streaked grin. "But milord Archangel, *major Hecaton Mezeta* says I've been booted down to Tirefire the Lesser. I'm sorry, milord. I *really* wanted to stay in the Pantheon."

Jibriil's eyes went wide with rage and he kicked Karma in the chest to lay him out in the dust. "Subhuman wretch. Wallow in disgrace."

Karma closed his eyes as Jibriil spat in his face. The archangel seemed to want to kick him again, but instead, turned and walked away.

The others stayed kneeling until they were comfortable that Jibriil was out of sight. Temple law required them to prostrate themselves before a member of the triada, and they did not want to inflame someone as volatile as Jibriil. *He's the real wretch,* Taki thought in indignation. *How did that vile bastard rise in the ranks? How could the exarch be so blind to his faults? And just how many flaws does the exarch hide?*

"Come on, New—Natalis," Hadassah said to him. "The schmuck's long-gone. Let's just go to the shrine already."

Taki nodded to her, and looked over to Karma. "Right. Is he coming with us?"

Karma crossed his feet and linked his hands together behind his head, staring up at the dreary sky. Hadassah sighed and started to walk toward him, but Draco reached him first. Taki tensed. *He's not going to kick the man while he's down, is he?*

"Come on, Gillette," Draco said, and extended a hand. "If you claim to be a Tirefire, you'd best get to peeling. I'll show you how."

Karma looked somewhat taken aback, but slowly reached out to accept.

✱ ✱ ✱ ✱

Before he could reach the kitchens, Taki was again abducted into a closet by Hecaton Mezeta and not permitted to leave. Her fingertips felt like a small iron vise against the tender cartilage of one of his ears, and he would have yelped in pain if not for the fact that he wished to preserve some semblance of dignity in front of her. Even doing that was difficult, however. In such close quarters he could smell the faint odor of lavender and burnt cordite suffusing her hair. His heart started to race wildly and he flushed.

"Don't get your hopes up, virgin. I'm not about to molest you," she said and flicked him on the face right over the gash that Lucatiel had given him. The stinging sensation brought forth tears. "And if I catch your eyes anywhere below my neck I'll put them out."

"Yes, ma'am," he said, swallowing nervously. What sort of horrific arrangement would she force on him this time? He would not be duped again, he resolved. Still, his career was effectively over, so what damage could she possibly do at this point? The greatest hero in the Dominion was dead and his territory ceded to the Imperium by now, and it was his fault.

Hecaton let go of Taki's ear. "Are you familiar with the houses of the diacheiristes?"

"I know they're the most trusted and powerful vassals of the basileus," Taki said. "But I know them not personally, if that's what you're asking."

"Then it's your lucky day. You're about to meet one of them."

"Who?"

"Amilia Gillette. Otherwise known as the Minister of the Exchequer. Also, the reason lil' Karma is such a lovely turd."

"What? What does she want with me? I'm not an officer or a noble. I'm a nobody."

"You're completely correct," Hecaton said, beaming. Taki glowered at her. "But I've known her for quite a while. Let's just say she did me some favors and I did her some favors. Since you all are like my dysfunctional, barbarian children, I tend to talk about you all. She heard you weren't just *pretending* to read like most of the scribes in Athenaeum, and that you could probably count to greater than ten. So she wants you to come over to the capital and work for her for a while."

"Am I... being transferred to the praetorians?" Taki asked, his heart picking up again. A transfer to the Minister's personal guard would be an answer to his silent prayers. An impossible second chance for his crippled future. Most of all, it meant no more kitchen duty, fighting with legendary enemies, or being sent back to places like New Petrovic. Elation welled from within. And yet, he also could not stop thinking about the faces of the others, particularly Lotte. He wondered to himself how he would break the news. *No, it's not important.* He clenched his teeth to drive back the thought. He needed to think of himself, after all.

"Of course not," Hecaton said with a callous chuckle. "You're too useful to me. I'm just loaning you out for the time being."

Taki's fantasies of success broke to pieces before his eyes. "What am I, your catamite?"

Snapping back at anyone, much less a superior, was unlike him. But even more so was the fact that he didn't regret it as much as he should have. Rudeness to his betters was punishable by a whipping and would delay promotion. *Then again, I'll never be promoted, so what's the point?* Hecaton laughed, loudly this time.

"That term implies we're friends," she said. "Now, be quiet and take these passes. They're to prevent the deathwatch from shooting you, and let you get on the next caravan out to the capital. Once there, you are to go to the old Grande Bretagne where you will be given further instructions. You are of course forbidden from discussing this with your squadmates. Understand?"

"Yes, *madam*," Taki said, wanting to be away from the cramped confines of the closet, and most of all, away from Hecaton. He was about to try and squirm out of the closet, but he thought of Lotte again, and also of Jibriil. Taki paused. Hecaton was a woman, at least on the outside. She would understand the unjustness of what the damned corrupt archangel was putting his captain through. Perhaps the major's spiteful nature could be put to some use. "One last thing, then. I'll do whatever dirty work you want, but in exchange, you'll grant me a boon." It was a directive, not a request.

"Pfft," Hecaton snorted. "Who do you think I am? Satan Claws?"

"You know more than you let on, Major. You know that the archangel Jibriil is coercing and abusing my captain. I want him stopped. He clearly fears you, so do something about it."

Hecaton wagged a finger. "Let's say I went up to the archangel and threatened him. Would that help Lotte out, truly? Or would he simply displace his wrath against me onto her? Would his unwanted caresses turn to beatings?"

"Then kill him instead! You have the power, don't you, Major? She's suffering!"

The fact that Taki had just requested the murder of an archangel of the Temple was not lost on him, but he was too indignant to care. And even if Hecaton were averse to killing Jibriil, Taki would ask her to make it so the archangel would never walk again, never see again, never feed himself again, and definitely never bed a woman again. *If I had the major's power, I'd show him what suffering really was,* he thought vengefully.

Hecaton knocked her forehead against his. "You still fail to understand something, boy. You assume that we women have not the will to protect ourselves, nor that we have the smarts to recognize a blackguard for what he is. Your captain bears her burden solely to protect your dumb asses, and if some white-armored templar tried to swoop in and save her, she'd cut his godrotting head off. If you wish to help her so badly, leave her be and work to bring your unit success."

Taki tried desperately to hold onto his wrath and failed. The godrotting major was right, of course. If Jibriil died, then the squad would be at the mercy of Michail or even worse, the current Yuriel. He had just tried to undermine everything Lotte had paid for in pain and humiliation. The thought filled him with shame. He swallowed and straightened his back. "Aye, Ma'am. Forget I asked."

"Now, git out! You smell like bad lo bak gao," Hecaton said as she opened the door and shoved him out. Taki found his footing again and shook his head. Despite the fact that he'd failed in his task, he had to give himself credit for attempting to extort Hecaton Mezeta and living to tell the tale. The thought filled him with hope. *Remember what that Imperial told you. You can still change things from within, and this is your opportunity to do so.* He started plodding back to his quarters to change into traveling clothes, and glanced back as an afterthought. Curiously, the major had not left the closet yet.

* * * *

Athenaeum was one of the world's oldest surviving cities, and if the legends were to be believed, the birthplace of rule by mob decree. Like many other large cities around the known world, it had been blasted away during the Fall and slowly rebuilt to its current state in the ensuing centuries. Vengeance-driven fights between cursed children had subjected entire populations to the most twisted fates imaginable by the inhuman mind. It was said that when the fusion warheads fell from the skies like heavenly fingers touching the stricken lands, those underneath wept with joy at their impending deliverance.

The Argead capital was built on the side of a small mountain overlooking a deep-water harbor. The harbor made the city a center of trade across the Dominion and its neighbors, especially the caliphates to the far south. In the first stages of Athenaeum's restoration it had been a cluster of shanty houses enclosed by a barrier of rusting shipping containers and razor wire. In the modern era it boasted many a gleaming white concrete edifice harkening back to its storied past. The metal crates and hovels never truly disappeared, and ringed the city like a crumb-ridden beard.

Two days after his encounter in the closet, Taki passed through the gates and was immediately struck by the sheer dirtiness of the place. Every surface within the Cloud Temple was aged and pitted by the harshness of the mountains, but the capital was simply a squalid mess picked over by festering dogs. Rubble and decaying offal mounded in the streets, and wherever he went it smelled like a latrine. Though he was hungry when he arrived, he could not bring himself to purchase from the street vendors. It was a shame, because he had always wanted to try the famous harspud kebab.

Taki stood in front of the Old Bretagne hotel, feeling grimy and sour from his journey. It was a stately place, with a roof done in tile rather than thatch or daub like so many others, and even had some surviving glass windows. He wondered if the Minister would meet him in a room with those windows, for surely she was a wealthy woman. Working for her might not be so bad. Perhaps she would notice his skill and override Hecaton's wishes. With a noble behind him, he would then have the power to help Lotte. He would even buy out his squadmates if they were extra nice to him. With a jaunty smile, he entered the building.

Showing his passes to the courtiers bought him an escort to a third-floor suite that he entered with trepidation. The shag carpet looked almost alive and seemed about as trustworthy as quicksand, though he knew that fear to be unfounded. Still, he watched his footing with care. So preoccupied was he with not being swallowed whole by a predatory rug that he almost missed Amilia Gillette staring quizzically at him from her seat on a couch by a sweeping set of glass bay windows.

"I assume you're Natalis," she said. "Don't worry, the floor won't eat you. I, however, might."

Taki stiffened at the sound of her voice before clumsily dropping to one knee and bowing his head. Her skin was as darkly hued as Karma's.

"Milor—" He cursed himself inwardly. "Milady."

"'Minister' will do, Natalis."

"Minister, I arrive as bidden. What service would you have me render?"

"Can you actually factor?"

"Yes, Minister. I am the purser of my unit and can perform multiplication and division for a legion."

"If I gave you a round of Browning Machine Gun and told you to divide it amongst a company, how would you do so?"

"The major receives three Old Nayto Standard. The captain, two. Assuming three lieutenants in a company, each receives five rounds of Luger. Sergeants get a round each, or ten reloads in the same caliber. Corporals, five reloads apiece. You will have a surplus of four reloads left to go to the company paybox for later."

Amilia narrowed her eyes.

"It seems Mezeta didn't deceive me, after all. Report to the archives. Ask the librarians to show you the transaction records of the three major ordnance exchange guilds for the last ten years. With this information, I want you to conduct an experiment."

"An experiment?"

"Yes, an experiment. Milligrad doesn't materialize out of the ether, so this is entirely a fiction. But I want you to plot out what would happen if it did. Use the figure of two million rounds of Luger injected into the currency pool. I want to know how badly the guilds would suffer, in particular. How much debt they would call in, and from who. Do you think you are capable of this exercise?"

Taki frowned. It was within his faculties to do so, but why would she waste his time on such fanciful speculation? *Don't question the noble. Just do as she asks, and you'll be rewarded,* he thought to himself. He raised his head. "I am."

Amilia nodded, and for the first time Taki saw what could have been mistaken for a smile on her face.

"Good," she said. "And I want to make something very clear. While you are in the capital, you are under my employ. I will compensate you fairly, and well. In exchange, you will not utter a word to anyone about this, Natalis. This is just a bout of frivolity, after all."

* * * *

Taki wrapped the knit scarf around his neck and made sure it was snug. Doing so would keep the drafts out and keep him from accidentally catching flame from his candles. The still air within the Vallianos archives was throat-scratchingly dry, and the ambient temperature hovered near frost level. If he set himself or the books on fire, no help would come for him this deep in the subterranean stacks.

He had now been poring over the accounts for days, tracing the flow of money from Athenaeum to the Cloud Temple and back. Like any other part of the Dominion military, polaris were compensated through block payments of ammunition. Part of the monthly shipment was expended to fulfill battle obligations, and any surplus left over was distributed to the soldiers to keep as their pay. While milligrad was the uncontested standard of currency, there was also substantial traffic in reloaded cartridges, and this actually made up the vast majority of transactions. It made sense to him. Warriors used a lot of ammunition in the commission of their duties. With an ingrained reluctance to fire the shiny "good" ammunition, that meant a lot of trading of milligrad for less sought-after varieties. Most of it ended up back in the hands of the guilds, which were in turn the main creditors for Dominion nobility.

"Corporal Natalis, it is refreshing to see your enthusiasm," Amilia said as she approached from behind. Taki started, nearly knocking over a candle and catching his hair on fire.

"Minister," he said, remembering to kneel.

"Rise. Have you gotten closer to confirming my suspicions?" she asked, not bothering to continue the pleasantries.

"Yes, Minister. Based on the accounts I've reviewed, a sudden influx of 'grad by an independent source would lead to chaos. The ordnance guilds would see their reloaded products rendered almost worthless overnight. In their panic, they will probably immediately start calling in debts, or at least refusing to lend. This will place the nobility and vassals, who engage the Guilds' services the most, in an untenable position. They would either be unable to defend themselves, or forever cut off from necessary funding."

"Is there anyone who would be untouched?"

"Possibly a few members of the diacheiristes. The basileus would suffer, but would not turn insolvent. Of course, with the Imperial Liberation Army at the walls, everything might turn out differently."

"Very good. Can you have a report to me by the morning?"

"It's already complete," Taki said, gathering a sheaf of papers and presenting them to her. She hurriedly skimmed the pages and let out a satisfied grunt.

"Then I release you back to the Cloud Temple, Corporal. Tomorrow morning, you will be given travel passes for the journey back. You may return to your lodgings. Remember to extinguish the candles."

She started to turn to leave.

"Minister," Taki said, despite all of the voices inside insisting that he simply depart as ordered. It was stupid of him, but he needed to know. "Are you planning to crash the guilds?"

Amilia stopped, slowly turned, and stared at him. He had not asked her if she were merely planning to destabilize the nation's currency. What he was asking was if she planned to usurp the basileus. Wrecking the economic foundation upon which all Argead lords rested their security was only productive if someone else stepped in to take control. Someone with power and the bullets to lend. Beneath her heavy robes, she wrapped her fingers around the grip of the small but powerful revolver held against her hip.

"And what if I am?"

Taki blinked. Now he had done it. He had disregarded every piece of advice that had kept him safe and comfortable for the last sixteen years and confronted possibly the second most powerful person in the country. Strangely, he felt relief, more than anything else.

"Do you think you would be a just ruler?" he asked. Amilia's grip tightened on the revolver. Taki could easily overwhelm her in combat, but he lacked preparation and weapons, and she had the advantage of surprise. A well-placed round of .357 magnum could take any man down, even the exarch.

"And what constitutes justice to you, Corporal Natalis?" Her finger touched the trigger and tightened.

"A little while ago, I was sent to Kosovo, to aid the duke against rebels. He was supposed to be this big hero, but we were made to help his vassals kill an entire village of innocents. We could do nothing to stop it, for he was within his rights. Though it is blasphemy to say this, if the rebels hadn't killed him I'm pretty sure one of us would have. While I don't presume to know what justice really is, I now know what it's *not*. I've always just gone along with everything because I didn't care either way, as long as I was comfortable. But I can't do that anymore, not if I want to sleep at night. I want to help change something."

"Even if that means betraying your overlords?"

"I'm no traitor. But my overlords have to earn my allegiance."

"Those are dangerous words, Corporal. Keep them close to your heart."

"Understood, Minister."

Amilia nodded. Her exhalation swirled tendrils of condensation in the frigid air. She let go of the revolver and brought her hand up to her mouth in thought.

"Come with me, then. I may as well show you the rest," she said.

They exited the archives together, and emerged into the muggy night of inner Athenaeum. Amilia was not given to conversation, Taki realized. He was fine with that, as it was enough effort already to calm the fluttering of his heart. Before joining Tirefire the Lesser, he would have never imagined voicing his thoughts, much less to one of his betters.

As they navigated increasingly twisted roads and alleys, Taki realized that he was gradually going underground. The capital was an ancient place, and previous empires and kingdoms had extensively developed the warrens underneath. The first three hundred years of fallout from the Gotterdammerung had made life on the surface impossible, after all. Eventually, they arrived at a nondescript but rigid set of steel doors. There were no guards in sight. Amilia rapped briefly on a knock plate, and a small panel slid open to reveal a man's eyes. He looked at the minister, slid the window shut, and opened the door.

The inside was underwhelming, though clearly massive in size. Just rows of stacked boxes under dim fluorescent lighting, and only a handful of sentries bearing the crest of House Gillette on their armor. Taki noticed, however, that they all carried functional, pristine Avtomat 74's. Enough firepower to bring down a company of knights, and highly illegal for commoners to possess. The guards stood at attention while Amilia motioned for Taki to approach. As he did, she unlatched the top of one of the wooden boxes and lifted its cover for him to see. His eyes widened as he looked at fifty thousand rounds of golden milligrad.

"It's not milligrad," Amilia said. She handed him a round of 9-millimeter Luger. "But it's very close."

"I must admit, Minister, I can't tell much of a difference," Taki said, rolling the cartridge in his palm.

"The Ursalans have always enjoyed superior knowledge of the old world. However, with the recent wars we've seen more refugees coming over the borders. Among them were skilled alchemists who have developed ways to refine our manufacture of ammunition to this point. We can now make and draw brass into casings, coat lead with copper, and most importantly, cut powder smoke down to a quarter of what it usually is."

"Much better than half-grad," Taki said, handing the bullet back to her. "This many in circulation will make most of the reloaded rounds completely worthless. It will also drive the value of milligrad down. The guilds will cease to exist."

"And when we dump these into the markets, I will have most of the lords in my debt, including the basileus. I think you can put together the rest."

Taki nodded. It was a more potent plan than any attempt at seizing the Mitripoli by force.

"With utmost respect, why have you shown this to me?" he asked.

"You're a low-ranking soldier in a disgraced unit. If you were to speak about this with your commanders, they would trepanate you because you'd have gone mad. And then, I would have others in my employ finish the job. Do we have an understanding?"

"Yes," Taki said, smiling despite himself. "Yes, we do."

"Good. I must remain here for a time. One of the men will see you out and back to the gates."

Taki was about to rise, but something stirred in his heart. Something he knew was wildly, impossibly dangerous. Something he couldn't fight.

"Minister, must I return to the Temple so quickly?"

Amilia tilted her head quizzically.

"You have done enough for me, and exposed yourself to great risk. To ask any more would be unjust."

He sank to both knees and touched his forehead to the ground. It was an abject and pitiful gesture, but the only thing he could think of at the moment to disrupt her focus.

"I beg you to reconsider! I want to help you do more. I want to make a Dominion I can be proud to serve again. I don't care about career, or reputation, or even my honor anymore. Throw my life away freely, so long as you put me to use. Please!"

Amilia was silent for what seemed to Taki to be an eternity. Finally, she bent over and lightly touched her fingertips to his head.

"You have a habit of speaking dangerously," she said. "So, Natalis, could you kill a king? Could you bear that damnation?"

Taki shivered. "Gladly."

"Then perhaps you can be of use. We will create that Dominion you desire so much."

11

"You know what, I think I'll go back to Kosovo and ask the Prince of Maladies to just kill me after all," Draco said. His mastery slowed by bitterness, he sloppily gouged an eye from a large potato in his hands and set to work on peeling the greenish skin away. The latest crop was practically bubbling with solanine and he swore it was leaching into his skin. His guts rumbled and his head hurt. Though the others had dismissed the theory, he suspected that Imperial sympathizers were unearthing the roots too early and letting them sit in the sun to poison everyone.

"But what if she's all like: *'Jawohl! Zen it is death by peelink zee potatoes,'* hm?" Hadassah asked. She poked him in the ribs with a finger, making him swat back at her hand.

"Then it wouldn't be any different from what I'm doing now, and I'd be in much sexier company."

"Go stick it in a goat."

"Compared to you, a goat is more personable and possibly comelier."

"Then what are you waiting for? No human woman deserves the burden of rearing your pus-faced, lazy-eyed, smegma-haired children. Not even the prince, who literally tried to jam one of her eastern pigstickers up my stinkstar and twist it."

"That sounds beautiful. Tell me more."

"Ugh!"

"Emreis, you may jape about death, but do realize that we've been sentenced to *hang?*" Lotte asked, rolling her eyes at him. Both corporals stood bolt upright.

"What?"

"You heard me. We're supposed to hang, but since there's no one to do the job, the punishment's been suspended indefinitely."

"How is that allowed?" Draco asked, grimacing. "I mean, I actually don't want to be hanged, but it makes no sense. Why are we still here? Aren't we entitled to a *speedy* execution?"

"We're losing. Kosovo wasn't the only province to go over. Everyone but us is holding a fort on the northern border or dying of fever and distemper. There's no wood to spare for a gallows, nor anyone to build them."

"So, basically, we have to keep screwing up, and we'll live forever," Hadassah said.

"A fate worse than death. Just my rotting luck," Draco sighed. "Also, why is *she* here?"

He pointed a bulbous tuber at Hecaton. The major reclined alone on a bench, resting her head on an outstretched palm. She smoked a pungent cigarillo which she languidly ashed into a nearby tin cup. For his impertinence, she flicked a dried bean at Draco's forehead. Inexplicably, it stung as badly as being shot. At least, that was how he imagined being shot in the face would feel. Draco reeled, his eyes tearing.

"I requested her help, now that Natalis is away and Gillette is not so used to our regular job," Lotte said.

Karma glowered miserably. Compared with the others, he was a neophyte with a peeling knife. Innumerable small cuts on his fingers smeared red on the wet starch of his conquests.

"I think I might prefer dogs eating my balls," he muttered. For this, Karma earned a bean to the lip. He gasped in pain, covering the swelling on his mouth.

"Don't forget, the 'H' is for 'Annihilation!'" Hadassah's spite was rewarded with a bean to the cheek.

"Just where the hell *is* Natalis, anyway?" Draco huffed. "He never showed up here after turning his gun in."

"Off at Athenaeum, visiting family. He has a grandmother who's on the verge of death."

"Wait, so all I have to do to get out of this is go and beat the shit out of one of my grandparents? Why didn't anyone tell me sooner? Why is this world so unfair?"

"And you call *me* twisted?" Karma asked, crushing a bloodstained piece of raw potato in his jaws for emphasis.

"*Ew, gross!* Major, flick a bean at him!" Hadassah whined.

"I'd rather she actually helped *peel!*" Draco said, wagging a potato at Hecaton again. "It's her fault we ended up doing this."

"You kids are abominably ungrateful these days," Hecaton drawled, swinging her legs over the edge of the table and sitting upright. "Anyway, you're not peeling these because of the Tirefire thing anymore. The exarch finally requested I change it to something more suitable to the dignity of the Temple. I couldn't refuse him in light of your recent failures."

"*Our* recent failures? We only lost Vergina because of that oriental twit who showed up at the last minute! Who *is* that guy, anyway?"

"Calling us 'oriental' is quite rude. That earns *two* beans."

One lodged in Draco's ear canal and the other knocked him over.

"Aha! So you *do* know him!" Lotte said, clapping her hands together in hard-bitten triumph.

"Yeah, Major, you owe us an explanation!" Hadassah said. "Is he your ex-husband?"

"He would have to be both incomprehensibly strong and incomprehensibly stupid to bed her," Karma muttered. His words earned him a bean in each nostril, plus one between the legs. He joined Draco in rolling around on the dirty floor in undignified panic.

"It's complicated, our situation," Hecaton said, uncharacteristically wistful for a second. "I certainly didn't think I'd ever see him again, or that I'd be slightly pleased to see him alive. But he is dangerous, that is an absolute certainty. As the blond idiot over there pointed out so indelicately, we're of the same extraction, and thus different from the rest of you. I can't guarantee that any of you would live if he fights seriously, but what I can promise is that none of his disciples will live if I do the same. Anyway, you all need to think of a new unit name. Or a number, I don't care either way."

* * * *

Taki sneezed into the crook of his arm just in time. For some reason, he was allergic to the down stuffing in Niketas Palaiologos's bedding, and thus got the sniffles whenever he made the man's bed. This made him wonder about nobles and other rich men who regularly used snuff to provoke the ostensibly pleasurable sensation of sneezing. It really wasn't that pleasant.

He had not expected, at any point in his career, to end up making the basileus's bed, cleaning the man's floors, and bringing the ruler of the Dominion his nightly cup of warmed aniseed wine to serve as a sleep aid. In Taki's wildest dreams, he had imagined himself defending the man against Imperial assassins as a praetorian guard, not maintaining his home as a manservant. Yet a manservant he now was, thanks to Amilia Gillette.

In actuality, he was the minister's new steward. The transfer had gone over Hecaton's head and straight to the exarch's desk, where one of the triada had signed it in the man's stead. Taki was to serve and protect Amilia Gillette, and would be paid the equivalent of three rounds of old Nayto Standard per fortnight: a major's regular salary. However, from the start, his day-to-day duty had been to fill in for the missing servants at the basileus's palace.

A short time ago, hundreds of thousands of high-quality reloaded rounds suddenly hit the ordnance depots. The results were as Taki had predicted. Anyone who wished to do business in the Dominion immediately dumped their supplies of unsafe, ugly, and dirty rounds in favor of the new ones, which were practically milligrad save for the smoke. Reports of the new rounds' increased and consistent lethality versus human and beast alike further bolstered their value. Even the value of milligrad itself took a dive, and the nobles panicked when their hoards lost most of their value overnight. The legion of servants who once cleaned the basileus's toenails for him deserted en-masse when he could no longer afford to pay them, and even his own steward left soon after. The cartridges simply weren't forthcoming. Amilia, however, would not let the last scion of the Palaiologoi go unattended.

Niketas had come into power a decade ago, and had already been targeted for assassination over a dozen times. Mainly by his family members, the whispers said. The Palaiologoi were an ancient lineage, more sacrosanct than any others, and prolific to boot. As the fourth son of the old basileus, Niketas stood little chance of inheriting the throne at the outset. Yet from an early age he had shown a knack for being indispensable to those smarter than he. It had only taken five years to eliminate his three older brothers, and five more years to dispose of his mother. The next to go were his aunt who was also his father's concubine, and finally four younger brothers. The men fell to poison and knives, and the women were sent to convents. In this time, he had accumulated many skilled companions, all of whom had expected a payout once he assumed the proper position. *And then I went and helped kill one of them,* Taki mused.

The small palace where the basileus lived was in constant need of repair and cleaning. Dust seemed to seep out of the walls and into every crevice possible, and it was a constant battle to keep the place presentable. One lone servant, even aided by prana, could not do a satisfactory job. And yet for all of his bluster in public, the basileus was a surprisingly lenient, though not social master. He never once berated Taki for lapses in cleaning or cooking, though Taki was far from experienced in those fields. Surprisingly, Niketas Palaiologos himself was virtually mute in private, mostly preferring to sit in an ancient ornate couch nursing a glass of cordial while staring into a fire. The limited conversations between Taki and Niketas were related to a direct expression of want or need. Wine, blankets, and sometimes a chaste massage. Taki had thought that the man would try to bed him, but nothing of the sort ever came to pass. The basileus did not even entertain courtesans, though he could likely afford them. The days had settled into contemplative silence, enough to make Taki sometimes forget what he had pledged to do for Amilia Gillette.

Today, Taki accompanied his master-by-default to a meeting of the diacheiristes: the inner circle. All of them had been hand-picked by the basileus, and were nobility of old families, some of whom had existed and ruled before Armageddon. It was the first time he had set foot in the Mitripoli, the seat of Argead power. Though it was a surprisingly cramped place to convene the leadership of a sprawling kingdom, it nevertheless made up for its small size with elaborate carvings, frescoes, and ornaments on every surface. Rather than excite the passions, however, the weight of such opulence usually seemed to stifle emotion. Yet, the basileus seemed at his most emotional today. With Taki standing uncomfortably at attention behind him, Niketas had been screaming at his inner circle practically all morning. It was easy to see why: things were rapidly falling apart from without and within.

"And who's next to turn traitor? Who's going to be the next one to whore himself out to the padishah? Is it going to be *you*, Manuel Comnenus?"

"I assure you, Your Grace, I have no loyalty but to your esteemed self! I am a disl—" the Judge of the Realm began to trip over his tongue.

"Oh, save me the *flattery!*" the basileus whined.

The human mind could become desensitized to anything, and that even included constant screaming. Taki felt his eyes grow heavy-lidded and he struggled to maintain his rigid posture. The high-ranking servant's outfit he wore helped in this regard with brace-like fittings that kept his back in perfect lordosis. Still, it was difficult, and he slipped into pleasant doldrums metered by fists pounding on mahogany.

"Exarch General Constantin Choniates, Supreme Commander of the Polaris, Lord Protector of the Cloud Temple, and Major Hecaton Kheiris Mezeta," a herald announced in a loud monotone. Taki's eyes flew open to hear the names. So surprised was he to hear of Hecaton's arrival that he forgot to feel embarrassed for falling asleep in the midst of the greatest concentration of power in the land.

The herald continued: "Know that you are in the presence of Basileus Niketas Palaiologos, Ethnomartyr of the Dominion, Protector of the Theotokos, Primate of Athenaeum, Supreme Commander of the Argead Military, and King in Exile of Constantinople, Alexandria, Libya, Adrianople, and All Egypt."

Oh shit, she sees me, Taki realized, as his gaze met Hecaton's. Her expression seemed neutral, however, as if she had forgotten who he was. For going over her head, Taki had half-expected Hecaton to zap him in public.

"Your Grace," Constantin said, "the Cloud Temple has come as bidden. We apologize for not arriving in a timelier fashion, as we were forced to ride the entire way."

"Bless the Trinity! At least I still have loyal subjects," Niketas growled. "Constantin! You're the only one who'll tell me the truth. What is really going on in the north? I want to hear it from your mouth, not the rasping, sucking orifices of these leeches!"

"Your Grace." Constantin exhaled, steeling himself. "We have taken significant setbacks in most of the realm. However, we are working on-"

"Did you take Kosovo back?"

"No, Your Grace."

"And Macedon?"

"The baron has turned traitor and sold his allegiance to the Imperium."

"And the Imperial army? Where does it camp now?"

"North, in Thessaloniki. If they succeed in pushing past the Hot Gates, Athenaeum will fall within a month."

"Do you see what I mean?" the basileus shouted to the diacheiristes around him. "Of all of you, why is it that *the mutant* tells me the truth and you all don't?"

If Constantin bristled at the label of mutant, he did not show it. Neither did Hecaton. The others remained silent, some cowed, some simply distracted.

"And that's why I called him here today," the basileus continued. "Because I won't let my nation be overrun by shit-monsters and heretics! Make note, Logothete! Constantin is the final member of the diacheiristes, and now that we are all assembled, I am invoking the final protocol of the Argead Dominion."

"My word," exclaimed one of the circle. "You want to open the Trident chamber?"

The basileus nodded. "We Palaiologoi are not the kings of the Dominion for nothing. We carry the divine mandate to rule, and the sign of God's decree to us on earth is that He left us His Hand! And I plan to use it to slap the shit out of the Imperium when they come knocking."

"Your Grace!" Constantin started to sweat. "The God Hand is a sacred relic! Any who use it stand to be destroyed themselves!"

"Not if I'm far enough away, and the Hand reaches far indeed. Constantin, your army will hold the Imperial dogs at the Hot Gates, and while they're bottled up there, I will have your best squad use the Behelit to guide the Hand and vaporize them all. This is my decree. I have followed the protocol laid out by the founders."

At this point, the metropolitan of the realm stood fuming behind his great, snowy beard.

"Your Grace. As holder of the Apostle Paul, and guardian of the protocol of Exo, I cannot allow this to happen. Even if the gates may be overrun and our bodies put to the sword, we *must not* stain our souls by releasing the Hand on this world as our forefathers foolishly did! Hellfire will rain for centuries *on our own soil!*"

"So you show your true colors after all, priest," the basileus growled. "Praetorians, arrest him! And confiscate the apostle!"

"Niketas, my child! I beg you to see reason!" the metropolitan protested. The praetorians keeping vigil at the door marched toward the dark-robed priest. Halfway across, they raised their rifles at him. "You are being corrupted! It's Gillette's fault! She pours poison into your ears. I beg of you to listen! The basileus of the Dominion has the responsibility to keep the God Hand hidden away from the world. Do not forget that!"

Two praetorians had the Metropolitan on his knees. One of them smashed the brass butt-end of his long Temple rifle against the old man's nose and broke his face. Blood and teeth splattered on the starry mosaic on the floor. The other roughly pulled the folds of the priest's robes away from a sunken chest and yanked at an object held on a chain around his neck. Taki raised an eyebrow as he saw just what the apostle Paul actually was: a small, dully-colored key.

"Gillette is the *only* one of you who has remained truly loyal to me to the end. Who among you has used funds from your personal treasuries to sustain me? Who here contributes to the costs of my servants and my fuel? That's right, none of you greedy parasites!" the basileus spat. "Take him away! Throw him in the dog pits!"

"Your Grace! Please see reason! Do not be swayed by her money and the pleasures it brings. She plots against you. She will be your downfall!" The Metropolitan sputtered and grasped vainly at cracks in the floor as he was dragged out of the nave. A thin trail of blood served as a wake for his passing. The golden doors slammed shut and his voice was heard no more.

"A truly regrettable turn of events. I urge you to show mercy to the poor, demented old man," Amilia said, shaking her head sadly. "At the very least, spare him the horror of being torn apart by mastiffs."

"Don't forget your place," the basileus warned her. "I shall punish him how I please. That goes for the rest of you. Now, Constantin, my attendants shall deliver the Behelit to your forces."

"Your Grace," Constantin said, bowing again. A quick look to Hecaton suggested that it was past time to start leaving, lest they be the next victims of their ruler's rage. The golden doors of the templon opened to allow egress, and they wasted no time leaving.

"We adjourn," the basileus said with a tired wave of his hand. "Gillette, I will speak with you later."

Taki bowed deeply while the discontented inner circle slowly rose and started to file out of the nave. He could not help but be troubled inside. What exactly was this "God Hand" everyone was so concerned with? How could anything alone destroy the entire Imperial Liberation Army? *Just keep your head down and listen,* he chided himself. *An opportunity will come up.*

* * * *

Much later at night, Taki had laid out his master's bedding, he set to work oiling the floors. He preferred to wear a loincloth alone while performing the task, and was about to disrobe before a knock sounded at the front door of the manse. He bounded down to the doors, opened the viewing slit, and saw Amilia staring back at him. Without needing to be prompted, he lifted the inner bar on the door and pulled it open to allow her to pass. She strode in and he knelt.

"Natalis, where is our master?"

"In the study, Minister. Let me announce your arrival to him."

"Do so, and be quick about it."

Taki rose to his feet and padded down the great hall and into the wing where the basileus sat, staring at a small cluster of glowing embers.

"Your Grace, I apologize for letting the fire die down," Taki said. "I shall retrieve more wood forthwith."

The basileus nodded.

"Also, Minister Gillette has arrived. Shall I show her in?"

The basileus nodded again.

He's been tormented like this for weeks, now. Taki noticed that the lines in the man's face had grown deeper since they had first met. More defined, as if the Imperial invasion was truly hollowing him out from the inside. Taki strode out of the study and gave Amilia a bow.

"In the study, Minister. I shall retrieve more firewood for you both," he said.

She grasped him by the hem of his sleeve before he could turn away.

"Do you still have what it takes to make a just kingdom, Natalis?" she asked.

Taki blinked. "Yes. I do. Whatever it takes."

"Then be prepared. Go get the firewood. The man loves to lose himself in thought. He would have been a good ruler if only he weren't such a fool whenever he opened his mouth."

Taki bowed again and exited out of the door he had let Amilia through. Wood had run short recently, and as a measure of desperation Taki had taken it upon himself to lop down some of the ancient, dying trees in the palace courtyard and use their trunks to feed the basileus's need for distraction and warmth. He strode over to the pile he had made, and hefted two split lengths, each about the size of a burly forearm. When he came back, he heard voices. He stopped, and sidled up against the archway into the study.

"I made a mistake, Gillette," the basileus said. "The old metropolitan, I shouldn't have killed him. I shouldn't have brought up the God Hand. What evil possessed me to desire its use? It's too much sin for a man, or even a king, to bear."

"But, Your Grace, we had little choice. The Imperium is at the gates. We must act, or lose everything we have."

"The exarch was right. I'm going to be cursed forever if I use this."

"Your Grace, do you have it? The Behelit?"

"Yes, on the table. I brought it out like you asked. But I've decided something in the meantime. I'll have it destroyed. It's fragile enough. When Natalis comes back, Amilia, we'll end this nightmare. We'll also go back to the Ooss and fill the trident chamber with sand. It's an accursed place, anyway. Men die horribly if they spend too much time in there."

Amilia sucked her teeth. "Then we will certainly fall to the Imperium. Are you prepared to be subject to their rule? Their Way that says that you are a mere commoner and not a king?"

"Yes, I am. Look at me. I'm pathetic. No wife, no heir, no companions. The padishah's hands are at my throat. My beloved brother Gul is dead, and my sworn vassals abandon me daily. The Palaiologoi are finished. Perhaps it was God's will, but I'll never know."

Taki's grip on the wood faltered and one of the sections clattered to the floor. He immediately swooped down to pick it up. He needed to at least make an effort to seem like he wasn't eavesdropping. Amilia looked knowingly at him.

"Ah, Natalis," the basileus said with a smile of relief. It was the first time Taki had seen him with any other expression but a brooding or angry one. "Just in time. Put a fresh log on and then when the flames are high, cast that thing into the hearth." He pointed at a palm-shaped, tube-shaped object sitting on the end-table next to his chair. Taki knelt and placed one of the logs into the embers.

Amilia shook her head and rose.

"Actually, Your Grace, Natalis will do nothing of the sort."

The basileus frowned.

"Are you betraying me, Gillette?"

"As you said, Your Grace, it is the end of the Palaiologoi. I intend to protect the Dominion, even if you do not. Remember the words of the first basileus: 'Don't give up the ship.' Trust me, Niketas, I will see us a better tomorrow."

"How dare you?" The basileus clumsily reached into his robes and drew a nickel-plated derringer. He pointed the muzzle at Amilia's chest.

Taki swung the remaining log and it collided with the basileus's forehead with a dull thunk. Niketas Palaiologos's head snapped back into the chair and then rolled forward on limp neck muscles. The gun clattered to the floor. Dilated pupils in the man's open eyes refused to shrink, and the bony contour of his chest remained still and without breath. The basileus of the Argead Dominion was dead and his line had ended.

"Perfect timing, Natalis," Amilia said. She rose from her seat and walked over to the end-table. "This is the Behelit, in case you were wondering." The short, squat object seemed almost innocuous in her hand.

Taki dropped the wood. He had forgotten his own strength. Forgotten that the basileus of the Dominion was still an ant in comparison to the lowest-ranked polaris, and was just as easily and thoughtlessly crushed. *I didn't mean to kill him.* Taki stared at Niketas's waxy pallor and fell to his knees. *Or did I? I don't know. It doesn't matter now. I'm a regicide. The lowest class of criminal. I should be drawn and quartered for this.*

"Don't worry, I still have use for you," Amilia said, as if reading his thoughts. "You won't be outed for his murder. This is an old building and there are many hazards to explain a sudden blow to the head. His death will be kept secret for now, especially since I have the loyalty of most of the diacheiristes, save for that bothersome metropolitan. His death was a most convenient occurrence."

"What would you have me do?" Taki whispered. He still could not bring himself to look at the basileus. There was a difference between pledging to kill a king and actually doing so. Part of him wanted to be gutted alive, despite all of his earlier convictions, and even despite the memories of Kosovo.

"I intend to use the God Hand in a negotiation with the Imperium. Right now, our position is weak because they mass at the Hot Gates, but an actual threat of detonation will shift the balance in my favor. The enemy will send his best soldiers to try to retrieve the Behelit, which you will carry into battle and deploy."

"Minister, I have little strength. If they send their elites…"

"I don't expect you to beat them, Natalis. When they find you, I want you to hand their commander this."

She took out a battered, palm-sized object covered in innumerable scratches and colored dull gray, and pressed it into Taki's hand.

"What is it?" he asked. It was solid, but felt slimy at the same time. Or perhaps it was just the sweat of his palm.

"A starspeaker. One of the last two in the Dominion, possibly the world. I have the other. When the time is right, I will send a message to the heavens, and celestial bodies will relay those words to the one in your possession. But have a care, for its remaining life is very limited, so don't use it without my permission. Do you understand?"

Taki nodded. He realized, at this point, that he was being used, just as Niketas had been. But being useful was the key to staying alive.

"Good," she said. "I trust you will not object to being sent back to your temple, then. You have done all you can here, but rest assured, I will have further need of your services."

All I can? I've just killed the rightful lord of the realm. Oh God, did all of my seditious thought lead to this? Can I take it all back? Please!

Amilia lightly tapped Taki on the cheek, as if reading his thoughts.

"Change requires sacrifice. If your earlier words were not mere bluster, then you will understand the necessity of what happened today."

Taki knelt, feeling more drained than reverent.

"By your leave," he said, and started to scoot away from her. For a moment, Amilia's expression softened.

"Here," she said, and handed Taki an en-bloc clip of .30-06 cartridges. His eyes widened at the amount. Just one of those could buy lodging for a month. Eight was blatant excess. "For the journey back to the Cloud Temple," she continued.

"This is too much, Minister."

She seemed to ignore his objection. "Tell me, Natalis. Is it true that your company recovered Karma Gillette alive?"

"Yes, Minister."

She gently closed Taki's fingers around the clip.

"Then give a few of these to my son, in whatever fashion you choose."

* * * *

Days later, Taki returned to the Temple. The starspeaker was secreted away over his heart, and though it was of little mass, it still felt like a lead weight yoked to his neck. Amilia had arranged to send the Behelit through separate channels, citing the risk of interception. Like his journey to the capital, Taki's return to the Temple was conducted under the veil of secrecy and thus he endured the indignities of the open road. Though he carried more milligrad in his pockets than he had ever possessed, he had realized early on that to try to spend one of the large battle-rifle rounds would only arouse suspicion. He subsisted on stale jerky and wild-gathered herbs, and drank from the least-muddy pools of water he could find along the way. In the end, he was thirsty, hungry, and footsore when he finally set foot the exarch's demesne.

"You look tired," Lotte said. Taki looked to her in surprise. Had she been waiting for him to arrive? She cracked a smile and rose from her seat on a decaying wooden pallet. She seemed thinner than she had before, and one side of her jaw bore the telltale signs of a healing bruise. Seeing this filled Taki with guilt and he wiped at moist eyes. She wrapped an arm around his shoulders and drew him close.

"Captain, I—" He wanted to tell her everything. That he was not only a traitor but a regicide to boot. That he had left her and the others to the stingy mercy of the triada while he had lived in luxury in the royal manse. She stifled him with a fierce hug, and held him like that for a while. They walked back to the kitchens in silence, and Taki found the urge to belt out his crimes to the world fading with every step. How foolish he had been to wish for a transfer. The capital was a lonesome place of callous intrigue, suffused with solitude and fear. The Cloud Temple, on the other hand, was a miserable rock constantly beset by chill and rain, and its denizens little more than prisoners and thugs. But it was home.

12

"I never thought I'd live to actually see the end of a nation," Draco said as he inspected the arsenal laid out before him. "But here it is. Living proof that we're about to go tits up. I mean, why else would they let us put our filthy mitts all over this stuff?"

Around the squad, racks of Temple Guns gleamed in the eerie flicker of prism-reflected torchlight. They were deep within the shrine, far past where even the sextons would go to access milligrad. Earlier, the neokoros on duty had reacted in aggravated disbelief when Lotte presented him with a signed missive from Amilia Gillette to authorize unrestricted access to the consecrated inner sanctuary. Even now the man periodically ducked in unannounced to "check on progress" and make sure the group wasn't stuffing their pockets with spare parts to sell to other squads.

"Speak for yourself. I don't grope and fondle every gun in sight like a horny baboon. I only finger the pretty ones," Hadassah said, marveling at the smooth lines of the new rifle she clutched like a newborn. The Springfield she held was a fabled piece of ordnance even in ancient times and was prized for its accuracy and ruggedness. Without the need to manually cycle a bolt like on her Nagant, it fired as fast as she could pull the trigger. If rumors were to be believed, the special sight attached to the gun was worth even more.

"You know that thing's worth more than your life, right?" Draco said. "If for some reason we win, you'll have to return it."

"I'll tell 'em I lost it in a boating accident. I'll even cry a little too. No one takes my arms."

"Then they'll send you to the mines forever, and make your shark-toothed, beady-eyed, knuckle-dragging children work off your debt long after you're dead."

Hadassah punched him in the arm. "My hideous children can beat up your hideous children any day of the week, including and especially on Shabbat."

"You'll eat your words when the Prince of Maladies and I have our own little squad, strengthened with hybrid vigor."

"I hate to break it to you, but she's obviously shagging her brother."

"I'll not have you slander my woman again. Pick your seconds and meet me for pistols at dawn," Draco said, practicing his stance with the glinting single-action revolver he had picked up to replace his old LeMat. He disliked having fewer shots than before, but the cartridge it fired was far superior to any black powder offering.

"Emreis, are you really throwing down the gauntlet over imaginary wives?" Karma asked with a derisive grin.

"She's a real woman, unlike your hand," Draco scoffed.

Taki ignored the exchange to focus more intently on the object of his consternation. He held the Behelit gingerly, as if pressing too hard on one of its surfaces would cause it to spontaneously combust. He knew that was impossible, but it did not stop him from worrying. Hecaton had given it to him earlier. *"You'll know what to do when the time comes,"* she cackled after shoving the device into his hands. He imagined her saying the same thing to a small boy while giving him a can of petrol and a book of matches.

"Can you operate it?" Lotte asked, peering at it over his shoulder as she bent over. With such a monstrous name, they had expected the device to be some sort of squishy, writhing contraption oozing evil from every disgusting pore. The disappointing reality was a metal and plastic box attached to a tube with glass lenses on both ends and two buttons on top.

"It's simple, actually. Just flip this switch on the side and press these." From one end of the tube, a concentrated dot of intense red light shone on the floor. "And it does this. The legends say these were used to blow holes in fortresses or sink ships from far away. But mine doesn't even heat water. The only thing I was told was to point it at the Imperial army, but if this is the extent of its power, it won't do anything."

"Maybe it…gets more powerful if there are more people around? Or perhaps you need to have some serious killing intent?" Lotte scratched her head.

"I've tried that, actually. But still no change."

"You did *what?* Who the hell did you want to kill so badly? Do I even want to know?" Draco said, clutching his revolver to his chest. "You know what, never mind, *don't* tell me..."

"Okay, so if it doesn't do anything lethal, then it means the Behelit isn't a weapon itself, but probably a *pointer* for a weapon," Karma said. An ancient surplus cigarette smoldered weakly and hung from his lips. Again, Taki thought of the Major dispensing flammables to children.

"A pointer for a weapon?" Lotte said. "Like some kind of sentient sword, or a suit of armor that fights for you? Also, Gillette, are you really *smoking* in a place full of *gunpowder?*"

Karma shrugged. "What's the problem?"

Lotte glowered and made as if to kick him. "If you need something to suck on so badly..."

"Yes, Cap'n," he said, and stamped it out.

"I know!" Hadassah exclaimed. "It summons Godzirra!"

"I doubt it," Taki said. "But I've been thinking the same thing, Gillette. This is ancient technology. Back then they had access to some pretty horrific things. Robotic skiapods, mechanical colossi with cannons for arms, and even devices that compressed the power of the sun into a bomb that could destroy a city."

"How do you know about this stuff, anyway?" Draco asked.

"I read about it in the archives."

"Hey!" Draco snapped. "No taking over my role in this story, eh? I'm the learned goon here."

"But I don't know what ancient horror *this* is going to unleash or become," Taki said. "If it's powerful enough to repulse an army ten times the size of our own forces, then it stands to reason that we'll probably get wiped out, too. I don't want that to happen. In truth, I don't know if I can push the button when the time comes. Perhaps you should have it, Captain."

Lotte crossed her arms. "No, you were the one it was given to, not me. There's got to be a good reason for that. All I can say is that as your commander I expect you to perform. When we get up on that hilltop I don't want you freezing up."

"Yeah, we all trust you," Draco said. "You've been peeling potatoes with us without complaint. If that doesn't make you a member of this squad, then nothing really does. Besides, you still owe us more writing lessons."

"But I could be responsible for all of your deaths," Taki said.

"Well, at least we'll die rich," Karma said.

Taki shook his head. "You're not taking this seriously. What do I have to do to convince you?" *Besides tell you about how I killed the basileus? I'm not ready for that. I'm not ready to debase myself that much.*

The door to the inner stacks burst open with a sound not unlike a rifle round going off and everyone flinched. Mailed boots clomped on stone, accompanied by the swishing of expensive robes. Taki realized who had just arrived and his stomach turned. He had almost expected the archangel Jibriil to arrive, but not the entire triada at once. Lotte greeted them on bent knee. Taki awkwardly shoved the Behelit into his satchel and genuflected. Draco and Hadassah hesitated, but did the same.

"What is the meaning of this?" Jibriil snapped. "How did you get in here? This is the personal property of the triada!"

"Milord, I have a declaration from the minister of the exchequer written and sealed by her hand," Lotte said. She produced the scroll for him and Jibriil snatched it away.

"Nonsense. She has no power here!"

"She does," Michail said, and terminated Jibriil's rebuttal with a wave of his hand. "These relics are part of the nation's treasury, and everything within the shrine is the property of the basileus in turn. We merely hold the sacred articles in confidence. Remember that, Archangel Jibriil."

"Still, these mongrels should not be defiling such holiness with their slimy hands," Yuriel said. "And they should definitely not be given the honor of taking the Behelit into battle. My Lord Archangel Michail, I beg of you, give it to a *worthy* company. Any other will do, just not these losers."

"Much as I would like to, Archangel Yuriel, I cannot override such a sacred dictum. Nay, I merely came here to ask Captain Satou a question."

Lotte bowed her head. Michail stepped forward, and to everyone's surprise and chagrin, crouched to bring himself to her eye-level.

"Milord, please, you need not abase yourself for me," Lotte said.

Michail half-smiled and patted her on the shoulder.

"I see that your corporal has the Behelit already. It has already chosen him as its master, and none may take it from him hence. But I must tell you that to bring it to battle means certain death for the wielder, and likely his friends. Life in exchange for power is the rule. Can you bear it? Can he bear it?"

"It's obvious he can't!" Yuriel insisted.

"I'll take it, in that case," Jibriil said, and started toward Taki. The Archangel's progress, however, was abruptly stopped by Michail's ornately-engraved pistol pressed against his forehead. Jibriil backed away, trembling and frothing.

"*I have told thee,* the Behelit chooses its own master," Michail said. "To interfere with its will invites doom on us all. Take not my words to mean esteem for this blasphemous group, my fellow archangels. It is far better to sacrifice their lives in the service of the Dominion than it is to sacrifice ours. They will perish in flames, and we will lead the Temple to glory. A fair trade."

"Milord," Lotte said, "do you wish to know the name of the brave corporal who has been chosen?"

Michail regarded Taki with a pious, wide-eyed stare, and shook his head. The triada filed out, and the door closed behind them. Lotte continued to kneel, and though her face remained stony, she curled her fingers tightly into a fist.

"Did he…" Hadassah sputtered. "Did he just tell us all to die in a fire?"

"You know," Karma said, "we *could* have Natalis press the big red button *after* we've all run away."

Lotte frowned. "Gillette, that's…"

"That's like saving our own lives by stepping on his corpse," Hadassah said. "Let's do it!"

"I'll immortalize you in my histories," Draco said, clapping Taki on the shoulder.

"And I, uh, really appreciate you taking one for the team," Karma said, with a grave thumbs-up.

Taki rolled his eyes and shook his head.

"You're all assholes," he said.

"Agreed," Lotte said. "There will be no abandoning each other. We go in united, and perish the same. But for now, steal everything you can."

A short while later, after they had shoved gleaming ammunition into every available pocket and pilfered as many spare gun parts as they could carry under their clothes, the squad emerged into the dusty chaos that had enveloped their home. The air was clogged with smoke and grit, most of it issuing from the gates one level below. A fresh river of fighters marched out from the grounds and onto the rudely cobbled path leading to the rest of the country. Blue flags of the Cloud Temple and the colorful banners of every company of foot flapped in the wind atop pikes and halberds. Anthems of the Dominion filtered through the air, coupled with the exhortations of priests that for every Imperial killed in battle, a sin would be cleansed. Periodically, a wagon carrying heavy cannon and shot would roll through, accompanied by much cursing as the loads shook and swayed dangerously from side to side.

"Look," Draco said to Taki. "The main batteries are up and running now. They're preparing for a siege." He pointed to the cannon turrets flanking the exarch's tower and festooned with prayer flags. The guns, ancient howitzers, could rain havoc on anything trying to climb the winding road leading to the Temple, for its entire three-kilometer length. His scanned the crowd, settled on a gaggle of gray-robed begging priests, and spat derisively in their general direction.

"That's still heresy what you're doing," Taki said.

"Listen, Natalis. These so-called men of God exhort us to kill in His name every moment, but when the starving times come they'll be eating the lion's share of the rations and turning all of the water stores into piss. When the Imperials start gutting us in the alleys the priests will harass our corpses for alms. So on top of having to defend our burning homes we also have to indulge their sanctimonious bullpocky? Is that really just?"

"I…" Taki began. As much as he didn't want them to, Draco's words were beginning to make sense.

"Noel!" Hadassah shouted at a diminutive woman wearing an armored wimple and riding atop an indigo-painted main battle tank that rumbled slowly through the gates. Surprisingly, despite the noise, the woman waved back. After a short while, the massive rolling temple disappeared in the dust coming off the road to the Hot Gates. "See? It *does* work!" She swatted Draco in the arm.

"Fine, fine, you were right. I can't believe you remember that," Draco said, rolling his eyes.

"I'll take your apology in the form of foot massages for a month."

"I can't abide feet. They're disgusting and they smell."

"Okay, Princess D."

"Speaking of smelly feet, I hear the exarch's going to be taking part in the battle down on the ground, along with the triada. Those godrotting idiots would've taken the exarch down with them had they a Behelit," Draco huffed.

"Good! We should just pass the damned thing to the archangel Yuriel, then," Hadassah grumped. "She can shove it up her—"

"Hold your tongue," Lotte admonished with a swat.

"I meant the bitchy one, not *you!*"

"When's the attack?" Taki asked.

"Day after tomorrow, dawn," Lotte said.

"Fuck it. Start drawing up your wills," Draco said, smiling sadly. Lotte put a hand on his shoulder and squeezed it.

"Polaris of the Cloud Temple!" Lotte said. "The mighty Imperium stands at the gates, intending to take our country, our homes, and our lives. We are outnumbered and outgunned. Our nation sends us on a suicide mission we never asked for, and our names will be forever erased from the histories if we succeed. But I promise you one thing in recompense: the enemy will curse us for the rest of their lives. They will remember how we turned their easy day into a nightmare, and we will laugh at them from hell. Are you with me, men and women of the Dominion?"

In response, Taki fell to his knees and vomited on the cobbles. Draco raised an eyebrow and looked at the others, who wore similarly confused expressions. Lotte's determined expression started to waver. Finally, Karma broke the silence.

"Well, it's worth a shot, I guess…" he muttered.

* * * *

Later that evening, Taki barely managed not to have his life ended by another lumbering tank. Like any other army encampment, the Dominion side of the Hot Gates was a sprawling, smelly mess where dust choked the air so thickly that it formed nostril-plugging clods in midair. He recalled reading about how more soldiers tended to die of disease than wounds sustained in battle. As he gingerly hopped over backed-up latrines cut into the dirt right next to communal drinking troughs with a single ladle for a thousand men, he was inclined to agree. Tents studded the grounds in almost random order, some large and ornate to house the better and richer companies of levy troops and mercenaries, and others merely simple affairs that tended to freeze inside at night. In almost all of them, however, one could find the writhing bodies of naked troops and their camp followers. So embarrassed had Taki been to chance on one encounter that he had tripped over a bundle of pikes and fallen right into the path of a rumbling metal behemoth.

He rolled out of the way just in time to prevent his head from being crushed by the treads. Taki considered shouting at the inconsiderate driver, but decided that opening his mouth would be useless and dangerous. The infantrymen escorting the rust-bucket looked surly and were probably itching to administer a gang-beating.

The important thing was to find Lotte. She had left him a message earlier requesting his presence near the canteen, ostensibly to discuss the best locations for deploying the Behelit. Though he thought it strange that his captain would want to talk alone rather than involve the rest of the squad, an officer's wishes were not to be ignored. Dusty and still annoyed by his brush with death, Taki arrived at a small tent near the canteen and waited. Nearby, he heard the strains of fiddle music and smelled the odor of roasting pork. Life went on, regardless of impending battle or not.

"Hail!" Karma said, and approached. On his arm was a young woman wearing an airy linen skirt and a yellow blouse topped with a jade shawl. Taki raised an eyebrow at the sight. He was pretty sure Karma and Hadassah had become romantically involved, though none had said for sure. So what was Karma doing with a camp follower on his arm? *Should I stay out of it? But Dassa's my... I wouldn't call her a friend... Well, I don't know about that.*

"Gillette," Taki said, "have you seen the captain?"

Karma gave a conspiratorial wink. "I actually left you that letter."

"You did? But it had her signature on it. You didn't..."

"Forge it? No, she signed it willingly but allowed me to write what I needed to get you to come out here."

"For what purpose?" Taki narrowed his eyelids. *Some kind of intrigue?* The last thing he needed right now in the face of impending death was to be caught up in another plot. *Oh God, is he acting in the minister's stead? She's his mother, after all. I have to be careful.*

"Relax, Natalis," Karma said. "We—I mean no harm, and intend no foul play. I just heard that you were a virgin, and I thought it unjust for you to perish without ever experiencing a woman's touch. It is one of the few things we tainted ones are given the right to enjoy, no?"

"Aye," Taki said, regretfully. "But what can I do about it right now?"

"You're a dense one, aren't you?" Karma chuckled. The camp follower eased off his arm and curtsied to Taki. "Meet Andromeda. When she heard your tale, she couldn't help but feel compelled to do you a favor. And, some 'grad also helped."

"Greetings, milord," Andromeda said, and Taki blushed. Her long black tresses enchanted him, but most appealing to him was that she seemed devoid of the hard-eyed look that most camp followers seemed to develop over the years.

"H-hi," Taki said, awkwardly. "Are you sure you're okay with this?"

"Relax, Natalis," Karma chuckled. "This is a gift we all got you. Even Captain Cake chipped in. We're not all bad people. Not all the time, anyway."

"Master Karma is an honorable man," Andromeda said. "Now come with me, milord. I'll relieve you of your burden and give you a nice memory to take into battle."

Taki blinked, and allowed her to take his hand. Karma waved jauntily and disappeared. Her touch felt unreasonably intoxicating, and his heart thundered in anticipation. Andromeda opened the flap of her nearby tent, and ushered him in.

Though the outside was simple canvas, the interior was lush, with a lining of velvet and fur, and a generous-sized mattress set out on an elevated wooden pallet, complete with goose-down pillows. Even the sheets appeared to be of high quality, and Taki could not see any obvious lice or fleas studding the surface. A nearby armoire even sported a mirror of polished steel, mostly devoid of imperfections. Taki half-expected Andromeda to simply start taking off her clothes, but instead, she gently eased him to the edge of the mattress and sat him down.

"Master Karma tells me this is your first time," she said.

"I've seen a woman without her clothes," Taki mumbled.

Andromeda giggled, although not maliciously. "It's nothing to be ashamed of, milord. It means you're free of pox, and you'll have a gentle touch. I like those qualities in a man."

"Well," Taki said, "I'm glad?"

Andromeda gently turned his face toward her and pressed her lips to his. Taki felt a band around his chest constrict and drive the air out, and he grew lightheaded at her touch. She pressed on, and started to slip her blouse off. *Finally,* Taki thought, as he swelled with anticipation. *Finally, I'll be rid of my curse! Thank you, Karma! Thank you, everyone! I forgive you for everything!*

"I'm telling you, he totally finished in his britches," sounded a faint voice in the periphery. Taki's ears pricked up. Sometimes, he regretted having better senses than normal humans.

"You're underestimating his virgin resolve. Endure for my sake, Onani-Master Natalis!"

"Shush! You're too loud! He'll hear us for sure!"

"I spent too much on this to lose to the likes of you, Emreis."

"Eat a dick, both of you! I wanna see 'em *cuddle.*"

"Dassa, are you actually getting into this?" Someone chortled. "You're a bloody romantic, aren't you?"

"You creeps are killing my delicate lady-boner."

Taki leapt from the edge of the bed and stormed over to the tent flap, through which he could now see the impressions of three bodies pressed against the canvas. He grasped the edge of the cloth and whipped it aside. Hadassah tumbled in first, followed by Karma and Draco into a pile of limbs. Taki clenched his teeth and his eyes moistened.

"I hate you all! Go die in a fire!" he shouted, and bolted from the tent, leaving a confused Andromeda behind to also glower at the trio.

* * * *

Taki ran to the edge of camp with his face burning and his nose leaking. He almost barreled head-on into a Pantheon lieutenant, but did not stop to apologize. His pride had been grievously wounded, and he wanted most of all to run away. From his squad, from Andromeda, from the Behelit, from Amilia Gillette, from impending death. When he ran out of breath, he finally crouched in between a pair of barrels and dry-heaved while tears fell from his eyes. He wanted to find an endless pit and jump into it until he could curl up into a ball in the gullet of the fallen Lucifer, trapped in eternal ice at the center of the earth. Judas had it good there: he didn't have to deal with this much humiliation.

"Natalis?" Lotte asked from behind. Taki turned and glared at her fiercely. She scrunched her brow and approached. "What's wrong?"

"You know what's wrong, Captain! I thought… I thought you all were trying to *help* me, but—" He sniffled and sucked a stalactite of snot back into a nostril.

"Oh no, what did they do?" Lotte sighed, and crouched down beside him.

"Begging your pardon, but don't play ignorant with me. Gillette showed me the letter with your signature on it."

"That? He told me he wanted to give you something nice because he felt sympathetic after how the triada treated you. I assumed he wanted to buy you a courtesan, and I gave him leave to do so. Did this not happen?"

"Oh Captain," Taki sighed, and wiped his eyes. "He did, but they were all trying to…to *watch* me! And they were taking bets on how long I'd last."

Lotte rolled her eyes. "*Idiots.* I don't suppose I can convince you that they actually meant well? Karma showed me what he was going to spend. Seven rounds of thirty-ought-six: enough to buy the only girl in camp without the pox. But it looks like they all shot themselves in the foot, yet again."

"He spent that much?" Taki brought a hand to his mouth to hide his grimace.

"And now he's out the full amount. But that's their fault, not yours," Lotte said with a knowing smile. She stood and offered her hand. "Walk with me for a bit. I want to stretch my legs after a rather dry and uninteresting meeting with our commanders."

Taki nodded, and rose. Unlike Andromeda's silky softness, Lotte's grip was callused throughout. Lotte felt warmer, though. They walked in silence past mounds of night soil left by the cavalry and grog lines redolent of sweat, until she came to an outcropping at the northern edge of the camp, and motioned for him to sit down beside her.

"You can see the Imperial camp in the distance," she said, and pointed far north. Taki strained his eyes. Despite the puffiness around his sockets, he could see flickering, almost ethereal specks of torchlight in the otherwise uninterrupted darkness. "And that outcropping is where you'll use the Behelit." She shifted her finger to a rest over ledge overlooking the pass.

"Right over the bottleneck?" Taki asked. "Won't that be heavily contested?"

"Our side will pay dearly for every step. History says that whoever controls the hills near the pass wins the day. So that's where we'll be tomorrow."

Taki swallowed and shivered, despite the balmy night air. He looked over to Lotte.

"Are we doing the right thing?"

"Who can say? In the fire of battle lies purity. I've always found my truth there. But I can tell that you might think differently these days."

"I...I will follow your orders no matter what. You are my commander, and no one else."

"Thank you, Taki Natalis," Lotte said. She inhaled and ran a hand through her hair. "So, were you at least able to lose it?"

"Lose what?"

"Your virginity. Did you do the deed?"

"No. I just kissed her. Now I feel bad for frittering away Gillette's money."

"Was it your first?"

"Yes."

"Damnation, what a waste," Lotte said, wistfully.

Taki hung his head. "You're right. I should go apologize to him, after all."

"No, I was cursing the fact that your first kiss was blown on some camp follower."

Taki blinked in confusion. "Who else would I have given it to?"

Lotte leaned over, lifted his chin with her fingers, and pressed her lips to his. Taki stiffened in surprise, but quickly melted. A stray lock of her hair fell in front of his nose and tickled him with the scent of gun oil and leather. Andromeda smelled of flowers, and Lotte of warfare. His heart throbbed in his chest and his eyelids fluttered shut as they had before, but much more intensely now. When Lotte broke the kiss off, Taki's lungs ached, his vision blurred, and his stomach twisted as if wrung by her hands.

"If only...If only you were older, I'd have—" she said with a note of bitterness, and looked away while clenching her teeth. After a few moments, she faced him again. "Well, it's not much, but I hope this puts some salve on the wound."

"Captain..." he whispered, and reached for her. His lips burned. His skin tingled madly, from the top of his scalp to his blistered soles. It was a horrific and yet exquisite sensation, this irrational, overpowering desire.

"Don't expect more, Natalis," she said, and rose to stand out of his grasp. "I'm your commander. I still own your ass, and I expect you to die when I say so."

Taki swallowed on a dry throat and snapped back to reality. She was right, of course. A relationship between them was mere fantasy, especially when tomorrow was their last day on earth. She had merely shown him a hint of sweetness to assuage his disappointment, so that he would not be jaded forevermore. No wonder Hadassah and Draco revered her so much. No wonder Karma had chosen her over Jibriil, and if the archangel was representative of who lorded over the best companies, then Taki didn't want to be in one of them anymore. He rose and saluted. With all that he'd seen, the prospect of dying for the exarch, for the triada, or for the Dominion was stupid and rage-inducing. But for Lotte, and even for his companions, he'd go out with a smile on his face. "Yes, ma'am!"

Tomorrow, Taki would perish a mere corporal in the worst unit in the Cloud Temple. And he was satisfied.

13

Thermopylae burned again before dawn. Bristling pike heads glinted in the light of smoldering Imperial war machines as Lacedaemonian phalanx punched steel into the bodies of their enemies. They buckled against charges by screaming Imperial halberdiers who tried to cut a path for their armored war-dozers to advance without being swarmed by infantry and saboteurs. Behind the phalanxes, Argead tanks sent up great plumes of exhaust as they maneuvered back and forth, trying to hit counterparts on the Imperial side. Errant shells plowed into the battle-lines, sending columns of men flying on both sides.

Cossack skirmishers melted in and out of Imperial formations, and picked off Dominion officers with well-placed head shots. Their efforts were answered by mortar rounds from the mountainside. Clay-covered shells splashed gelatinous fire on plate-armored shock troopers and cooked them in their carapaces. As soon as the artillery fired, however, their crews were melted by a deluge of molten lead from above. Bulbous, patchwork balloons hovered in the sky like distended waterskins, tethered to the ground by long lengths of rope and chain. Suspended under each distorted shape was a gondola where Imperials stoked fires to keep themselves afloat and keep their deadly payload hot.

"Now that's just unsporting," Draco sighed as another river of fire spilled from above and crashed to the ground on the Argead side. A column of Thracian peltasts dissolved under the onslaught and fled despite the curses of their officers.

"I want to peg it," Hadassah said. "I'm pretty sure they're committing some kind of crime against nature, like dentistry, or shaving the pudenda!"

"Never mind their devilry! Focus on what's in front of you," Lotte shouted. She glanced back at her squad who sheltered in the crater with her.

They had mobilized hours beforehand, seeking to get an early start to the overlook. They had gone with the Wolf Pack and Pantheon as well as a company of Cretan musketeers. In total, almost five hundred fighters. From the moment they had set foot on the rocky hillside they were at a disadvantage, for the high ground was already swarming with enemies. Pantheon engaged Varangians early on, only to discover that spetsnaz were embedded among the heavy-armored fighters. Gunfire quickly turned to elemental discharges punctuating aerial duels to the death. The Wolf Pack was forced to attempt a flanking maneuver to bail their companions out, leaving Lotte and her soldiers on their own.

They pushed on with half of the musketeers in tow. Now they were less than a hundred meters from their destination, but were pinned down at the far end of a sedge field. Janissaries had taken over an Argead artillery tower and turned the cannon and ballistae around. Shells and bolts raked the ground and tore the hillside to muddy pieces, while cavalry harassed them from the sides with charges and feints. An ancient shepherd's wall of piled stone and a few miserable holes provided the only cover.

"Emmy, spot for me! I'll see if I can take out the gunners inside," Hadassah said. A four-pounder ball sailed overhead and its wake kicked loose pebbles against her head. She spat in annoyance and slapped the bottom of her magazine to assure that it was seated properly. Draco cautiously rose and snuck his spyglass over the jagged rim of stone.

"I wouldn't do that," he said, panning his view across the field. "They have enough men operating the guns to replace whoever you kill. If we become enough of an annoyance, they'll just blow up our cover and we'll be screwed." Further ahead, a group of ten Cretans behind a fallen tree decided to charge. Half of them rose and fired over the barricade, while the other five made a dash for another crater. Hundreds of lead balls from a load of canister shot smashed into the men and left only their boots. Draco withdrew his glass and crouched down again.

"So we're stuck here? Until what? I refuse to pee in such cramped quarters," Hadassah said.

Hoofbeats thundered nearby and she shouldered her rifle. Through its scratched reflex sight, she eyed a quintet of charging Imperial kataphracts whose lances aimed to skewer the squad. She cackled and tenderly squeezed her trigger. Bullets roared from her barrel and smashed into the lead man's breastplate. He dropped his lance, grasped at the tiny hole in his armor, and fell gracelessly from his horse to the mud. The second round Hadassah fired slammed into another kataphract's helmet with a resounding clank and he tumbled backwards. By this time Taki and Karma had unslung their carbines and were ready to fire.

"Kill the horses!" Lotte shouted. The Argead flanks had fallen, to allow a cavalry charge so deep into their lines. Burst of fully-automatic fire pierced the chain armor on the kataphract mounts and the massive chargers toppled to the ground along with their riders. The Imperials were fully prepared for this possibility, however, and easily wriggled out from under their stricken horses. Spiked pole-hammers in hand, they charged on foot.

"Allow me!" Draco said. He bounded forward to roll under the sweeping arc of a hammer, and whirled around to smash his fighting iron into his attacker's neck. The force was enough to shatter vertebrae underneath steel, and the man dropped. Another attempted to stick Draco with a sidesword, but missed. Draco swept his enemy's legs with the fighting iron and brought the man down on his back. Before he could get up, Draco smashed a charged fist into his helmet. The impact cratered steel and splattered brain tissue through the faceplate. The remaining fighter dropped his hammer and drew a double-barreled scattergun from its scabbard on its chest. Draco zigzagged to dodge the first load of shot, and drew his revolver. Before the second round could go off, six rounds tore into the kataphract's chest and dropped him where he stood. Calmly, Draco returned to cover and methodically ejected the spent rounds from his pistol.

"Major! Can you somehow protect us from the cannon?" Taki asked, as he replaced the depleted clip in his Bastard with a fresh one. Deflecting the last charge had won them some respite, though it would be short.

"But it's fun to watch you dodge cannonballs," Hecaton drawled. To Taki, she appeared to be not so much hunkering down under fire, but languidly sunning herself while sipping from a flask of rotgut.

Does she just have fun, no matter who gets killed? he wondered.

"What about smoke? You used something similar when we were at Vergina," Lotte said.

"Oh? This little guy? But he's all I have left," Hecaton said, drawing a small frog fetish from her pocket. Though miniscule, it had been crafted with exacting detail and an emphasis on vulgar, bulbous protrusions. From its open mouth protruded a fuse instead of a tongue. A lascivious grin to invite malfeasance. "I'll let you have it for a hundred rounds of Old Nayto!"

"Send the bill to Babu!" Lotte said, snatching the fetish away from her Major. "Company! I'm going to throw this as far as I can. Invoke your best sutras and be ready to charge the front. When you get to the tower, storm them from the flanks. Smash them to pieces! Are you ready?"

Glowing blue *Thureos* fields surrounded bodies and shrouded eyes. Lotte lit the fuse, and satisfied that it was sparkling vigorously, hurled the frog with all of her might over the broken wall and into the field. A few seconds later, a small thump rang out and dark purple plumes shot into the air, almost tangible in their thickness.

They charged the field. Lotte ripped the canvas away from a heavy load she had carried all this way and unveiled what she had taken instead of her usual shield: an ancient belt-fed machine gun, ornately graven and heavily altered to allow a user to fire from the hip, and one of the archangel Michail's most valued treasures. The air throbbed around her as she pulled the trigger and sent bursts of heavy fire toward the cannon tower. The heavy ammunition blew fist-sized holes in concrete and killed men crouching behind. Chaos erupted within the tower as soldiers crushed each other in a rush to leave.

Karma was the first to reach the battery. He quickly tossed a brace of stick grenades through the front slit, before darting around to the back entrance. Green-armored soldiers spilled out of the doorway as the charges went off, only to run into Karma's swords. Draco and Taki swooped in from the other side to trap the Imperials. They emptied their guns into the confused men, drew their steel, and plunged into the fray. Lotte now joined Karma, and set to work with her flamberge.

Before long, the squad stood amidst dozens of bodies, panting heavily. Draco grimaced and squeezed a handful of his hair, which dripped red around his boots. Taki tried in vain to blow into his cupped hands to warm them and shake off a layer of frost left by casting sutra. Staccato cracking of pistol fire rang out from within the tower as Karma and

Hadassah cleared the place of any last holdouts. After a few minutes, the two emerged from the smoking darkness, coughing and sputtering.

The surviving Cretans arrived with Hecaton in tow and set to stacking bodies and extinguishing fires so that the tower could be used as their strongpoint again. Lotte flicked the gore off of her sword and fastened it back to her harness, then plopped down on a bale of straw outside. Since the battle at the citadel, she had been more conscious of conserving her energy.

"Everyone rest and eat," she ordered. "We've won this field."

The others muttered their agreement as they sat down on ruined pallets and clumps of straw around a small cookfire. Karma had located some salt-cured beef earlier, while Taki set to work cutting up a head of cabbage he found nearby. With the help of a dented cookpot nearby, they soon found themselves with a salty stew. Hecaton, of course, took the lion's share.

"Much obliged for the break, Captain," Draco said. He sipped steaming broth from a helmet.

"You earned it with your valor, Emreis," Lotte said. She took a chunk of beef from his improvised bowl and plopped it into her mouth.

"Are we really about to extinguish the light of a hundred thousand souls?" Karma muttered. He topped off the magazine on his rifle with a few rounds, and gingerly fed it into the action.

"Didn't you say it would be cool to watch?" Draco asked. Karma drew his charging handle back and let it slam home.

"A few pints of blood are necessary mortar for any kingdom, but an ocean? I wonder."

Draco smiled. "Perhaps you aren't a total psychopath after all, Gillette."

"Hey now, don't kill my mystique."

Lotte stood and looked at the sky with trepidation. "We should move now. You lot reload and check your blades and plate for cracks. We'll not be made fools of this time, especially if we're going to get vaporized for our trouble."

Taki spoke. "Can I ask one thing, Captain?"

"Yes, Natalis?"

"Seeing as we might all perish here, can we change our squad's name back to the old one? I know it means potatoes, but it's kind of grown on me."

"Are you godrotting serious?" Lotte asked through grit teeth. Hadassah looked at him incredulously as she brushed a stray lock of muddy hair from her face. Karma dropped his Bastard into the mud and cursed as he retrieved it.

"Yes, Captain," Taki said with a smile.

She grimaced, buried her face in her hands, and then laughed out loud.

"Fine! Any objections?" Lotte said with a grin. She wiped at a glob of mud on her face, only to end up smearing red on her jaw.

"Nope. Just regretting that there's no historian to record it," Draco said, chortling despite himself.

"Oh, fuck everything. Sure," Hadassah said. Karma rolled his eyes and nodded.

"Very well. Then we will resume battle as 'Tirefire the Lesser'. Put it in the ledger, Major," Lotte said.

"Idiots," Hecaton sighed, and tossed her cigarette into the mud.

＊ ＊ ＊ ＊

Taki did not want to look over the lip of the rocky cliff to see the battle below. At such a height, he feared being taken with an irresistible urge to throw himself off rather than complete his mission. From what he could see, the front lines remained static, though increasingly filled with burning vehicle hulks compared to the morning. A cloud of rubbery-smelling smog clung against the coast and blocked his view of the water. The seething mass of the Imperial Army clogged the shoreline and the lowlands in the distance.

Any final misgivings he possessed about unleashing certain, suicidal destruction were stifled by the sight of the quarter-million-strong Imperial vanguard. No matter what Aslatiel had promised him earlier, Taki knew that when invading armies trampled through fields and homes unopposed, it meant only rape, pillage, and murder. The massacre at New Petrovic would be repeated again and again, and the rub was that it would all be justified in Imperial eyes. Soldiers, on the other hand, went to war knowing death was part of the job. *Mass-murder I can take pride in. Ha! I'm so fucked up.*

"Natalis, it's up to you," Lotte said.

"Yes, Captain. Deploying now," he said. He pulled the Behelit out of a satchel and thrust it at the Liberation Army below. Fingers brushed over the rubber of the buttons and he tensed his abdominal muscles in anticipation.

"I advise you not to do that, young man," Chronicler said. A smirk thinned his lips and gave him the appearance of a predatory fish. Taki's eyes widened and he clutched the Behelit to his chest, as if trying to hide mischief from a parent. The others readied their weapons, now aware of the rest of Alfa Gruppe emerging from the shadows.

"Of all the bad luck...It's the wife." Draco sighed as he spied Lucatiel. She circled warily, and her swords glinted with infused prana. Their points traced random, glittering paths through the air to deny her enemies the chance to predict her attacks.

"You know, girls don't like to be stared at. If you want to ask her out then just do so already, mouthbreather," Hadassah said. She shifted her grip on the handle of her war-pick and spat on the leather wrapping to keep it sticky against her fingers.

"Don't make the mistake I did. *Never* stick it in crazy," Karma said, earning a quick stomp of her heel on his foot.

"*You again,*" Hecaton said. Her eyes narrowed at her former husband.

Chronicler was behind Taki, blocking out the light of the horizon. The boy's outline broke and blurred against a miasma of writhing shadow, as if he were being digested. Like a father would gently pry a toy from a newborn's fingers, Chronicler took the Behelit. He peered closely at the device with curious disdain.

"Give that back," Taki whimpered. Chronicler ignored him. "I said—" he continued, but stopped. The quavering of his voice filled him with hot shame. The fact that his legs refused to move also angered him. Was he truly that pathetic in the end? He had openly confronted a minister of the Dominion, and yet he could not challenge some wizened old man? He did not wish to insult Amilia Gillette with such incongruity.

Taki's brow furrowed in concentration and he stared at his legs. He ordered one of them to move. It twitched at first, and then took a step, dragging his body along. *Just like a newborn, dammit.* But he was almost out of Chronicler's shadow. He shifted his efforts to the other leg. He needed just a few more steps, going one leg at a time.

He lurched forward, coordinated like jelly escaping a sieve. Once out of the old man's eclipse, he quickly found his old strength. He drew a dagger and leveled the point at Chronicler's face. Taki still trembled, breaths painful as frostbite and heavy as lead. His arm burned to heft the little blade, but this only made him strengthen his grip in response. Chronicler blinked.

"Most children know better than to point a weapon at me. What is your name, *basang?*"

Taki pushed back the desire to kneel and shut up. No, he was not a subservient child anymore. No, he did not have to raise his hand to speak let he be chastised. No, he did not have a career, a future, to consider.

"Corporal Taki Hagiochristophorites Natalis, of 'Tirefire the Lesser.' And you are my enemy. So I will point whatever I please at you. *Sir.*" It had come out somewhat higher-pitched than he had hoped, and he was sure his voice had cracked a bit, but it was better than silence.

Chronicler laughed and his remaining eye opened fully to reveal a ringed pupil. When he saw it, Taki collapsed to one knee, his earlier resolve now completely forgotten. It was only logical that he toss away his weapon and offer his neck so Chronicler might see how sincerely sorry he was. A scream erupted from his chest and he swallowed it back. After all, he did not want to anger anyone. He had his standing to consider. He was a good student. Good students sought forgiveness for their sins.

"Well spoken, young man," Chronicler said with an indulgent smile. "However, I cannot honor your request. You will be happy to know that there is no need to massacre you and your companions. Your bravery is noted, however, and I will mention your name to the padishah. Corporal Natalis, a hero of the Dominion."

He turned and started to stroll away. Taki shivered wretchedly and started to sob. His gut roiled and he vomited brownish green on his leggings. It tasted of sweat and failure. He wanted to simply lay down and sleep, to forget this nightmare. *At least you're a hero,* Hecaton's voice whispered snidely in his ear. *A hero like the duke,* he thought. *Someone who made a deal and survived.* He remembered Pristina. Remembered New Petrovic.

"No!" he hissed. The damnable major had it all wrong. He was no hero. He had seen what a "hero" of the Dominion was capable of. He was a killer, and a coward. But he was not, and would never be Gul

Hekmatyar. His teeth chattered. *How dare she? How dare he? How dare I accept this?* He squeezed his eyes shut and grasped his saber tightly, opening all of his prana gates. Clarity washed over his consciousness and he shakily rose to his feet. The air around his body started to mist and haze. *"A hero?"* he roared in the old man's direction. *"Just who the hell do you think I am?"*

Aslatiel's mouth opened in warning when the ground under Taki's feet shattered. Taki blinked out of sight and re-emerged no more than an arm's length from Chronicler, with steel leading the way. He aimed right at the base of the neck, where Hadassah had once poked him for reference. With a furious shout, he drove the blade home.

Chronicler rolled his eyes, parried the blow with the palm of one hand, and planted the other on Taki's chest. A thunderous report shattered the stillness and the boy flew back through the air like a doll flung by an angry child. A mist of blood erupted from his orifices as he tumbled freely before coming to land on a patch of evergreen.

"Alna shuu, Shastirch!" Hecaton bellowed. The sky blackened into a mass of thunderheads and instantly plunged Thermopylae back to night. Chronicler clenched his teeth, his chest constricting as if his breath was sucked from his body. Gouts of ejaculated lightning streamed from above and lanced the fields. One of them caught Hecaton fully within its discharge. Instead of being burnt, she seemed to draw vigor from it before she leapt at Chronicler with incandescent fists. She cared not for the fate of nations, but to see him execute one of *her* subordinates was a mark of the deepest disrespect.

"Attack!" Lotte shouted despite empty lungs, and fired a gout of lead at the Alfa. Gleaming brass shells and pieces of belt-link flew from the ejection port but did not land on the ground. They danced in midair, laws of gravity and magnetism pushed to the wayside. Aslatiel dove away from the stream of .50 caliber rounds while the others blasted away at Lotte and forced her to roll out of the line of fire. Karma's spatha sparked and rang against Lucatiel's jian as they clashed on the edge of the cliff, twin-swords against twin-swords. Irulan tried to flank Karma, who merely doubled his quips about women chasing him. Cackling, he danced through the air to avoid lethal steel wire and a hail of bullets and knives.

Lotte brought her machinegun up to defend herself from slashes of Aslatiel's kriegsmesser before swiping at him with its mass. She tried to smash his face in with the barrel, but instead he caught it with his bare hands. Undaunted, she jerked it to line up the muzzle with his chest and squeezed the trigger. He twisted to avoid the discharge and wrenched the gun away. It sailed over the cliff edge, lost forever. Lotte drew her flamberge and hefted it with feet firmly planted on the ground. Aslatiel nodded to her. She nodded back and took a swing at his head.

Hecaton and Chronicler brawled, each of them piling hammer-blows on each other without regard for defense. Two juggernauts matched in skill and now reliant solely on strength and endurance. Their hits pocked the stony ground with deep craters, vaporizing rock and sending deep splits into the mountain face itself. For every blow Chronicler landed, he paid dearly with a lash of electricity. Lightning seared him mercilessly and caused his body to lurch when he touched her. Hecaton, however, buckled and gasped under every crushing punch and kick. Boxing gave way to grappling, where Chronicler had the advantage. Taking Hecaton by the arm, he savagely spun and threw her. She sailed through the air and almost took Lotte's head off. Before she could right herself Chronicler blinked right up against her and planted a foot on her stomach. Prana exploded from his heel and flung her further. Her eyes bulged and she sailed over the edge of the cliff. Energy lanced from her body as she fell to the battlefield below and was swallowed by smoke and fire.

"Fuck! Major!" Lotte swore as she pushed Aslatiel back. Draco realized what had happened as he glanced off the edge.

"You asshole!" he shouted, and charged Chronicler with his fighting iron. Nonchalantly, Chronicler caught the weapon's head in one hand and pulled. Draco flew and smashed into a boulder. Armor and bone crunched as he broke stone to pieces with the impact. Lotte let out a roar and her flamberge swung for a decapitation strike, only to come to a clanging stop against Chronicler's forearm. Her eyes widened in surprise, and he smiled. A thin line of blood made its way down from a small cut and dripped from his elbow. He gripped the blade and wrested the sword from her hands, and lightly tapped the pommel against her chest. Her plate armor crumpled like tissue under the impact and she hurtled through the air into a tree trunk with a sickening thud.

Hadassah dropped her war-pick and grasped at the hilt of the longsword impaled in her midsection. Her pistol fell to the ground with a metallic clank, its slide locked back and magazine empty. One of the Alfa men, an albino, jerked his arm back and pulled the blade away, splattering gore on the dirt and spinning her to the ground. She reached for a grenade only to feel his boot stomping on her wrist. He leveled his pistol at her head, and she stared back at him, refusing to close her eyes.

* * * *

From the chaos below, a dark, massive shape shot up in the air and crashed to the ground. The detached, flaming turret of an Imperial main battle tank smashed into Chronicler's head. With its massive smoothbore gun gripped like the shaft of a hammer by an enraged, sooty Hecaton, twelve tons of steel swallowed Chronicler whole. Hecaton lifted the shattered steel from the crater she'd made, hefted it again and swung at Aslatiel. He flew through the air, propelled by the overwhelming force of the giant club against his attempt to block it. Lucatiel screamed and charged only to be punched in the gut and sent rolling in a heap. Karma lunged at Irulan and smashed the pommel of his broken sword into her head. She collapsed, as did he a moment later.

With a snarl of disgust, Hecaton released the burning, twisted mass of metal. Chronicler shot up from the ground, tackling her in a chokehold. His arms were covered in blisters of blood and bubbling lymph, and his head was missing some of its hair. She raked him with current again, but he drew his fist back and slammed it into the top of her head. Hecaton collapsed and did not move again.

Taki groaned and coughed as an object collided with his blood-crusted brow. How he was alive was a mystery. He was pretty sure his heart had ruptured, but it was not important right now. He tilted until he saw what had bumped him. It was the Behelit. He took it, pressed the buttons, and aimed it at Chronicler's chest. A brilliant, pulsing red flower of light lanced out and the device buzzed and clicked in mechanical joy. Even if whatever it summoned didn't destroy the entire Imperium Army, it would at least take their most dangerous soldiers out of the fight, and especially the old man. Perhaps the Ursalans would have better luck. They seemed the lesser among monsters now.

Chronicler dashed over, kicked the Behelit out of Taki's hands, and lifted him off the ground by the throat. Hecaton growled and spat as she attempted to claw her way to them.

"Strange that you survived that. Perhaps there is more to you than meets the eye," Chronicler said, tilting his head in curiosity. One of his hands drew back, fingers pressed together and pointed straight for a penetrating blow. "Regardless, I will correct my mistake now."

The starspeaker in Taki's belt pouch buzzed to life. A woman's voice and a disembodied melody filled the silent devastation all around.

"Ooh, baby do you know what that's worth? Ooh Heaven is a place on Earth."

"I think…it's for you," Taki said, bubbling bloody froth. His expression inscrutable, Chronicler relaxed his spear-hand, took the small relic, and pressed a flashing button.

"Who is this?" he asked.

"I am Amilia Gillette." Her voice possessed a disembodied quality, but the heavens had aligned well enough for her words to be clear. "I am a minister of the Argead Dominion, and wielder of the God Hand. I assume this is the Chronicler?"

"I have the Behelit, Minister. Does this inconvenience you?"

"No, it does not. The device has already broadcast your coordinates. The God Hand is ready for launch from the holy sepulcher of Ooss. It can arrive at its destination within five minutes. The reach of the purging sutra within it covers far more territory than even you will be able to traverse. If you do not do as I say, you and the entire Liberation Army are dust."

Chronicler released Taki from his grasp, and the boy fell to the ground in a sputtering heap. Hecaton regained her feet and lurched over to Taki's side. He tried to speak with her, only to be shushed. Warmth and relief suffused his body with the transfer of her prana to him, and he realized that she was uncharacteristically attempting to save him. *So she can kill me later?* He laughed, and it was painful.

"Where is your master, the basileus?" Chronicler asked.

"His Grace has perished in an accident," Amilia said without a hint of irony. "As such, his exarch and nobility have sworn fealty to me. I will not, however, presume to call myself basileus until the appropriate mourning period has passed."

Chronicler was silent for a moment, before bursting into grim laughter.

"If only we had a zakhiragch like you back in my homeland, Minister. It seems we are at an impasse. If I do not do as you say, I and many others will die. But you will also lose your last line of defense. The Padishah will send more soldiers, and you will hang by your guts as surely as the moon evades bullets. So how do you propose we resolve this disharmony, *Your Grace?*"

"I am ready to surrender the Dominion to the Osterbrand Imperium. However, I will only do so with stipulations. Withdraw your army and call your master to the table, or your next visitor will be a mushroom cloud."

The starspeaker went silent for the last time. Chronicler grimaced and tightened his grip to crush it into slivers that glimmered as they fell through his fingers. He stared at Taki for a moment, as if debating whether to kill him. Hecaton tilted her head, as if inviting him to try. Chronicler sniffed, and turned away. He strode over to a battered Aslatiel, who stood painfully at attention despite the blood staining his torn tunic.

"Alfa Gruppe, cease hostilities. Assist the enemy wounded and withdraw to the staging area. I must speak with our master."

"Chronicler, I never grow tired of seeing you upstaged by crafty women," Hecaton said in their shared tongue. She wiped a streak of blood from her lip into her forearm. She squatted and lit another hand-rolled cigarillo, puffing on it as smugly as she could. *"I'm surprised and yet disappointed. You're still just someone's lapdog, even as old and crusty as you've become."*

The old man curled one of his hands into a fist, but relaxed it in the same breath. *"Unlike you, my dear wife, I am no traitor. If you're going to spend your life running away, then at least make offerings to Golden Peach's soul."*

Hecaton stood and spat a gob of scarlet on Chronicler's boots.

Taki's eyes widened in terror – would the two start their horrific brawl yet again? This time, he would not survive. He'd already cheated death so many times that it was heresy to survive again. He gritted his teeth and prepared for the end.

"Never say her name again," Hecaton whispered. "Don't make me brain you! Git out!"

Chronicler was flinty-eyed, but he turned to leave.

Taki let out a ragged breath. So uneasy had he been during the exchange between the two ancients that he had failed to notice Aslatiel looming overhead with sword unsheathed. Taki flinched on instinct, recalling their first encounter. Instead of going for a decapitation, however, the man knelt and extended his free hand to touch Taki's face. As Taki felt fingertips brush gently against the healing wound on his cheek, prana started to flow, and the lancinating pain in Taki's chest began to subside.

"We meet again, Taki Natalis."

"Are you angry at me, Aslatiel van Halcon?"

"Quite the opposite. It's obvious that you've changed since we last talked, and that you've also had a hand in changing things around you."

Taki grimaced and looked away. "At too high a price."

"Yet you have your integrity intact. That's rare in this world."

"Integrity means little without strength. And I lack it, sorely."

"Then start by improving your swordsmanship," Aslatiel said. He gracefully turned his kriegsmesser onto its side and presented it to Taki, blade facing politely away from the intended recipient. "We owe you a new blade, anyway."

His hands trembling, Taki accepted. It felt light and strong, balanced on his fingertips. "Thank you." He looked back up at Aslatiel. "Why are you doing this?"

Aslatiel smiled and opened his mouth to say something else, when an enraged Lucatiel pounced and began to drag him away by the scruff.

"Bastard!" she snarled at Taki. "Stop seducing my brother. I've got your number! I've got your ass!"

Taki blinked in amazement, and then started to blush. "I'm not doing anything!"

Lucatiel leveled one of her pistols at him and sent two rounds into the soft earth at his feet. "Man-whore!"

Aslatiel could only shrug. Taki clutched the kriegsmesser to his chest and started to laugh. It was a bizarre ending to what had been an impossible day.

14

The field hospital stank of putrefying bowel. The groans of the wounded melted onerously together into a single, uninterrupted dirge. It had been less than a day, and already the survivors knew that their homeland was lost to the Imperium. Everyone had seen the padishah arrive earlier on board his shining golden-crimson flying carriage. As the sublime relic had descended on the battlefield in the thick of the Liberation Army, the cheer could be heard all the way on the Dominion side. Although actual negotiations with the new basileus—called "The Usurper" by some—were still ongoing, the conclusion was inevitable. The official counts were not ready yet, but the whispers were of two thousand Argead dead. The Imperials had supposedly lost nearly double that number, though by the high spirits in the opposing camp, one would think they had lost only the least-loved officers.

Despite the shock of defeat, most Argeads only wanted to go home. Preparing their homesteads for the winter was a task that most of the men fighting that day needed to get back to. Empires rose and fell, but the seasons did not wait. Taki counted himself among the lucky ones from the battle, for at least he was able to walk, albeit slowly and burdened by a nagging ache in his trunk with every breath. The others were still fresh from the surgeons' ministrations and confined to bed. He had been helping change their bandages. It was a welcome distraction from the fact that he had nearly wiped two armies off the face of the earth on the orders of the Usurper. He sat at Lotte's bedside, attentively dabbing blood away from a weeping gash on her forehead.

"Natalis," Lotte said. She sat up in her cot, her expression sleepy. The shock of seeing her rise despite elephantine doses of laudanum from earlier nearly made Taki knock over a stack of linens. For the second time, and now up close, he could see just how many scars she wore on her back. Tracks of white and pink with the stars of old bullet and bolt wounds. A map of the battles of her life.

"Captain, you shouldn't be up, you need to rest—"

She shushed him.

"I feel better now. I'm a quick healer. How is your chest feeling? The major told me that what the Chronicler did to you has killed many more powerful men."

Taki glanced down at his own body. Nearly his entire torso was covered with dark purple bruises. "Just a little soreness, that's all. I'm more concerned about how everyone else is doing. I heard Draco's leg got broken, and…"

"…And it's a little greenstick fracture. I'll be walking tomorrow, whether the sawbones like it or not!" Draco said, pulling aside the dividing curtain hiding his bed. True to his word, his right leg was bound up in a bulky plaster splint. He busily pried at the edges with his fingers in an effort to scratch an itch underneath.

"Karma almost gave him a sponge bath by accident!" Hadassah snickered, also woken by the noise. Before she could say more, she turned pale and gagged. Earlier, the surgeons had forced her to swallow a potent elixir of garlic extract for prognosis. They could smell no leakage from the wound, so she was likely to live. So they had said, at least.

Draco shuddered. "I'd rather have a wanking from one of those Alfa."

"Blow me, Emreis. You'd be lucky to get a sponge bath from me. You need one, too," Karma said. He flipped Draco off with his unwounded hand.

"You lot…" Taki gingerly tied a new length of gauze around Lotte's head. "I almost got you all killed. Shouldn't you be angrier? Why are you acting like nothing happened?"

"Natalis," Draco chuckled, "Almost getting killed is part of this job. Or were you asleep for that part of the academy?"

Taki sighed. They still didn't get it. "I was working for minister Gillette in secret. That's why I was given that damned Behelit. I nearly threw away everyone's lives."

Lotte shrugged. "So what do you want me to do? Smack you? I don't think that's necessary."

"Yeah, and you won. The minister is the basileus now," Hadassah said. "So it all worked out in the end. We're going to hit her up for favors since she owes you one, and therefore, owes *us!*" She cackled and rubbed her hands together. Friction made the smell of garlic waft around the room again, and she stuck her tongue out in disgust.

"Aye," Draco said. "We're all up for a hanging anyway, so what's a little treason going to add? And maybe we'll be forgiven now, right? Basically I agree with Dassa."

"My, good sir. You're matured impressively since our last meeting. Maybe you'll be able to socialize with women who aren't completely insane," Hadassah said.

"Oh be quiet, you damned garlic-chugger."

"In truth, Natalis, we all suspected you were up to something, but we trusted you," Lotte said. "You've fought alongside us and bled with us. Or was your bluster about reclaiming the unit name all for show?"

"Even though we've lost? Even though the Dominion is no more?" Taki asked. "I might've cost you all your futures. What if we're all forced into the streets tomorrow?"

"Calm down," Karma said. "Changes don't happen overnight, even with new overlords. We'll simply have to take things as they come. More than likely, we'll be back at the Cloud Temple in a fortnight, but hopefully not peeling potatoes. After all, why should the exarch care now?"

"I'm pretty sure we'll be peeling," Lotte said. She took one of Taki's hands in hers. "In any case, I've been thinking, Natalis. You may have been forced to join us, but you've become our friend. You also have talent and guts. So even though the rank may not mean anything when the Dominion Army is dissolved, I'm using my authority to promote you. You are now Cornet Natalis, an officer candidate of the junior grade. Congratulations," She smiled. "Sorry, I don't have the official insignia on me, but I'll update it on the ledger as soon as I can."

"Now you have to take us all out for drinks!" Hadassah said. "Better have saved up, *sir!*"

"It's customary! After all, if you're going to be ordering us around, you have to get us sauced up," Draco said. "Or we'll frag you for sure."

Taki grit his teeth, tried not to cry, and failed miserably.

****

A week later, Tirefire the Lesser was back in the same dank, smelly room they had started in. Freshly washed tubers rolled from a chute into a large wooden tub, and the door periodically opened to let the scullion through to pick up the remnants. Torches flickered dimly overhead.

Taki panted to lessen the heat scorching his palate. What he had just tried to eat tasted and smelled unlike any other food in the world to his knowledge, and it was damnably good. The others seemed to agree, since now they all violated an earlier pact to never eat potatoes again.

"Emreis, how the hell did you think of doing this?" Taki asked as he went for another deep-fried sliver of potato.

"Well, you know, there was this hearth and potholder that we never actually used all this time, so I figured we'd start a fire for warmth," Draco said as he dusted some salt on his portion. "And since it wasn't a problem to get some old oil and a pot, I reasoned I'd try to fry up some meat for a snack."

"Yeah, except the cooks are stingy bastards and wouldn't even give us bones," Hadassah said.

"Right, so potatoes," Draco concluded. "And this actually makes them bearable!"

"Except for the whole one you tried to dunk," Karma said as he used a wire sieve to fish out a handful of the sticks from the bubbling oil in the pot. He dumped the golden bounty into a metal bowl and passed it to Lotte, who greedily stuffed a pair of fat wedges in her mouth.

"It was still good, but cutting them up makes each bite taste richer," Lotte said, licking grease from her fingers.

"I have to give Emreis credit, then. But why in the name of God are we still peeling?" Karma asked.

"Remember what you said, smartass? About how changes don't happen overnight even with new masters?" Hadassah retorted.

"I know what I said, but this is just ridiculous. I mean, Niketas Palaiologos is *dead*. He's the only one who got offended by the whole 'Tirefire the Lesser' thing, right? Why does my mother give a shit?"

"If Niketas actually knew about it we'd all have hanged a long time ago," Taki said. "It was the triada who issued the sentence, and the alternative was being flogged. Like, every day."

"So tell them to lay off with the punishment detail, *Cornet* Natalis!" Hadassah said, flicking a potato skin at him.

"In case you've forgotten, I'm still a lowly scrub in a unit of ill repute."

"Then make the exarch intervene, jeez!"

"That would be even more impossible," Karma sighed.

"Gillette, if your mother is the basileus, doesn't that make you some sort of…I dunno, crown prince or whatever?" Draco asked.

"I wish. No, the pruny hag is a stickler for the rules. I'm property of the Cloud Temple like the rest of you, and don't inherit any titles or holdings."

"Then we need to get rid of your powers so you can stop being a creepy wizard and become a respectable man. I heard a circumcision does the trick," Hadassah said. A clump of potato skins hit her on the face. "Look, aren't we under Imperial rule, anyway? Doesn't the basileus have to follow the padishah's orders now? Just write to the guy!" she groaned, wiping starch from her hair.

"It's not that simple," Lotte chimed. "Aside from letting the Imperial army travel freely and allowing their educational corps to set up, Dominion law still prevails, and the basileus is still the supreme authority of the land. That means we still follow the Triada's rules. And their punishments."

"So basically nothing's really changed. Figures," Draco lamented. "At least we don't have to fight those godrotting Alfa again."

"Oh, now that you don't have to kill each other on sight, the Prince of Maladies is totally available!" Hadassah said. "If you want, I'll totally take her shopping and see if she likes you back. I'll totally talk up your few good points. Maybe."

"Isn't that a bit sexist to assume she likes shopping?" Karma asked.

"Every psychotic killer bitch I know enjoys shopping, you peon."

"Anyhow, there's no way we'll see them again," Draco said. "They're probably already storming Astarte by now. The holy primate's got an ass-kicking in his future, that's for sure. We were just a little stumbling block on their true campaign. Just as I told you before, Natalis."

"I still can't help but feel like this is against the rules, somehow," Taki said, tilting his head at the bubbling pot.

"You're one to talk, Cornet 'I helped depose the basileus,'" Hadassah said.

Taki disregarded her quip and watched the flames dance along the bottom of the cookpot. "Actually, do we even know where the chimney goes?"

The door burst open with an accompaniment of screaming curses and orders to get on their knees. Taki had barely turned his head to face the threat when a buttstock punched into his gut and he fell back. No less than five men barged into the room, muskets and swords at the ready. Lotte's eyes widened when she saw what they wore.

"We're unarmed!" she shouted. She raised her hands and lowered herself to her knees. "Squad, do not resist!" she continued. A knife edge pressed against her throat and a pair of groping hands tore her dagger away from her belt. There was no mistaking who the intruders were: Black Cross.

Hadassah suddenly tackled Karma from behind while he raised his hands. A heartbeat later, one of the men fired and blew a hole in the wall where Karma's head would have been. Stone crumbs dusted their bodies. "Cease fire, dammit!" she cursed as they pointed their guns at her head.

"*By order of the exarch you all are under arrest!*" a lieutenant bellowed. He leveled his sidesword at Draco, who had been about to eat another piece of potato. Draco grinned nervously and dropped the fry.

"What are we being charged with?" Lotte demanded.

"Treason and sabotage."

Taki swallowed to fight the hollow feeling in his chest. He had already accepted that Amilia Gillette, the Usurper, would eliminate him one day. If there was one crime that could never be forgiven, it was regicide. He deserved to die for his role in ending the Palaiologoi. Taki smiled sadly to himself and shook his head. He felt no regret, and better yet he had no family to disgrace. He had long-ago given up his future, and now it was time to yield the rest.

"The others are innocent, I am the one you're aft—" he started to say.

"Sir! Here's the source of the miasma!" One of the Black Cross swung the frying pot away on its hinge and pointed to the fire.

"Well put it out, then!" the lieutenant growled. One of the Black Cross came in from the kitchen with a bucket of water and sloshed it over the fire. While the flames died, their hissing embers only filled the storeroom with more smoke. "And take those damned potatoes as evidence!"

"How did we commit treason and sabotage? This is a *kitchen!* We're just *cooking!*" Lotte snarled.

"Captain, lies won't save you this time." The lieutenant sniffed. "You were clearly driven mad with resentment and constructed this chimney flue to vent directly into the quarters of the agia triada while they recovered from battle. Only by the grace of God and the sharp senses of the exarch did they avoid succumbing to smoke poisoning."

Lotte's lips parted slightly and she stared at him. She quivered, her face painted with disbelief. She hung her head, but a moment later, started to laugh so hard that she toppled to the floor. The lieutenant scowled as she beat the stones with her fists and convulsed in merriment.

"Take them all to the brig. We'll hang them in the morning after a sound flogging."

"That's bullshit!" Draco cried. "Why the *hell* does this chimney go directly to the supreme commanders of the Temple? How would we even know that? Who the *fuck* designed this idiotic place?" A baton crashed between his shoulder blades and knocked him to the floor. Hadassah yelped as they dragged her away by her hair. Karma tried to push his way over to her but was answered by a buttstock to the groin. He fell back, groaning loudly

"Stop! I'm the one you want!" Taki shouted tearfully. "I know you're here on the orders of the basileus! Just shoot me and be done with it, but *don't hurt my friends!*"

"Why does the Usurper care about *you?*" one of the Black Cross said as he mashed Taki's wrists together.

From the kitchen came a deep thump and the unmistakable ozone of electrical discharge. Men's shouts and gunshots erupted only to yield to oppressive silence. The lieutenant whirled around and thrust his side-sword at a figure standing in the door. Metal twanged in protest at a sudden stop, caught between thumb and forefinger belonging to Hecaton Mezeta. She sneered at the lieutenant and then tilted her head at the door. He let go of the sword and bolted out, followed by his subordinates.

"I heard you lot were making fries. Where's my share?" Hecaton asked. She lit a cigarillo and squatted with her elbows balanced on her knees. Lotte raised her forehead from the cobbles and looked blearily at her major.

"We didn't invite you. But you can have mine," she said with a half-smile.

Taki sniffed and blinked away tears of relief. He knew it was wrong to feel grateful to Hecaton, but what she didn't know wouldn't hurt her.

"As long as they're still warm. I won't abide cold leftovers. Now, I don't know what happened here, but the triada are all a pube-hair away from croaking and Constantin is furious. I've never seen him so pissed. It's great!" Hecaton cackled. "And to think I was growing bored of this place. Well, maybe I'll stick around for a bit longer."

"I'll look forward to it," Lotte said.

Hecaton grinned. "Silly barbarian, you'll rue those words one day. My old bones feel another storm coming soon, and it is all our *joss* to be swept up again and tossed about. Frankly, I don't think any of you will survive, though you're welcome to try."

Taki remained silent. By now, he knew that the old woman's words carried a weight beyond that of idle, derogatory banter. Upheavals and crises loomed in his future. And yet he'd already endured the worst of what fate—joss, as Hecaton put it—had to throw at him, even if he hadn't exactly triumphed over much. In the scarred and spiteful world he lived in, perhaps survival was good enough.

Keep going for a preview chapter of the sequel, <u>Swords of the Imperium</u>!

Visit www.carsonchoi.com for updates, announcements, and bonus material!

There, you can follow us on Twitter, like us on Facebook, join our mailing list, and be the first to hear of deals and new releases.

Finally, if you enjoyed this book and want to see more in the series, leaving us a review on Amazon is the single best way to let us know.

Coming Soon: Swords of the Imperium

1

Hadassah Mikkelsen licked the flat of her knife and smiled sweetly. "He's being difficult. Let's cut off his head, take his key, and open the chest already."

"I don't want to hang for fragging an officer," Draco Emreis said. He unwound a length of hempen rope from around his fists and drew it tight. "If we all rush him at once, we can hog-tie him instead. Besides, who's to say the key's actually on him? What if he hid it somewhere?"

Karma Gillette smacked the wide end of a leather-wrapped cudgel against his palm. "I bet he shoved it up his rear. It's like a hidden compartment for men."

"I'm *definitely* not checking that," Hadassah said.

"I'm in command," Captain Lotte Satou said. "I'll check."

Draco looked surprised. "Captain? You sure?"

Lotte nodded grimly and spat into her right hand. "Mikkelsen, hold him down. He'll feel more comfortable if women do the deed."

Taki Natalis clenched his jaw as he swept his squad with the muzzle of his pistol. With his promotion to cornet came the privilege of carrying a side arm within the Temple. The Herstal he had been given was a third-rate castoff pockmarked by rust, but it *worked*. Taki was grateful to have the weapon, especially while backed into a corner and facing unspeakable acts. The only problem was that he only had a single dirty round to his name. "For the *last time*," he said, "I'm not holding out on any of you! We are *out of bullets. That* is why you haven't been paid."

"Then go to the shrine and get more!" Draco flipped his hair in indignation. "I'll hold your hand if you're scared of being robbed."

"You think I haven't checked? There's no more 'grad in our coffers. Hecaton Mezeta's the one who fills our stores. She's been missing for a *fortnight!*"

"Don't we have savings?" Hadassah said. "Just give us our friggin' pay! I thought we were *friends!* Why do you have to be so *mean?*"

"I'm not being mean!" Taki replied. "And *you're* the one who wants to cut my head off or rape me or both!"

Hadassah sniffled and wiped at her nose.

Taki rolled his eyes. "Don't you dare!"

Karma shook his head. "Are you really making a girl cry?"

"Don't you feel bad about yourself, Natalis?" Draco asked.

For a moment, Taki considered shooting himself and trying to bleed all over everyone before he died. Hopefully, he'd make Hadassah throw up and Draco slip and break a rib. He wasn't Lotte—he couldn't simply beat them all to death—so suicide was the only alternative. He raked his fingernails against his scalp. "Oh, fine! This will definitely get me knouted, but fuck it. I'll open the box and show you all, if you stop trying to murder me."

"But I wanted to check!" Lotte said. Her fingers gleamed stickily in the torchlight.

Taki ignored her and holstered his gun. He knelt down, grasped the brass handle of a worn wooden chest, and dragged the chest over the stones until it was in full view of his squad. Then he reached into his leggings, grimaced, and produced a tarnished old key.

Hadassah gasped. "Was that in…in your *bung*?"

Taki shot her a vitriolic glare and turned the key. Slowly, he opened the lid.

"Damnation." Draco tossed his rope away.

"You all owe me an apology!" Taki's voice cracked, but his scowl held firm. The balding felt interior of the chest was completely bare. He slammed the lid shut. "I can't believe you all tried to brutalize me! You *know* I can't show you lot what's inside!"

"All right, we're sorry!" Draco looked at the others. *"Why am I the only one abasing myself here?"*

Taki crossed his arms.

Draco flinched. "You want me to kowtow to you? I'll do it, so long as you stop looking at me like that."

"That's enough," Lotte said. "I'm very sorry, Natalis. I shouldn't have let things get to this point. But the issue still stands! We need funds. We're hungry."

Taki sighed and sat back on the paybox. His expression softened, if only slightly. "Captain, you know the answer."

"Right. I'll sell Emreis to a cathouse."

"*No*. We have to find and talk to *Mezeta*. Without her, we starve."

Draco's eyes widened. "Wait a second. Let's not do anything rash! Leave her lordship out of this, aye? We can all get by for a bit longer. After all, these are blessed times. We're no longer in the kitchens, and most of all, that woman's gone and fucked off to God knows where! My virtue is a small price to pay for it. I'll make a *fine* courtesan. You know how good I look in a dress. I'll call myself…Dulcinea."

"Draco's delusions aside," Karma said, "didn't Mezeta vanish because of a promotion?"

"Yes, and it's just like her," Draco said. "She's the opposite of human decency! An ungrateful hag! Her Grace the Basileus appoints Mezeta the exarch's direct successor and what happens? The woman deserts!"

"Wait." Hadassah chewed a nail. "You're saying that being nice to Hecaton Mezeta makes her vanish? We've been going about this all wrong for *years*."

"No, and I'll tell you exactly why you're wrong," Draco said. "We're just stupid barbarians to that woman. We're not her loyal Polaris of the Temple. We're just shit-flinging monkeys she uses to troll the higher-ups for the sake of her ego. And even after we singlehandedly repulsed the Imperial horde while flying *her* standard, her way of saying thanks is to neglect to pay us. If trying to screw her and trying to appease her yield the same result, then I'd rather keep plotting her death. *If for nothing else, then for the sake of my dignity!*"

Hadassah cuffed Draco's cheek. "You're turning purple. And did you really just call me what I think you called me?"

"If she'd only dubbed our squad 'The Dung-Chucking Gorillas,' we'd all have been spared blasphemy charges and wouldn't have had to do nothing but peel potatoes for two whole years."

"So you *did* call me a poo-toucher! I *demand* satisfaction!"

Taki winced at the memory of punishment duty. Hecaton Mezeta was the squad's commander, but she acted more like its owner. She led in a style that was equally mean-spirited joke, blatant sedition, and part of a greater, if completely incomprehensible, plan. "Captain," he said, and shot Lotte a warning glance. "Enough dithering. Tell us what to do before we all resort to cannibalism."

Lotte groaned. "Do you have to always be so forthright?"

"Yes. I'm a commissioned officer of the Polaris of the Temple. Aren't *you?*"

"More sass, and I'll spank you."

"Go ahead. You'll all starve in the end, anyway."

Lotte looked wounded for a moment. "Fine. I think I know where Mezeta is. Come with me?"

Taki glared at her. "Is that your order, milord Captain?"

"If you're going to be that way, then yes," she said. "It's an order. Mikkelsen, come with us. Gillette and Emreis, go round up dinner. Here's the last of my funds." She took out her revolver, swung out the cylinder, and held out an unfired cartridge.

"Captain," Karma said, "I mean no disrespect, but there's a reason we're so poor right now. We've been eating market meat and fresh eggs at *every meal.* If we just restricted ourselves to the mess hall once a day, we'd save—"

Lotte mashed the lead nose of the bullet against Karma's forehead and twisted. "I'll kill us all before I eat another potato."

Karma shuddered, latched on to Draco's arm, and dragged the man away.

"Captain," Hadassah said, "did you have to be quite so flirty with the man? And are you sure old Hecaton hasn't just abandoned us for real?"

Lotte shook her head. "I'm afraid not. There's a stench coming from her quarters."

"I'm *not* toting her body." Hadassah crossed her arms and spat.

"It's not corpse flowers," Lotte said. "Now move along."

* * * *

Hecaton Kheiris Mezeta, formerly a major but now a lord principality of the Cloud Temple, had hung a cheery "Do Not Disturb" sign on the door of her office. The office was not only barred from within, but also protected by a retribution mandala. Taki discovered it when he attempted to force the door open with a shoulder check and ended up unceremoniously sprawled on the floor.

"Milord Principality!" Lotte shouted. "Open up! We know you're in there."

There was no response.

"You weren't kidding about the smell," Hadassah said. She scrunched her nose up at the smoky, cloying odor wafting out from the doorframe.

Taki groaned and slowly rose to his feet. He wiped away a thin stream of blood from his left nostril and reached out to cast a sutra. Before he could follow through, Hadassah kicked him in the back of a knee. He stumbled, lurched around, and pushed her. She riposted with an elbow to his gut, and the two wrestled.

"Out of my way," Lotte ordered. She knelt with palms upturned in supplication and started to invoke a sutra. *"The mind commands the body, and it obeys. I am become Walking Death. I eat the hearts of my enemies, wear their skins, and become cuter."*

Hadassah looked up from her efforts to drive her thumbs into Taki's nostrils. "Captain? What are you doing? We can't—"

Lotte inhaled and let out a roar before she lurched face forward at the door. Light lanced out from the wood to reveal a previously hidden mandala that blurred and dissolved under the assault. The door buckled and shattered like plate glass struck by a juggernaut, and Lotte careened in before coming to a stop in the center of the office.

Someone cackled. *"Om mani padme hum."*

Taki extricated himself from Hadassah's leg lock and limped into the office after Lotte. When he saw what lay within, his face scrunched in horror.

Hecaton sat atop her desk, cross-legged, with the tops of her feet flush against her thighs. A circlet of desiccated clover blossoms rested loosely across her brow, and she wore a robe of dirty, sweat-yellowed linen with a wooden begging bowl balanced in her lap. Before her, melted stumps of candles pooled wax across the wood and over the edge to form a stringy, multicolored waterfall.

"Milord Principality," Lotte said, out of breath, "I apologize for the intrusion and the door, but we were all concerned for you."

Hecaton smiled magnanimously. "My child, are you ready to shave your head and become a nun?" she asked.

"No. What's all this about?" She motioned with her head to the rest of the office. Stolen laundry lines crisscrossed above with deep-ochre-stained undergarments hung haphazardly in the fashion of prayer pennants. Books and scrolls were strewn around the floor unopened, their pages ripped from the bindings and spit-glued into lewd sculptures attached to the walls. Incomprehensible red squiggles danced across the walls, as if children had been given buckets of paint and promised protection from their parents' wrath.

"An offering, first." Hecaton pointed to a large, pewter spittoon overflowing with ash. A handful of fresh joss sticks pierced the gray mound. "I *am* a twice born, you know. I'm one who's entered the stream. If you give up your worldly desires and meditate every day, you can too."

Lotte looked at the other two. "Natalis, use your power."

Taki hesitated.

"Well, go on," Lotte said. "Eastern gods *eat the smells.*"

"You're sure, Captain?"

"Don't question her orders," Hadassah snapped. "Just do what she says! Wanna fight again?"

Taki shook his head. He edged closer to the spittoon with his arm stretched out, as if trying to avoid contamination. He flicked his fingers at the end of a joss stick but shook so much that the summoned flames missed their target entirely. The stick glowed feebly after a few more tries.

Lotte sighed. "Milord, there's your offering."

Hecaton nodded sagely. "Now, all of you clap twice and keep your hands pressed together. Bow at the waist and hold for ten seconds. I won't make you kowtow, since you're nonbelievers."

"Enough sacrilege!" Lotte said. "*You* answer *us* now. Why have you refused all contact, even from the exarch? What are you *doing* here? Have you fed *Babu?*"

Hearing his name, a rotund, tiger-striped tom half leapt, half pulled himself onto the desk next to Hecaton and let out a yowl. Hecaton shot an imperious glare at the tom, and he responded by flopping down in her lap. "The basileus has offended me greatly. So I will not see her cronies until she kowtows to me and retracts what she has done." She scratched Babu's ears, and he nibbled the folds of her robes.

Lotte frowned. "You are a principality of the Temple. You are the next in line to guide the flock, and you lord over even the Agia Triada. How in the hell does that displease you?"

"I didn't want it. I just wanted an egg—"

"Whether you wanted it or not is irrelevant. Besides, an increase in rank means more pay, more prestige." Lotte stepped forward around the repurposed urn and put her forehead to Hecaton's. "It means Her Grace wanted to *reward* you."

Hecaton merely licked the tip of Lotte's nose in repose. "That tastes like a lie!"

Lotte planted her hands on her hips. "Are you done playing dress-up? Can we move on?"

"You're insulting my people."

Hadassah waved. "Isn't a promotion just the kind of thing you want, though? You know, to be in control so you can piss around with people's lives and such?"

"All I wanted in life was to bake bread," Hecaton said. "My father and brother were bakers, you know. They were making scallion dumplings the day I went to the bihara. And now...*I don't remember how they tasted!*"

"Scallion dumplings are easy," Hadassah said. "I'll even be cute and teach you how. Does that make you happy?"

"No! They're made in a specific way, and none of you barbarians could possibly appreciate their refinement."

Lotte jabbed a finger at Hecaton's nose. "You're being rude."

Hecaton clasped Lotte's finger in her hands and peered at the tip while sucking her teeth. "Lieselotte, child, listen to me. I'm sorry, but you have leprosy."

"No one has leprosy!" Lotte snapped her hand back. "Now, with all due respect, shut the hell up and listen to me! You're acting like a godrotting child! If you're so unhappy with Her Grace's esteem, you can just *leave!* No one's keeping you here against your will. Go ahead and resign right now *so we can get paid!*"

Hecaton blinked. "But I don't want to. I like being around you dumb kids. Sometimes I think of you as my own."

"If you truly think that about us, milord Principality, then please respect our need to eat. Or else we'll all starve and possibly die."

"You can always eat the exarch. He's very fat and doesn't run fast."

Taki saw something wild cross his captain's face, and bile surged up his throat. "Beg pardon!" He stepped between the two women but avoided touching either. "If the basileus offended you, why don't you send a letter to her? Or even better, you can go *visit* Her Grace!"

Hecaton grinned and leapt from her perch to twirl around. "A splendid idea, my little regicide! We're off to see the basileus, the wonderful basil of

Oz! And if she doesn't do what I want, I'll shove this promotion up her *ass!*"

She kicked the spittoon over and took Taki by the hips to whirl around in a clumsy, parodic waltz. Tears formed in Taki's eyes, and a thought crossed his mind: *It'd have been better to starve.*

"It's decided," Lotte said. She shook her head. "Accompany the principality to Athenaeum."

Hecaton grinned and pirouetted while Taki scurried away. "Yes, come with me, my loyal onions, minions, or whatever you are! Company, to arms! And let us bask in obscene incandescence!" she said as she skipped airily out the door and left her choking subordinates in a cloud of ash.

"Wait, Captain," Hadassah said. "If we don't go with her, maybe she'll get lost and die in a ditch. After all, she's gone raving mad. We shouldn't squander this opportunity to be rid of her!"

Lotte cuffed the redhead gently across the cheek. "Idiot, this is a lucid moment for our tyrant. Now get your damned guns and off to the capital with you."

* * * *

Taki chanced a breath through his nostrils and immediately wished he hadn't. Effluvium coursed slowly down channels on either side of the boulevard he walked down and sent up an indescribable odor that cut his senses like a rusty shiv. Greenish-brown, the oily shit backed up everywhere and simply pooled on the cobblestones, making him step gingerly to avoid splashing it on his leggings.

The Argead Dominion, to which all Polaris of the Temple pledged their lives, was now a country only in name. A month earlier, the Osterbrand Imperium had overrun the borders in a sudden, brutal conquest. The surviving peerage of the Dominion now numbered less than a dozen, having been slaughtered in battle or hanged in front of their keeps. The assassination of the childless Basileus Niketas Palaiologos had further destabilized the faltering nation, and his successor had been forced to offer terms despite an improbable Dominion victory at the capital's doorstep.

Because of that narrow win, Athenaeum had been spared a siege and thus was exactly the same as Taki remembered it: the smell of human waste intermingled with roasting harspud. Hecaton traipsed gaily ahead, still clad in her sweaty prayer robes, which dragged on the cobbles and smeared dust and filth in her wake. Taki shook his head at the sight and glanced at Hadassah, who was busy play-acting as a tourist and seemed indifferent to the smell.

"What?" she asked.

"Nothing," Taki said. He scrunched his nose up. "Well, what do you think of it? The jewel in the Dominion crown?"

"Disappointing. I expected more rubble and bodies falling from the rooftops. Or at least more fires. There hasn't been a single screaming woman or roasting child. There's nothing to loot, either."

"Why are you so preoccupied with looting? And with death and carnage?"

"Because I love shiny things and I'm not afraid to kill for them. Aren't I too perfect?"

"You're a criminal."

"We both are. Except I didn't, you know, kill the last of the Palaiologoi or nothin'." Hadassah slid a finger across her throat and let out a gruesome rattle.

"I didn't..." Taki began, but his words died in his throat. *I didn't what? Mean to do it?*

"Did you drown him in the tub? Or shank him on the shitter?"

"Nothing of the sort! Just...just shut up! Please!"

She wrapped an arm around his and squeezed. "Don't get me wrong, Natalis. There are lots of people out there who had it in for the old basil. And maybe some who'd call you a hero or a savior. So don't be glum. The rest of us don't think ill of you, and even though you won't fess up to it, we know."

Taki blinked and unclenched his jaw. He let out a breath and murmured his thanks. "I appreciate it. I really do. I just need time to figure out some things."

Hadassah smiled. "Did you put something up his bung?"

Taki frowned and wormed his way out of her grasp. "Forget it! If you're just going to jape at me, then I have no further words for you."

"Your problem is that you're too damned uptight. You're so focused on your own stupid virtue that you end up being an ass most of the time."

She took a too-large bite of a harspud ball impaled on a stick and started to pant.

"I hope you get the shits from that."

"Speaking of which," Hadassah said, "where's old Mezeta gone to?"

Taki swore and frantically looked around. The old woman was nowhere to be seen. He sprinted up to the edge of the square but realized quickly that finding her would be impossible in the crowd. He jogged back over to Hadassah, who hadn't moved an inch and was still chowing down like a yokel. "Damn you! She was just here! If you hadn't distracted me…"

He squatted and ran his fingers through his hair. Now he'd done it. The old hag had gone insane, slipped away, and would kill the new basileus for fun. He'd be a double-regicide now. Cries and gunshots erupted in the distance. The two Polaris looked at each other and took off running.

It wasn't long until they came up to the wrought-iron gates of the Mitripoli, only to be confronted by a line of bayonets and muzzles. Nearby, Hecaton stood with her hands on her hips, seething. A battle line of praetorians with rifles barred the way to the palace. From behind marched up a platoon of city garrison with brightly painted shields and spears, backed by crossbowmen. Taki raised his hands in surrender. There was no escaping now.

"Milord Principality," Taki said. "What happened?"

"One of them spat on my robes," Hecaton said. "I took offense and made them pay. Now the others will learn some proper respect. Because fuck turning the other cheek."

"Why didn't you wait for us?"

"You two were having fun. I didn't want to be a burden."

Taki rolled his eyes. "No, you wanted to ditch us and start a meaningless fight."

"Maybe?"

"What's the meaning of this?" Amilia Gillette said. She stood on the opposite side of the iron fence with her arms crossed and her brow furrowed. The ivory robes of the basileus contrasted with the brown of her hands and face and the silver of her hair. When she saw Hecaton, she sighed.

"Your Grace!" a praetorian shouted. "You must get to safety!"

Amilia shook her head. "Lower your weapons, open the gate, and resume your posts. I've been expecting this one and her entourage. I'll see you inside, Hecaton Mezeta. Be a dear and wipe your feet."

The praetorians slowly withdrew, disbelief written on their faces. One of them grudgingly unbarred the entry and pulled the gilded doors open. Hecaton strode nonchalantly inside without a word to her subordinates.

Taki slowly let his arms fall to his sides. They burned from being held up for so long, and he rubbed at his shoulders. He glanced at Hadassah. "Far be it from me to question the captain, but was it actually smart to bring Mezeta here? She's gone batshit!"

"It doesn't matter," Hadassah murmured. "She's going to do what she wants, with or without us. We're just her peons along for the journey. Now here, have some balls." She offered her snack to Taki, who finally, glumly, took a bite.

When they trudged into the throne room, the exchange had already begun.

Amilia, slumped on the brass eagle throne, regarded Hecaton with a bemused expression. "And for what purpose did you assault my men?"

"I want to escape the cycle of death and rebirth," Hecaton said. "Material attachments prevent me from doing so. Make them go away."

Amilia sighed. "I'm the basileus, not the Buddha, and definitely not God. Did you really waste your time coming here to hear that? Drop the bullshit religious act. It's self-indulgent."

"You've offended me, and I've lost my appetite," Hecaton said.

"Good. I wasn't going to throw you a feast, anyway."

"Then I ask you this. Why did you make me heir to the Temple without my consent?"

"You make me sound like a rapist, and I resent that," Amilia said. "Exarch Constantin was a fair defender of the land in his prime. However, now that we are under Imperial control, it is time for new leadership. The old man's way of doing things nearly cost us our lives, though I don't aim to punish him for it. But I need fresh blood to replace stagnant."

"Then why don't you make one of the triada take his place?" Hecaton asked, pacing all the while. "Or hell, just make lil' Karma do the job? He's *your* unlovable spawn."

"The triada are idiots and blowhards. I'd execute them if I weren't concerned about rebellion. And Karma may be my son, but he is eminently unqualified for any position of power and prone to treasonous leanings. I often entertain the thought of having him killed. Prophylactically, you understand."

Hecaton grinned. "You are one of the few barbarians who understand good parenting!"

"Stop trying to flatter me and change the subject. I want *you* to run the Temple and appoint a new command. I want you to make us strong again."

Hecaton threw her head back and laughed. "No."

"I expected you'd say that. I'm prepared to offer you almost anything within reason in return for your acceptance. *How much?*"

"A million bullets and a pony."

"Will you take installments? The animal can be delivered immediately."

Hecaton glowered. "You don't do sarcasm, do you? I want nothing, and I won't accept."

"Then I order you to, on pain of death."

"Good! Just when I think you're getting boring, you prove me wrong again. If someone like you had been in charge a long time ago in my homeland, things would have turned out differently for Shastirch and I."

"All I hear from you is gibberish," Amilia said.

Hecaton inhaled deeply, exhaled, and smirked. "I know what you're trying to accomplish. Sadly, it's impossible. I am a 'twice born.' Do you know what that means?"

Amilia shook her head.

"Unlike most of you peons, I've been a human once before. This is my second birth, and because I've been such a good little arahant, I get to shoot lightning out of my cooter. Choniates and the triada are *barely* twice born, and they'll just return as vermin when they die. Only the twice born among my people can manage this much power. I haven't seen it anywhere else, and I've traveled much further than you think I have. So I can't turn your Polaris into a bunch of little knockoff Mezetas. Not that I'd ever want to, anyway."

Amilia snorted. "Although I respect your power, you also display shocking levels of ignorance."

"Oh? Do explain."

"My order has nothing to do with your ability to control the elements or act like an arrogant ass. It has everything to do with preserving the people of this nation. And to do that, we will need to resist Imperial whims. We need to preserve our way of life."

"*You're* the one who offered the country on a platter," Hecaton said. "Besides, I've traveled their lands, and compared to the Dominion way of life, they're practically enlightened. No Imperial will accuse you of being a witch just so they can stone you and steal your house."

Amilia chuckled. "You act as if I haven't been accused of witchcraft before and haven't gotten my accusers boiled for slander. I offered a conditional surrender because my choices were to either sign a surrender treaty or reduce my own country to ash with the God Hand."

"That might have been preferable."

"I should have pressed the button then, but only for you."

Hecaton stamped a foot. "Why don't you nuke me right now?"

"Because it'd be a waste of a good relic. You're not that important."

"Clearly I must be, if I'm your only guard against the Imperium overtaking this shitty culture."

Amilia made a fist. "Mezeta, I despise many things about my own kingdom, and that's why I wished to change it. But the way the Padishah sees it, each and every one of us is mere fodder for the machine of conquest. The man blathers on about parity between sexes and the primacy of merit through deed, but the reality is a shit pile. Men and women and queers all carry the same spear and turn into the same mincemeat to take some unimportant hill. Even *you* will meet that fate in his world."

"So be it. There's always someone stronger."

"And I aim to be smarter. So, will you accept?"

Hecaton rolled her eyes. "I'll think about it, if it gets you off my tit for a sodding second. Now, I need to piss."

She sauntered out of the chamber unbidden.

Amilia shook her head, rose from her throne, and dusted her robes off. She glanced at Taki and Hadassah. "I doubt the principality will return. In the meantime, I'd like a word with you, Cornet Natalis."

"Your Grace." Taki bowed deeply and tried to stifle his own trembling. *She wants to eliminate the evidence. Now is as good a time as any.* For once, he was glad that Hadassah was with him. *At least she'll get axed too.*

"There've been rumors of late," Amilia said. "Idle slander that I seduced a young Polaris of the Temple and that, in a foolish attempt to gain my favor, the young man killed our former liege."

"I know very little of these matters, Your Grace," Taki said. He swallowed. Sweat droplets formed on his brow.

"As basileus, it is my sacred duty to uphold the law and bring justice to the murderer. If it so happened that an ambitious but misguided young man raised his hand against Niketas Palaiologos, then he should be hanged, drawn, and quartered, and his parts sent to all corners of the Dominion to serve as an example for traitors."

Taki clenched his jaw. "Yes, Your Grace." *This is the end.*

"So you basically used him, and now you're gonna turn him into wieners?" Hadassah said. "That's pretty shitty of you."

Amilia cracked her knuckles. "Were we not alone here, you'd be flogged to death for your insolence, girl."

Hadassah seemed unfazed. "I just speak plainly, Your Grace."

"Just consider yourself lucky to be beneath my notice. As for you, Cornet Natalis, perhaps I'll speak plainly too. You're becoming a liability. But, as your wench pointed out, it would be untoward of me to simply have you killed."

"I'm *definitely* not his wench," Hadassah said.

Taki coughed and sputtered. "What will happen to me, Your Grace?"

"The safest thing for both of us would be to cut out your tongue, have you branded on both cheeks, and sever your thumbs before depositing you on the Ursalan border. You'd avoid execution, in any case."

Taki went pale. "P-please, Your Grace..."

"Luckily for you, another option has presented itself. For now, you'll simply need to wait...and to not do anything stupid."

Taki dug his nails into his palms. His knees wobbled, and he found it impossible to stand.

"I hope you understand my situation. I'm not a monster." With that, Amilia rose from her seat and pointed to the door.

Taki lowered his head and stared at the tiles on the floor. They formed a mosaic of Orestes tormented by the Furies: punishment for the murder of his betters. And yet because the deed had been instigated by a god, Orestes had been unable to even take shelter in any temple. Until he'd made impossible amends, his fate was always to suffer. Rendered in exacting detail with tiny precious stones, the ancient hero's face was caught in an eternal scream.

* * * *

Hecaton stood at the highest point of the Mitripoli, letting the wind whip her hair into disarray. Her prayer robes had been dumped on to a beggar in a side alley, and now she sported a gold-accented tunic that she'd swiped from Amilia's chambers. Wearing it was treason, but edicts were meaningless atop the fort's steeple. Athenaeum also smelled slightly better where she was.

"*Udaan uulzsangui shuu, Sirin*," Chronicler said. He perched on a buttress nearby, just out of arm's reach.

Hecaton tensed for a moment to hear her sworn nemesis speak her truest of names. Had anyone else addressed her with such familiarity— such intimacy—she'd have struck him down where he stood. Chronicler, however, was no stranger. She let out a sigh of resignation and continued to stare out over the city. Of the two of them, Chronicler was always the more physical, and trying to run from him would only result in more taunting. It was always better to cut the man down with words, anyway.

"I've made precious few mistakes in my life, Shastirch," Hecaton said, using the name deepest-graven on Chronicler's heart. "But marrying you was the worst by far."

"Have a care for my health, Sirin. Setting my heart aflutter like that is bad for my qi."

"Aren't you a little old to be scrambling on the rooftops like some idiotic basang?"

"The same could be said for you. That gray hair of yours is far too dignified. A head of shocking pink might fit better."

"You looked better wearing it, Shastirch. Now, are you done wasting my time, or have you come for some sort of useful purpose?"

Chronicler blinked. "Actually, I just wanted to talk you again. In person. Without the inconvenient need to slaughter each other on sight."

"I can't imagine why," Hecaton said. "Aren't you sick of my face?"

"Do you know how many years I searched for you? How many years of humiliation I had to endure for mere fleeting glimpses and missed chances?"

"You brought that on yourself. I never wanted you to come after me. Our romance was over a long time ago."

Chronicler laughed. "It wasn't out of sentimentality, I assure you. I wanted to take you back to the Ring for judgment. But now, I'm not so sure that's a good idea."

"I had my reasons. And I find it hard to believe the Sarang would allow you to abscond simply to look for me."

"Perhaps I wished to escape my service as well."

"Then we're both traitors without any right to return."

"So, what do you plan to do from now on, Sirin? Continue being a sellsword?"

"I'm thinking about carving out a swath of land for my own. You know, crown upon a troubled brow and all that. If you wish, you can be my consort. But no sex. I'm too dried out for that."

Chronicler laughed. "The offer sounds tempting, though I know you are merely mocking me."

"I really wasn't. How about you, Shastirch? Will you continue to be the padishah's dogsbody until senility?"

"I like to be on the winning side. And I have no intention of staying as a dogsbody."

"Hah! Now, that's the man I once knew. So when are you planning to assassinate your master?"

Chronicler shrugged. "I wasn't. I find him fascinating. He's certainly charismatic, as far as centuries-old demons go. He was actually around during the Fall, you know. Now he feels like it's his responsibility to lift mankind from the ashes. Through conquest, of course."

"Come, Shastirch, you're not saying you believe in his cause? World domination? How *trite*."

"It's not trite when he has the power to actually achieve his goal." Chronicler's eyes flitted from side to side. "He's set his sights on the Ring, and I intend to help him take it. Against his armies, even a thousand twice born don't stand a chance. And again, I want to be on the winning side."

Hecaton glowered. "What did he promise you in exchange for betraying our home?"

Chronicler shook his head. "I want to save it. I will rule in his stead there and make sure that what happened to us never happens to others."

"So, a dogsbody to the end."

"Call it what you want. I'll ask you one final time, Sirin. Will you join me and bring order to the Ring?"

Hecaton turned away. "No. You embark on a fool's journey. Try not to die on the way."

"The same to you, my dear. I advise you not to get in my way."

With that, Chronicler leapt off the top of the steeple and was gone.